A Death For Ripley's

After entering the apartment, Camellion closed the door, but since he had broken the latch, he couldn't relock it. Suddenly the door was kicked inward and two men rushed into the room. The man in front carried a Czech Vz25 submachine gun. The man behind held a U.S. AMT Combat .45. Both men raised their weapons when they saw Camellion.

It was a simple matter of Camellion's having the edge—not only had he known what to expect, but he was faster. Both Backpacker auto mags boomed. When man or beast is hit by a Lee Jurras-designed bullet, impelled by 300 grains of powder, the results are predictable.

Both .44 Magnum projectiles struck the men in the chest, flattened out, tore tunnels two inches in diameter through their bodies, and exploded out their backs. No two men died faster.

The one, with a big, bloody hole in his chest, dropped the Vz25 machine gun and pitched backward, the .44 projectile that had shot out of his back rocketing straight at a third man, who had entered the room behind him. However, the bullet never reached the third man; instead, one of those stranger-than-fiction accidents occurred. The .44 Magnum bullet tore directly into the muzzle of the .38 BSW revolv the .44 slug wedgin at the end of the ba exploded in the m apart like ripped c

THE DEATH MERCHANT SERIES:

#41 in the incredible adventures of the
DEATH MERCHANT
SHAMROCK SMASH
by Joseph Rosenberger

PINNACLE BOOKS   LOS ANGELES

DEATH MERCHANT #41:
SHAMROCK SMASH

An original Pinnacle Books edition, published for the first time anywhere.

First printing, October 1980

ISBN: 0-523-41019-0

Cover illustration by Dean Cate

Printed in the United States of America

PINNACLE BOOKS, INC.
2029 Century Park East
Los Angeles, California 90067

Out of Ireland have we come
Great hatred, little room
Maimed us at the start.
I carry from my mother's womb
A fanatic heart.

—W. B. Yeats

Special Note

While this book is fiction, the war in Northern Ireland is very real. For the sake of naturalism, there will be terms and phrases that are actually in use by both sides in Northern Ireland, such as "Romanism," "damned bloody Protestant," etc.

We use these terms for realism only; they are not meant to be an insult to the religious beliefs of our readers.

Joseph R. Rosenberger

SHAMROCK SMASH

CHAPTER ONE

Although Richard Camellion and Christopher McLoughlin had a lot to discuss and had their own private compartment on the train, the trip from Dublin, Ireland to Belfast, Northern Ireland, was as exciting as watching a turtle race.

Rail service in Ireland is about the same as the service offered by Amtrak in the United States—totally inefficient, with the old coaches wobbling from side to side and the seats in need of repair. There wasn't any club car. There wasn't a snack bar. No employee of the Irish railway system went through the cars selling sandwiches and hot and cold drinks at exorbitant prices.

In the case of the Death Merchant and Chris McLoughlin, there was only boredom and the danger that there might have been a leak, that the deadly Irish Republican Army might know they were coming to Belfast. Who could say that IRA assassins weren't on the same train, waiting to gun them down? For that matter, Camellion and McLoughlin had no assurance that Ulster Volunteer Force gunmen weren't on the train, determined to blow them away.

There was the additional risk that they might be stopped, questioned, and searched by the IIB, the Irish Investigation Bureau, Ireland's FBI. The British passports of Camellion and McLoughlin were valid. The weapons they carried were not. It wasn't that Camellion and McLoughlin were afraid of being detained for any length of time by the IIB. A word from the British Foreign Office and they would be released. But the secret would be out, that Camellion, traveling under the name of "Warren Jasper Ringgall," and McLoughlin, using the alias of George Allen Weaver, were agents of SIS, the British Secret Intelligence Service. The main secrets would remain intact, however Camellion and McLoughlin were both contract agents of the American Central Intelligence Agency and they were going to Northern Ireland to find out how the commu-

1

nists, particularly the Soviet KGB, were smuggling firearms and explosives into Northern Ireland.

It took almost half an hour for the engine, an old-style coal-burning locomotive, to back the train into the central station in Belfast—a huge hangar-like shed grimy from years of smoke. There was a twenty minute wait as the passengers lined up (or queued up as they say in England and Ireland) and slowly shuffled to the last coach, from whose right rear door they would step down to the concrete.

For Camellion and McLoughlin, jammed in like sardines among other people, this was the point of maximum danger. Directly behind them was a couple who, in their sixties, had the appearance of farmers. A young couple, with two eight- to ten-year-old children, was in front. Appearances didn't mean anything. In the religious war between the Roman Catholics and the Protestants in Northern Ireland, teenagers—even children as young as twelve—tossed bombs and pulled triggers.

Battle-trained realists, Camellion and McLoughlin didn't underestimate the danger of their position. Until they were freed from the train, they were helpless. Both men felt relief when at length it was their turn to be helped down the three steel steps by the conductor and his assistant. Then they were on the concrete and, with other people, walking toward the gate that opened into the long station, a silly thought floating into Camellion's consciousness. *Why is it that people de-plane, but never de-train or de-bus? Another of life's little mysteries from the Department of Useless Information.*

Their hands deep in the pockets of their Irish-styled trench coats (they had bought the coats in Dublin), they moved through the gate into the train station, which was almost a block long.

Camellion's right hand was wrapped around the butt of a small .22 Astra auto pistol. A .32 Mauser HSc autoloader rested snugly in a left ankle holster.

McLoughlin had a TDE .380 ACP pistol in his trench coat, and a 9-mm Sig-Sauer autoloader in a right ankle holster.

The Death Merchant didn't have any doubts about Chris McLoughlin as a backup. Not only was the tall young man an expert in karate, but he had seen plenty of sudden death in Vietnam. He had survived numerous ambushes, had the instincts of a natural-born survivor, and was not prone to panic. A businessman, McLoughlin designed and sold knives and

2

other defensive items, which he sold in the United States through his company, Armament Systems Products, Unlimited, based in Atlanta, Georgia. McLoughlin, however, was more adventurer than businessman. For that reason, he was with Camellion—for excitement and a love of danger. The $50,000 that The Company would pay him—only if Winglewax-4 succeeded—was a further inducement.

A babble of voices greeted Camellion and McLoughlin inside the station. There were rows of hard wooden benches, most of them filled with people. On the north side of the station were magazine, souvenir, and fast-food stands.

"It's a quarter of a block to the front of the station," McLoughlin said in a low voice when no one was close to them. "I'll feel a lot better once we're in a taxi and on our way to you-know-where."

"That makes two of us," grunted the Death Merchant. "Out here we're like clay birds in a shooting gallery."

Watching everyone and everything, Camellion and McLoughlin hurried along, Camellion on the left, McLoughlin on the right. There wasn't anything they could do about the rear. They didn't have eyes in back of their heads, and they couldn't be constantly looking over their shoulders, not without arousing suspicion. There had to be almost half a dozen plainclothesmen of the RUC, the Royal Ulster Constabulary, in the station, sizing up the crowd. At any rate, an IRA ambush was not very likely. The IRA didn't even know that they were coming into Belfast. *Even if they did, they don't know what we look like. . . .*

Twenty feet more, and Fate proved to the Death Merchant that there are no guarantees in life. Camellion's eyes were raking over an open tea shop—the kind in which the counters form a square, with stools on all four sides—when he saw a young man get up, turn in his direction, and reach into the left side of his coat with his right hand—the kind of motion an individual would make when reaching for a gun. Too much of his hand was under his coat.

Instinct took over, intuition and experience. Camellion realized that if he warned Chris about the man, he would automatically jerk his attention to the left and lose a few seconds. There had to be more than one assassin—*at least one in front and maybe one to the rear*.

"Ambush!" Camellion warned McLoughlin. "In front and to your right."

Just as the man—twenty-five feet in front and to the left—

3

pulled a .380 Enfield revolver from a shoulder holster and began to swing it upward, Camellion's right hand came out of his coat pocket. Darting to the left, he "body" fired when the Astra pistol was at waist level, the loud, sharp pop sounding like the crack of a bullwhip. Almost simultaneously, there were five more shots, all within a split second of each other.

The man Camellion had fired at didn't get off a shot. A silly, surprised look came over the man's face when the .22 long rifle hollow-point Astra bullet struck him in the chest. He dropped the Enfield, tripped over a stool, and fell sideways against a woman getting to her feet.

Two more men fired from the front, one using a P38 Walther, the other triggering a British Smith & Wesson .38. Twenty-five feet to the right, one man was in the door of a telephone booth by the wall, between two gates. The second man was on the outside, next to the phone booth's east side.

Two more IRA gunmen fired from behind Camellion and McLoughlin. Both were standing to one side of a magazine rack by the station's north wall. The fifth shot came from McLoughlin's TDE pistol.

The slugs from the P38 and the BSW .38 missed Chris and Camellion and struck a man ten feet behind and slightly to the right of them. Crying out in pain, the man went down, his head cracking loudly on the tile floor. Simultaneously, another man three feet to the right of the bystander who had been hit, groaned and pitched sideways as projectiles from the two men by the magazine rack cut into him.

McLoughlin's .380 TDE bullet stabbed into the IRA assassin who was standing inside the phone booth and getting ready to trigger another round from the Walther. The man was sagging when the perceptive Camellion swung to the right and fired at the man by the side of the phone booth, just as the man triggered a round at Chris McLoughlin, who also ducked to the right. The IRA gunman's bullet missed him by a foot or more, kept right on going and struck the back of a woman running for safety—a hundred feet behind him.

The Death Merchant fired twice, the two .22 hollow-points slamming into the solar plexus of the man. The BSW .38 revolver dropped from his hand and he slid to the floor, tiny trickles of blood oozing from the corners of his mouth.

The Great Victoria Street Railway Station was thrown into an uproar, everyone thinking the same thing: *the Catholics and the Protestants are killing each other*. Women screamed. The lines of people at the gates, waiting for departing trains,

4

dissolved like smoke before a strong wind. Some people had the sense to throw themselves to the floor. Others ran blindly in all directions.

No one was surprised, actually. The railroad station was a popular target of the Irish Republican Army, as was the nearby Europa Hotel, even though it was protected by a wire fence and numerous security guards. The only decent hotel left in the besieged city of Belfast, the Europa always shook and shuddered when a bomb went off in the Great Victoria Station. This time, the Europa was lucky; the IRA was only using firearms.

It was terrified bystanders who prevented the two IRA gunmen by the magazine rack from tossing slugs at Camellion and McLoughlin. Now and then, when people weren't blocking their view, the two IRA gunmen caught brief glimpses of Camellion and McLoughlin, and vice versa. But within fifteen seconds the area was clear, and the Death Merchant and McLoughlin, weaving and ducking back and forth, cut down on the IRA gunmen, who were trying to reach a door at the northern end.

One of Camellion's .22 slugs caught an IRA terrorist in the side of the neck, just below his right ear. The man yelled, a yell that was quickly cut off as an ocean of blood flooded his throat. The second man, trapped, turned and fired a quick shot with his Polish P64 SL pistol, the 9-mm bullet missing Camellion just as McLoughlin's .380 slug popped the gunman in the chest and kicked him backward. A moment later the Death Merchant fired, his .22 bullet boring into the man's rib cage, tearing through his lung and lodging against the center of his sternum.

In less than two minutes five IRA gunmen and three bystanders had been killed. Camellion and McLoughlin hadn't been touched. Not yet! They still had to get out of Great Victoria Street Station. British soldiers and uniformed members of the Royal Ulster Constabulary would soon be pouring into both ends of the station and coming through the north side doors. There was only one direction open to Camellion and Chris—south, through one of the gates and onto the ribbons of steel tracks.

Guns in hand, they sprinted toward the nearest gate whose wooden slats were raised, shouts of "Halt!" coming to them from a hundred fifty feet to the west. Darting and zigzagging, they raced through an open gate, several L1A1 rifles cracking to the west, 7.62-mm slugs missing them by inches.

5

Camellion and McLoughlin paused only long enough to take their second pistols from their ankle holsters, Chris muttering, "Which way now—and what do we do about the soldiers?"

"They'll have Victoria Street covered," Camellion said. "Our only chance is New Kilmainham Road to the west. The soldiers? We say 'Feet, do your duty'—and run like hell!"

They started racing down the length of concrete between two trains that had been preparing to depart—until the shooting had started and the would-be passengers had scattered. No one attempted to stop them. Conductors, brakemen, switchmen, and baggage handlers, seeing the two men with weapons in each hand, either scrambled under trains, ran into freight or passenger cars, or made themselves scarce in other ways. People who had already boarded the trains ducked down behind windows, afraid of bullets crashing through the glass.

For that moment, the Death Merchant's main concerns were the British soldiers and the RUC police, especially the British Tommies, who were armed with LIAl rifles. The LIAl was actually the NATO FN light rifle—a dangerous weapon that could be fired on full automatic. Not even the Death Merchant could outrun a string of 7.62-mm projectiles.

Camellion and McLoughlin were almost to one of the locomotives when British soldiers, accompanied by half a dozen uniformed RUCs, came racing through two of the gates between the station and the train shed. They stopped and raised their rifles, then hesitated because several lift trucks towing jitneys loaded with baggage were between them and the two fugitives they presumed to be IRA gunmen. One Tommy did fire a short burst, but most of the slugs buried themselves in luggage; the rest glanced off one of the steel girders supporting the wide, curved roof. Before the soldiers could fire again, Camellion and McLoughlin dashed around the front of the locomotive and started to race west. They both saw the two trains being backed into the shed, one being pushed by a modern Diesel, the other by a coal burning boiler-type locomotive. It was the train being pushed by the Diesel, the one farthest to the west, that they had to beat. They jumped across the steel ribbons of tracks, their lungs demanding air, their feet crunching on the gravel between the ties. Both men were very much aware that if they didn't succeed in getting to the other side of the two trains, they would end up naked on a slab covered with sheets, and with bullet holes in their backs and morgue tags on their big toes.

They ran ten feet in front of another parked locomotive, raced across two more sets of tracks and, with fear pouring extra adrenalin into their bloodstreams, sprinted behind the end of the last coach being pushed by the coal-burning engine. They made it easily, with a dozen feet to spare.

They raced across three more sets of tracks and to the rear of the last car of the train being pushed back into the shed by the Diesel, the end of the coach so close that the coupling jaw and the end of the airbrake hose almost touched McLoughlin, who was a few steps behind the Death Merchant.

At the same instant, the British soldiers and the RUC policemen rounded the engine of the train a hundred feet to the east. But they were too late. The two trains were between them and Camellion and McLoughlin, both of whom were daring across the spiderweb section of the tracks. Beyond the tracks was an upward incline, then a twenty-foot-wide area of grass and weeds and the sidewalk of New Kilmainham Road.

"Get your TDE and Sig-Sauer out of sight," Camellion said to McLoughlin. He shoved his own .22 Astra and the .32 Mauser into his coat pockets and eyed the train ahead. It was slowly moving out of the station.

Breathing heavily, Chris glanced at Richard. "It's either over it, under it, through it, or we wait."

"Under it is out," Camellion said. "We'd have the time, but if we get these coats smudged, we'll attract too much attention when we reach New Kilmainham Road. We can't wait either."

"Let's go for it," Chris said. "We could be worse off. We could be dentists in the Soviet Union."

They hopped up onto the step-rungs and grabbed vertical railing handholds, Camellion taking the end of one car, McLoughlin the front of the coach behind. Quickly they crossed between the cars, stepping carefully on the coupling hookups. They reached the other side, jumped to the ground, and hurried on their way. The incline was only fifty feet away. They raced up the slope, reached the top, hurried down the other side, and began calmly walking north on the sidewalk. They had maybe five minutes at the most before the British soldiers and RUCs would have a clear line of fire at them.

Traffic moved up and down the road, but not a single taxi was in sight. It was Camellion who spotted the double-decker bus coming from the north, half a block away, on the opposite side of the street. He saw, too, that the bus stop was across the wide road, in the middle of the long block. To the south, at the intersection of New Kilmainham and Oxford Street, a policeman was directing traffic.

Ducking and dodging cars and trucks, Camellion and McLoughlin darted across the street, not concerning themselves with some drivers who had to slam on brakes to avoid hitting them, who cursed and called them "spalpeen" and other choice names.

When they reached the red- and yellow-striped curb of the bus stop, several people waiting for the bus gave them odd looks; but by the time the British soldiers and RUC policemen reached the top of the incline and began looking around for the two "IRA gunmen," the bus had pulled up and people were getting on, Camellion and McLoughlin among them.

The British Tommies and RUCs reached the sidewalk. The bus pulled away from the curb and headed into traffic, Camellion and McLoughlin seated in the bottom section, toward the center on the right-hand side. Neither spoke, pretending to be strangers to each other.

Now and then, from where they sat in the bus, they could see the dome of the imposing City Hall, but none of the busy docks. Industry and civic beauty seldom go hand in hand, but Belfast is the exception because of the natural charm of its situation on the banks of the river Lagan, where it flows into the blue waters of Belfast Lough. Yet there was a hideous side to Belfast, despite the green Irish hills surrounding the city. One could stand on the roof of the Europa Hotel and look over a red-bricked city devastated by terrible violence. Thousands of terrorists' explosive and incendiary bombs, along with ages of decay and neglect, had reduced much of the area to little more than rubble.

The Death Merchant was quick to realize that it would not take very long for the British soldiers and the RUC fuzz to put two and two together and come up with the bus. Within fifteen to twenty minutes, RUCs and British soldiers in patrol cars and in jeeps, all over the city and its suburbs, would be looking for them.

At least for two men in trench coats, one wearing a hat, thought Camellion. *That description could fit thousands of men. But it's an assumption that can get a man arrested, that can get a man wasted.*

Two blocks later Camellion and McLoughlin got off the bus, walked half a block east on Groomsport Street, and finally hailed one of the old-fashioned cabs so common in Belfast. McLoughlin no longer wore a hat. "Take us to City

Hall," Camellion instructed the driver, then closed the glass in the partition between the front and back seats.

"City Hall?" McLoughlin's voice had a ring of curiosity in it.

"We can change cabs in front of City Hall," Camellion said. "We'll take the next taxi to the Royal Victoria Hospital. It's on the corner of Falls Road and Grosvenor Road. From there we'll take a cab and head for Briscoe's place on Mervue Street."

He reached down, pulled up his right pant leg, and started to unstrap the telescoping aluminum cane he had strapped above his ankle. The rounded tube was only 7.8 inches long; when fully extended, it would be a full-sized walking cane of 38 inches.

Camellion slipped the rounded tube underneath his coat, and watched McLoughlin pull from under the right side of his trench coat a flattened black velour hat with a narrow brim.

"Don't put the hat on in here," Camellion said. "Wait until we're out and the driver is on his way. He might wonder about a man who got in hatless, but got out wearing one."

McLoughlin nodded. "I want to make sure it won't have that 'crushed' look when I put it on."

An amused smile flickered briefly over the Death Merchant's lean face. "Your remark about dentists in the Soviet Union. Run it by me again."

McLoughlin thought for a moment. "Oh, that!" He grinned. "You mean about the hardest job in the world—being a dentist in Russia."

"I don't get it."

"In the Soviet Union no one wants to open his mouth."

CHAPTER TWO

Built of red brick, the two-story, five-bay house was similar in design and appearance to the other houses on Mervue Street, which was part of a middle-class, staunchly Protestant neighborhood in north Belfast. There weren't a dozen men in the entire world who knew that Number 279 was the chief safe-house of British Secret Intelligence Service in Belfast. Likewise, only a handful of men knew that Sean Briscoe, the owner of the house, had been an SIS operative for thirteen years. A retired postal worker, Mr. Briscoe had the reputation of being a friendly man and an expert in chess. He was a member of the Belfast Chessmen, the leading chess club in Belfast, and often played in local tournaments. Now and then other members of the Belfast Chessmen would come to his home to play chess, a fact well known to his neighbors.

Nevertheless, the "slight traffic in chess players" was not a good enough explanation for Richard Camellion, who was already concerned about how IRA gunmen had spotted him and McLoughlin in the Victoria Street railroad station.

Edward Windrow, the senior SIS agent in the upstairs room, eyed Camellion with covert concern, his calm expression concealing his tension. "Your concern is appreciated, Mr. Ringgall," he said to the Death Merchant. "However, I assure you that this house is safe, as secure as we can manage."

"Perfect security doesn't exist," Robert Ford, another SIS agent, said rather stiffly, "not even in your American CIA."

"Look at it this way," Humphrey Grimes, the third SIS agent, said quickly. "Neither the Provos, the Officials, nor the RUCs have suspected this location in all these years. Why should they now? For my money, they won't."

"In theory, no one should have known about me and Mr. Weaver," Camellion said, his voice strong but uninflected. "But someone talked, and the IRA was waiting for us inside the station. That, gentlemen, is a fact of life."

"It sure wasn't ghosts shooting at us," Mr. Weaver—

11

McLoughlin—said, not even raising an eyebrow one suggestive millimeter. "And it wasn't spirits that we wasted."

Jesse Anson, the only CIA Case Officer in the room, cleared his throat. About forty years old, he was thin, of medium height, with thick blond hair and mustache.

"There has to be some logical explanation," he said firmly. "Only the CIA Chief-of-Station at the American Embassy and the SIS Chief at the British Embassy in Dublin knew that the two of you were coming to Belfast." He rushed on like a priest performing the last mass of a very long day. "I'm sure that neither one is in the employ of the IRA. By the way, your two trunks arrived."

"I'm not sure of anything, except that one day I'll be dead. Today, I am alive. The only question is what I shall do between those two points. A large part of what I shall do depends on how the IRA knew that Weaver and I would be on that train." Camellion unbuttoned his beige Harris tweed jacket, leaned back in the chair, and folded his arms, his peculiar blue eyes shifting to Sean Briscoe, then moving on to Anson and the three SIS officers sitting on the other side of the room, a number of thoughts flashing through his mind:

One of the most murderous areas on the face of the earth, Northern Ireland, with 5,451 square miles, is only slightly larger than the state of Delaware. Its population of one and a half million is two-third Protestant and one-third Roman Catholic. Belfast, the capital, is the chief industrial center.

The Irish struggle for independence dates from the British invasions of the twelfth century. Bitter rebellions and harsh repressions fueled the Anglo-Irish conflict for eight hundred years, with many of the religious and ethnic divisions in the current conflict stemming from the seventeenth century, when England colonized Ireland with thousands of English and Scottish settlers. As a result, the Roman Catholic population in the north became heavily outnumbered by Protestants, who assumed dominant political, social, and economic positions.

After guerrilla warfare by the Irish Republican Army and government reprisals, Southern Ireland accepted dominion status in 1921, but Northern Ireland chose to remain part of the United Kingdom. In 1949, the Irish Free State in the south seceded from the British Commonwealth and became the Irish Republic.

The current round of violence began in 1969, following Roman Catholic complaints of discrimination in housing, jobs, and voting rights, the Catholic civil rights workers' movement demanding justice. Protestant extremists responded to these demands with gang attacks and arson in Belfast's slums. The outnumbered Catholics then asked help from the Irish Republican Army (not to be confused with the regular army of the Irish republic, the IRA is an underground terrorist organization that is outlawed in all of Ireland). The war was on. To make matters worse for the Roman Catholic minority in Ulster, the IRA, during its convention in Dublin in late 1969, split into two factions: the Officials, who wanted to solve the problem by peaceful, political means; and the Provisionals, or Provos, who were convinced that only guns and bombs could solve the problem. To the Provos, victory meant a united Ireland, and they would settle for nothing less. As if to slap the Catholics and the IRA in the face, a 1973 vote indicated that eighty percent of the Northern Irish population qualified to vote favored remaining in the United Kingdom.

The war continued. By 1980 a total of fifteen thousand British troops were deployed in Northern Ireland at an estimated cost of 145 million per year. Great Britain was spending an additional $1.9 billion in annual welfare payments and investments in Northern Ireland.

As of January 19, 1980, 2,640 people had died in "the Troubles."

But the IRA was on the run. . . .

Camellion said, "What proof do you have that Liam O'Connor isn't a double agent? He may be feeding information to SIS, but he's still a member of the Officials branch of the IRA. To me, that means he's a Marxist."

Sean Briscoe, a tall, gangling man with a big nose and almost no chin, made an angry face. "You should get the facts, Mr. Ringgall," he said indignantly. "Some of the Officials are Communist. Most are not."

McLoughlin eyed the man laconically. "I was under the impression you were on the other side. Yet you sound like you're standing up for the IRA," he said, with gentle insistence.

"I despise the IRA as much as any Loyalist," Briscoe declared solemnly. "But I do believe we should be precise in these matters. It's totally inaccurate to lump all the Officials together under the heading of Marxist."

"A nice speech, and you're right," the Death Merchant said, unimpressed, "but it doesn't tell us anything definite about O'Connor."

"I'll answer your question." Edward Windrow got up from the window seat and sat down on a chair that was close to

Camellion. A short, ashen-haired man with a wide chest, he said patiently, "O'Connor has been giving us valuable information for years. As a member of the UDA, he's given us tips about the UVA. Only some weeks ago, because of—"

"Hold on!" McLoughlin held up a restraining hand. "Let's have some clarification of terms. What're the UDA and the UVA?"

Windrow's voice remained unvaryingly mild. "The UDA is the Ulster Defense Association. It's the largest of the Protestant paramilitary organizations."

"Whose main goal in life is to kill Catholics!" Robert Ford said drily, letting cigarette smoke drift from his nostrils.

"The UVF is the Ulster Volunteer Force," continued Windrow. "The UVF is the most active and the most violent of the Protestant paramilitary groups. It's regarded as the counterpart of the Provisional IRA. But understand that the UVF is not separate from the UDA. It's only a part of the Ulster Defense Association. The UFF, the Ulster Freedom Fighters, is still another terrorist group within the UDA. All three make no secret of their longing to meet the IRA in open battle on the streets of Belfast."

Humphrey Grimes leaned forward and placed his forearms on his legs, his folded hands between his knees. "Belfast reminds me of a large basket full of crabs," he said with a distinct Oxford accent, looking at the Death Merchant. "These people don't want the war to end. If one of the crabs tries to crawl out, the others reach up and pull him back in. Ask the Protestants and they'll tell you that the Pope is the enemy. The Catholics scream that anti-Catholicism is the root cause. The truth is that it's a three-sided war: the Protestant bigots, the papist bigots, and us, the British, caught in the middle.'

"It's enough to make a man an atheist," Ford said, poker-faced.

"Don't forget the people behind the scenes who profit," suggested the Death Merchant. "The center of world terrorism is Tripoli, Libya. That madman Qaddafi underwrites and directs a lot of terrorism in this part of the world."

"You're right, Ringgall," agreed Jesse Anson. "The IRA has a permanent representative in Tripoli. The IRA contact arranges for arms, ammo, and explosives to be smuggled periodically from Libya into Northern Ireland."

"No doubt that is true," Windrow said evenly, a trace of a smile on his thin lips. "However, we should like to remind you both that at least fifty percent of the arms captured in

14

Northern Ireland are of American design. More than half of them were shipped directly from the United States. Literally hundreds of Armalite rifles—no doubt stolen from American armories—have shown up in Belfast and other cities and towns in Northern Ireland."

Anson's face retained its masklike rigidity. The expression on Richard Camellion's face did not change. McLoughlin remained a sphinx.

Robert Ford added bluntly, "We have evidence that certain Irish—American organizations in the United States sent $823,000 to Northern Ireland. Another $213,000 was sent again between 1971 and 1973. We don't have the figures for the years 1976 through 1980. We do know that one of the two chief recipients of the money was Joe Cahill. He was the Provo quartermaster until his arrest in 1973 by the Irish Navy. They caught him smuggling arms and ammo into Northern Ireland."

The Death Merchant's mouth twisted slightly as he turned and looked at Jesse Anson. "We should make some kind of comment, wouldn't you say?"

Anson stared at the three British SIS agents. "The CIA is not responsible for lax laws that make it possible for Irish—American organizations to send money, supposedly for 'relief,' to Northern Ireland," he said grimly. "We are well aware of the various Irish–American organizations involved in this mess. We know about them from the files of the Foreign Agents' Registration Office in Washington. Furthermore, the Department of Justice vigorously prosecutes those Americans who illegally assist the IRA. Unfortunately, there's a certain well-known Irish–American U.S. senator who helps people accused by our Justice Department of smuggling arms to Northern Ireland. Sometimes this Senator's brinkmanship frightens even the IRA, especially his demand for overnight withdrawal of British troops." Anson paused momentarily, his eyes becoming hard. "You men know as well as I do that for generations, American politicians have made their careers by sticking their fingers into the boiling pot of Ireland, hoping to snatch political advantage out of other people's misery without burning their own hands. The Irish–American senator I just spoke of is a consummate practitioner of this art."

"And his name?" inquired Robert Ford.

"I don't feel it would be dignified to give his name," Anson said, "not to nationals of another country."

The three British SIS officers nodded, Humphrey Grimes

saying, "Your American senator who plays the Green Card reminds me of Randolph Churchill, who played the Orange Card in Ulster in the 1880s."

The Death Merchant sighed loudly to attract attention.

"Now that we have decided that the CIA is not responsible for all the laws passed in the United States, suppose we get down to business and try to figure out how the IRA knew that Weaver and I were coming to Belfast."

Robert Ford, a well-built man in his forties, shifted uncomfortably in his chair and slowly moved the fingers of his right hand across his forehead.

"I think I have a partial answer," he said hesitantly. "I recall that a week ago, when I made contact with Liam O'Connor, I mentioned that SIS was bringing two agents from Dublin to Belfast. I'm sorry. I spoke without thinking."

Chris McLoughlin made a noise of disgust. "Now that is what I call 'top security,' he said contemptuously.

Camellion's blue eyes jumped to Edward Windrow and Humphrey Grimes, both of whom appeared stunned by Ford's admission.

"Mr. Weaver is right," Windrow said harshly, turning to Ford. "Such a blunder on your part, Bob, is inexcusable. If we weren't so short-handed over here, I'd send you back to London for a reprimand."

"It was a mistake on my part," Ford admitted without any hesitation. "I'm sorry. I expect the breach of security to be put on my record."

"It will be." Windrow glanced through one of the windows at the deepening twilight, then got up, went over to both windows, and pulled the drapes tightly shut. McLoughlin, who was closest to the light switch, got up and turned on the single light bulb hanging from the ceiling by a twisted length of blue electric cord.

Camellion surprised Windrow, who was returning to his chair, and the other men, by saying, "Ford, you didn't make too big a slip to O'Connor. You didn't know our names or the day of our arrival, much less the train we'd be on. The leak didn't come about from anything you told O'Connor. There has to be another explanation."

"I'm glad you don't hold it against me, Mr. Ringgall," Ford said, sounding relieved.

Camellion stretched out his long legs. "We all make mistakes. What we must do is turn your slip of the tongue to our advantage." He looked at Sean Briscoe, who was sitting

16

quietly, deep in thought, puffing on his pipe. "Briscoe, you belong to the same Officials cell as O'Connor. Did he mention anything to you about two SIS agents coming from Dublin? Or did anyone else mention it?"

"If Liam O'Connor or another member had said anything about it, don't you think I would have reported it at once, even before you and your friend arrived in Belfast? Me boy, you've got to remember that the IRA, Provos and Officials, is no longer a ragtag army of boozy boyos."

"He's speaking the truth." Windrow's tone was guarded. "We thought we had the bloody Provo bastards on the run, and we had good reasons for such a belief. Mass arrests by our army had resulted in men and women experts in guerrilla warfare being jailed and not replaced. There was little or no leadership in Dublin, where the top IRA men live in comparative safety and plan strategy. Our intelligence reports indicated that Keenan McGuire—he's the head of the Provos in Ulster—is reputed to have called Rory O'Brady and other top IRA men in Ireland a pack of cowards. O'Brady is the head of the Provisional Sinn Fein Party, the political arm of the Provos."

Humphrey Grimes got up from his chair and began to pace up and down, saying in a low voice, "We found out how wrong our estimates were when the Provos murdered Lord Mountbatten and massacred eighteen British soldiers at La Mon. The biggest worry in London, as well as in Dublin, is that the IRA is no longer a bunch of drunken hoodlums fueled by romantic ideas of Irish nationalism . . . not anymore."

"Give us your present assessment of the situation," Jesse Anson said, knitting his brows as he engaged in some very rapid mental gymnastics.

Windrow gave the Americans the brutal facts: the new IRA was a streamlined fighting force made up of secret cells with a high degree of technical skill. The British Army and SIS were dealing with a well-trained, well-armed, capable enemy.

"It was Keenan McGuire who did away with the cumbersome battalions and brigades." Windrow looked apprehensive. "He dismantled them almost a year ago and replaced them with cells of not more than ten men. There's very good security, with only the cell leaders having links to the higher command. That kind of operation is hard to crack."

"We're lucky that we have Briscoe in one of the Officials

17

cells," commented Grimes. He sat down and glanced at his watch.

The Death Merchant hooked his thumbs over his belt buckle. "Do you have estimates on the total Provo force in Ulster?"

"Between a thousand and twelve hundred hardcore fighters," replied Windrow, scratching the end of his chin. "Fortunately they have little support among the rank-and-file Catholics, who think of them as murderous savages."

Ford said quietly, "Every outfit of any size has its quotient of psychopaths who kill for the love of killing, and the IRA has more than its share. At the same time the revamped IRA is more of a thinking organization than it previously was. Its members are more cautious; they plan more carefully and have tighter discipline. Another thing—"

The more the three SIS agents talked, the more Camellion and McLoughlin realized that The Company Center in Langley, Virginia, should have coded the mission: Impossible. Not only was the IRA highly organized, it had also acquired a formidable armory. The guerrillas had developed a homemade mortar, known as the Mark 10, that could hurl fifty pounds of explosives several miles. They made their own napalm bombs by mixing recrystallized ammonium nitrate with gasoline. They had learned to trigger bombs by remote control, using a radio device designed to operate model airplanes and boats.

To make matters worse for the British government, the SIS, and the British Army, IRA finances were in good shape, with funds flowing in constantly from Irish sympathizers in the U.S., from Libya, and from the Palestinian Liberation Organization in the Middle East. Like American gangsters in the 1930s, the IRA was also in the "protection" racket. Pubs and businesses all over Ireland and Northern Ireland paid for "protection" from violent attacks on their property. Kidnappings and bank robberies netted another $5 million annually.

More bad news was the secret report by Brigadier James Glover of the British Defense Intelligence Staff. The conclusion of this report was that the IRA campaign of violence "is likely to continue while the British remain in Northern Ireland." The IRA active service units, continued the reports, "are manned by terrorists tempered with up to ten years of operational experience, and we foresee a continued trend toward greater professionalism. Under the leadership of Keenan "The Bomber" McGuire and his aides, we can expect greater violence, more bombings and more killings."

"The report didn't mention the low morale of the British troops in Northern Ireland," Robert Ford said, making an angry face.

Chris McLoughlin's face wore a faint smile. "We didn't think the job would be easy. It seems to me that if anyone should know how arms and ammo are being smuggled in, that man should be McGuire."

"Tell us something we don't already know, Yank," Grimes said casually, but with a faint trace of mockery. "We've been trying to grab that maniac for the past five years. No insult intended, but I doubt if you and Weaver will have any better luck."

McLoughlin grinned innocently. "Our methods always work."

Jesse Anson frowned. All he knew about "Ringgall" and "Weaver" was that they were special contract agents for the Company. To him the situation was intolerable. Not only did he dislike contract agents, but worse, his orders from the Chief-of-Station in Dublin were to do exactly as "Ringgall" said. Anson decided not to comment.

"We believe that the shortest distance between two points is a straight line," the Death Merchant said pleasantly. "By this I mean that we reduce a problem to its basic components, then take a direct route, the shortest route."

Sean Briscoe shook his head and puffed on his pipe.

Trying not to appear amused, Edward Windrow looked calmly at the Death Merchant. "That's all very interesting, Mr. Ringgall. Where do you and Mr. Weaver intend to start?"

"With Liam O'Connor," Camellion said promptly. "I intend to have a heart-to-heart talk with him—as soon as you can arrange it."

"Tomorrow night at the earliest," Windrow replied. He didn't know why, but suddenly he had an uneasy feeling about Ringgall. A highly experienced SIS agent, trained in psychology, he detected a strangeness about Ringgall, an eerie quality he couldn't quite put his finger on. Yet the weirdness was there, and it was frightening.

All at once, Windrow felt sorry for Keenan McGuire and the IRA terrorists in Northern Ireland.

CHAPTER THREE

The smooth purring of the armored vehicle's Rolls Royce engine seemed extra loud in the stark quietness of the burned-out section of Massey—five square blocks in south Belfast that had once been solidly Roman Catholic. Here on Skerries Street, the houses showed the hideous results of the holocaust. On either side of the street, the buildings with their blank, burned-out windows reminded the Death Merchant of caves, or hives. Useless rubble . . . collapsed roofs, crumbling walls, and staircases that climbed up to missing second stories. Half-burned furniture sitting in debris-littered yards.

In the Beaverette M-7 were Camellion, McLoughlin, the driver, and Major Alex Shades, the latter of whom was a tough-looking man in his forties. He was the battle-hardened commander of Green Jackets Unit 4. When he smiled, which was seldom, his cheeks bulged up, turning his eyes into evilly good-natured slits.

"As you can see, the UVF did a good job on this section," Major Shades said matter-of-factly. "On the other hand, the Provos have put the torch to a lot of Protestant homes. Only a few months ago, some four hundred houses on Farringdon and two adjoining streets went up in flames after the residents were warned anonymously to get out. Another thing about the IRA is that often they don't wait for the date on the evacuation order."

Not replying, Richard Camellion continued to study both sides of the street. Dressed in tiger-striped fatigues, as were the other men, he reflected on how Edward Windrow had arranged for him and McLoughlin to tour some of the battle-blackened areas of Belfast; Windrow had also obtained identity cards that identified "Warren Jasper Ringgall" and "George Allen Weaver" as members of the British Defense Command in Belfast. With the blue ID cards was a red card that permitted them to carry concealed weapons.

The Death Merchant eyed the slowly moving column of

21

seven armored vehicles. Out in front, taking the point, were two Hubler VI armored cars, the 37-mm cannon in the turret of one car swung to the left, the cannon of the other to the right. Behind the two Hublers was the Beaverette, a cross between a troop carrier and an armored car. There was no turret. The sides and rear were 75-mm armor plate. The driver sat behind a "windshield" that was also 75-mm armor plate, his view of the road made possible by a five-by-sixteen-inch slit opening. To the right of the driver was a vertical slit and a U-coupling. To the coupling was mounted a Bren .303 light machine gun. The open top of the Beaverette could be covered by accordion-shaped armor plate that could be pulled up from the interior sides of the vehicle. Against small arms and heavy machine gun fire, the Beaverette was ideal. Against fire bombs—*this baby is a death trap. I'd just as soon ride in a furnace that's about to be lighted.*

On each side of the Beaverette was an eight-wheeled Harrington MK7 troop carrier, thirty soldiers in each large vehicle.

To the rear, behind the Beaverette and the two Harringtons, were two more Hubler VI armored cars, their 37-mm cannons pointed at opposite sides of the street.

A long brick wall in front of a gutted three story house, caught Camellion's eye. Written in chalk, in block letters, were the words:

> *Wrap the green flag round me, boys,*
> *To die were far more sweet,*
> *With Erin's noble emblem, boys,*
> *To be my winding sheet.*

"Fanatics—every bloody one of them, Catholic and Protestant alike," growled Major Shades, who had also noticed the poem. "The Catholics feel persecuted and the Protestants are afraid that the IRA will overthrow the state of Ulster. The result is that both sides act like they're under siege, and I guess they are. So far, all we've managed to do is push the two sides back into their own neighborhoods. They call those ghettos 'our frontier towns.' Crazy as loons, every bloody one of the bastards."

"It must be terrible for the children," remarked Chris McLoughlin.

"They're marked for life," said Major Shades. "By the time a child finishes grammar school, his attitudes are fixed and he sees Catholics or Protestants as a natural enemy, as the people who are going to burn them out and shoot and kill him and his parents. There's nothing you can do with a child after he gets out of school . . . nothing.

"You can't reason with any of them—either side. I remember the time we stationed ourselves around the predominantly Catholic areas and had to face the Protestants. The IRA would roar out of those areas in their cars. They'd throw petrol bombs, shoot up everything all around them, and then go back into their areas. And they managed to do this through our ranks! Now just imagine a situation like that with the British Army, maybe four or five on a patrol, standing on a street corner. A car flies through them, throws a few nail bombs within vision and hearing as it scoots around the districts, fires through a lot of Protestant windows, then rushes back in through the patrol into the Catholic area. Multiply that by a thousand, and you'll get what's happening all over Belfast."

"At least you British army boys outnumber the fighting units of the IRA and UDA," commented the Death Merchant.

"Yes, for all the good it does us." Shades went on to explain that the only worry the British didn't have was the Irish Republic's army, which was mainly a ceremonial force and was outnumbered by even the Royal Ulster Constabulary, not to mention the regular British Army units stationed in Ulster. It was the possibility of a full-scale civil war in Northern Ireland that was a dry rot in the Home Office in London. In the event of a civil war, it was more than conceivable that large numbers of fiercely proud and patriotic men in the Irish Republic's army would defect to the IRA.

Holding the steel ride-bars, Major Shades frowned in bitterness. "It wouldn't be so bad if the Provos and the Officials were poorly armed, although the Officials don't have the number and quality of weapons possessed by the Provos. The Provos have every kind of weapon imaginable, including the Russian AK47 assault rifle, the U.S. M16, and demolition supplies. Hell, everything from timed explosive pencils to radio-controlled detonators. And they know how to use what they've got. The Black Geese see to that."

"Black Geese?" McLoughlin raised an eyebrow.

"Hold it. We're coming to an intersection," growled Shades.

Slowly the column of seven armored vehicles approached the four corners of Skerries Street and Carncormick Avenue.

"Intersections are always dangerous," explained Shades.

"The IRA paddywhacks just love a crossfire at an intersection."

Close to the intersection, the two lead Hublers picked up speed. So did the other five vehicles. With precision, the entire column turned to the right on Carncormick avenue.

Major Shades turned and gave McLoughlin what was supposed to be a grin. "The Black Geese are Ireland's 'special birds,' " he said in his gravelly voice. "They're professional soldiers who have fought in every climate and trouble spot on earth . . . men like that murderous sonofabitch 'Bomber' McGuire, or Clyde Lynch, one of McGuire's lieutenants. McGuire was in the French Foreign Legion when he was only eighteen. He's seen action with the French in Vietnam and later in what was French Algeria. Lynch was once in the employ of some sand fly of a Sheikh in Arabia. Those two and only God knows how many others are up here in the north. You know why? Because they're convinced that we can be taken, that the British Army will lose in the end. You know something else—they're right!"

Major Shades then explained that the main difficulty of the British Army was that there wasn't any way it could be turned loose in an all-out punitive campaign against the IRA. The IRA had always known of this flaw and had made it an integral part of its strategy. Public opinion throughout the world wouldn't stand for reprisal executions.

"Look what happened when the press learned about our interrogation procedures," growled Shades. "We were made to look like sadists out of the Spanish Inquisition. That's when your Senator Edward Kennedy demanded the withdrawal of all British troops from Ulster."

"Don't say 'our' Senator Kennedy," the Death Merchant snapped. "That gas bag wouldn't make a third-rate dogcatcher."

"Somebody should tell him that Northern Ireland is a part of Great Britain. I wonder what he would say if a British politician demanded that the U.S. Army withdraw all its forces from the State of Texas?"

Shades lapsed into silence. The worldly-wise McLoughlin caught Camellion's eyes but wisely remained silent. The Death Merchant winked but didn't speak. Privately he agreed with Major Shades. Great Britain was destined to lose in Ulster for a variety of reasons: even though the IRA was outlawed in both the north and the south, the Irish Republic to the south would always serve as a sanctuary for IRA killers

24

on the run. This meant that the IRA forces wouldn't be diffused; they would only be transferred to different locales. There was the undeniable fact that the British Army was prevented from employing its full strength. Another strike against the British was that much of the population of Northern Ireland was sympathetic to the IRA and was prepared to give it full support. More importantly, the IRA was tightly controlled and could be directed in accord with a strategical plan. Time, the faceless It that was always against Camellion, was on the side of the IRA, which could perform its operations over a long period of time and on a rising scale, and in so doing wear down British opposition. Finally, even if the British Army could succeed in stabilizing the bloody situation in Ulster, the British had too small a force to carry out any prolonged occupation and still meet its defense obligations to NATO—*which explains why the Russians want to keep the blood flowing in Ulster.*

The houses on Carncormick Avenue resembled the burned-out Victorian hulks on Skerries Street. They, too, were gaunt, blackened monuments to that special kind of stupidity generated by religious bigotry.

Half a block ahead, to the right, they saw an old woman bending down by the curb. Wearing a long, dirty coat as protection against the spring chill, she was crouched in the gutter, catching water in an empty can. When she spotted the first two Hublers, she got to her feet, hurried up the walk to a fire-destroyed building, and stood defiantly in the doorway, shaking both her fists at the armored column as it passed by, and screaming in a high voice dripping anger and hatred: "God damn you Prot bastards to hell! Get your dirty British asses out of our country!"

Major Shades uttered a low, bitter laugh. "To the Catholics we're Protestant bastards, the 'invaders' from Britain. To the Protestants, even the Loyalists, we're ineffective bastards. They feel that we've had eleven years to drive out the IRA and haven't done the job. And by God, we haven't. That old bitch back there—you can't blame her. In all this filth and squalor, hate is the only antidote for despair."

"I'm surprised that people are still in the area," commented Chris McLoughlin. "Does that old woman actually live back there, in one of the buildings?"

"Probably. A lot of these wrecked houses have one or more occupants, people who don't have anywhere to go, people too proud to accept welfare—'stinking Queen's money' as they call it."

"And you don't try to drive them out?" asked McLoughlin.

"We don't have the manpower. If we did, we wouldn't. It would be too dangerous. The IRA also uses those houses."

On either side of the road, there wasn't anything but destruction, And where there weren't any hulks of buildings, there were lots filled with rubble. Many of the burned-out houses had collapsed. There were webs of pipes, twisted masses of wire, and hundreds of boards that, collapsed in a heap, looked like a giant's game of pick-up-sticks. There were bricks, hundreds of thousands of bricks. . . .

The Death Merchant knew the scorched earth policy would continue, for vacant buildings always breed vacant buildings, just as fires breed fires. Once an entire block is deserted, the surrounding blocks catch the cancer, and they too begin to empty. After a neighborhood is gutted, fires would appear in adjacent communities.

Yet it's the British who are the "sadists out of the Spanish Inquisition!" mused the Death Merchant. *The world demands that the British be gentle with IRA killers, with men who murder innocent women and children. I'm not bound by any such silly sentiments. The IRA has made a mockery of religion. They have turned their Hail Marys and Our Fathers into exploding bombs and burning homes. Their mass is the rattle of a machine gun, their Angelus a grenade.*

There wasn't a single human being in all of Ireland who knew it, and only Courtland Grojean, the chief of the CIA's Counterintelligence Section, suspected it—but the Cosmic Lord of Death and all his forces were about to be unleashed in Northern Ireland.

Starting tonight—with Liam O'Connor. . . .

26

CHAPTER FOUR

A quarter moon hung in a dark sky splattered with drifting clouds, and there was little traffic on the streets. There were plenty of British and RUC patrols. Three times members of the Royal Ulster Constabulary stopped the sedan and politely asked the driver for his identity card, which stated that he was Wilbur Grenfell, with the rank of Master-Sergeant in Special Unit 3 of the Queen's Fourth Guards. As any Irish schoolchild knew, SU3 was the intelligence section of the Queen's Fourth Guards.

Twice a British Army patrol stopped the car and demanded that all four men produce identification. Each time, the officer in charge of the patrol became very respectful when he looked at Robert Ford's card and saw that he was a member of M15 Branch 5, British Military Intelligence.

After the car had been stopped the second time and then had been waved on, Chris McLoughlin uttered a tiny, polite laugh.

"Ford, I gather that you SIS fellows never carry SIS ID cards," he said, his tone curious. "I noticed at the last stop that the officer mentioned M15. I assume your cover over here is British military intelligence."

"I doubt if you have 'Central Intelligence Agency' stamped on your passport, Mr. Weaver," Ford said slyly. "You and Mr. Ringgall are freelance journalists. We in SIS are like you CIA chaps. We never advertise who we really are."

Camellion nudged McLoughlin with his knee and, when Chris glanced at him, shook his head slowly from side to side. Later, the Death Merchant would tell him that it was considered bad form to discuss such matters even with intelligence agents of friendly powers.

"We're only five blocks from Liam O'Connor's house on St. George's Street," the driver said, giving Ford, next to him in the front seat, a quick glance. "The back or the front?"

"Take the alley. We'll go into the flat through the rear. You

27

wait at Point Seven, and we'll phone when we're ready for you to pick us up."

The driver nodded. Ford turned slightly, and said over his shoulder, "If he waited in front of the flat, a passing patrol—either one of ours or the RUCs—would stop and ask him a lot of questions."

"It makes sense," Camellion said, "as long as some trigger-happy Protestant doesn't mistake us for Catholics and use us for target practice."

"There's little danger of that," Ford replied congenially. "This entire area is as anti-Catholic as Martin Luther. If anyone sees us, and no doubt they will, they'll think we're UDA. It's to the south, past Grosvenor Road, Howard Street, and May Street that you'll find 'Fortress Rome.' In the outskirts, Gilnahirk and Andersontown are as Catholic as St. Peter's in Rome."

"I should think it would be recriminatory to ask if there are any mixed neighborhoods left in Belfast," Camellion said humorously.

"It would be, yes," murmured Ford. "There used to be numerous Catholic and Protestant neighborhoods. Then the troubles started. In predominantly Protestant neighborhoods, the Roman Catholic minority was soon burned out. In areas that were chiefly Catholic, Protestant homes went up in smoke. Now each side has its own ghettos. As you Yanks would say, it's a Mexican standoff. It's the same in Newry, Londonderry, Ballycastle, and other towns. Ulster is one big armed camp. But the worst is Belfast. All you two have to do is look out of your sixth floor window in the Europa and you can see the whole damned mess."

"The Europa is comfortable enough," Camellion said, "though I've seen better service in hotels in Addis Ababa."

"And you didn't have to worry about the hotel in Ethiopia being blown up," added McLoughlin. "We can't say the same for the Europa."

"Yes, I realize the disadvantages of your staying at the Europa," Ford said apologetically. "However, it's necessary for your cover, since you're both freelance journalists. If you were stopped and gave the address of one of our safe houses, you'd blow your cover to our army people, or to the RUCs. As we explained earlier, both the IRA and the UDA have their sympathizers in the RUC. Then too, all foreign journalists stay at the Europa."

Sergeant Grenfell turned the Mazda onto Mallow Street

and began to slow down as the vehicle approached the center of the block.

Robert Ford rolled down the window on his side. "I always count the garbage cans on the fight side of the alley," he explained. "That way I always know when we're in back of Liam O'Connor's building."

Grenfell turned the car into the alley and, at greatly reduced speed, headed the Mazda toward the yard in the rear of the apartment building where O'Connor lived.

"This is it," Robert Ford said within a few minutes. Grenfell stopped the car and the three men got out. By the time Grenfell was pulling out of the other end of the alley Ford, Camellion, and McLoughlin were halfway to one of the rear doors of the old building, their eyes straining against the darkness.

"A perfect place for an ambush," McLoughlin muttered under his breath, his right hand wrapped around the cold butt of a 9-mm Beretta pistol in his trench coat's pocket.

"Almost anywhere in Belfast is ideal for an ambush," Camellion said. "Northern Ireland is Vietnam all over again, only the jungle is concrete and bricks. But the killing is the same. Dying and death never change."

Once inside the building, they found themselves at the end of a long, gloomy hall lighted only by a single bulb set in a wall fixture. The building itself was Victorian, right out of the 1880s—high ceilings, high, curved baseboards, and walls coated with several dozen layers of wallpaper.

The three men came to the end of the hall, briefly surveyed the grimy foyer and the front door, then turned and silently started up the creaky stairs. All three had the feeling they were moving through a musty mausoleum, except for the cooking odors. The smell of boiled cabbage was strong in the air.

In a very short time, they were on the third floor and Ford was knocking softly on Liam O'Connor's door. A sturdy, middle-aged woman opened the door, a woman who had two narrow coin-slots of eyes that screwed up even tighter as she scrutinized the three men. Her stringy hair made it look as if she had been wearing a cheap wig that needed cleaning. Wordlessly, Mrs. O'Connor ushered them into a small living room, then quietly disappeared into another room of the cramped apartment.

Without smiling, Liam O'Connor got up from a sofa that had seen better days, looked expectantly at Ford, then stared anxiously at Camellion and McLoughlin, neither of whom Ford bothered to introduce by name.

"These are the two men from Dublin," Ford said, taking off his topcoat. "I mentioned them to you a week ago, or don't you remember?"

A tall, big-boned man with sandy hair, sharp features, and a prominent Adam's apple, O'Connor appeared puzzled as he watched Camellion and McLoughlin sit down on ordinary chairs. Neither man had removed his coat.

"I remember," O'Connor admitted in a thick Irish brogue. He sat down on the couch and began to fidget with his bony fingers. "What has that to do with this meeting? You said on the phone that it was a matter of great importance."

"Either the Provos or the Officials knew they were coming," Ford said in a none-too-gentle tone. "There was an ambush waiting for them in the Great Victoria Street Station."

Surprise, then anger flickered over O'Connor's wind-hardened face. A crane operator on the Dufferin Dock, his skin had the look of sun-hardened leather.

"You'd be accusing me, you would, of setting them up," he bit out, his Adam's apple bobbing up and down. "Is that what you believe?"

"We believe that the gunmen, whether Provos or Officials, had advance information about us," the Death Merchant interjected brusquely. "Someone had to talk. He tells us"—he jerked his head toward Ford—"he told you and no one else."

Camellion, watching O'Connor sink deeper into the couch and his mouth take on new lines of tightness, mentally analyzed the man's record. Liam O'Connor was one of the "invisible" members of the IRA, a Roman Catholic living in a non-Catholic neighborhood—a "fallen away" Catholic in O'Connor's case—posing as a diehard Protestant. A member of the Ulster Defense Association, as well as of the UVF, O'Connor was an SIS informer for one reason only—money. The British Secret Intelligence Service only half-trusted O'Connor and was always dubious about any information he turned in. The Death Merchant didn't trust him at all. *Who can trust a paid informer? But suppose his true loyalty is actually with the IRA? Where is the proof that he's not really a Provo, spying not only on the UDA and the UVF but on SIS as well? A very good theory—which is destroyed by the ugly fact that all the information O'Connor has passed to SIS has been proved to be accurate.*

Liam O'Connor's fixed stare did not retreat from the Death Merchant's penetrating appraisal.

"I admit he told me that two men were due to arrive from Belfast. Special Agents, he said. He didn't give names or descriptions. He didn't tell me the day you two lads would arrive. He didn't tell me what train you would be on. To say that I am responsible for the ambush is a lot of blarney."

"O'Connor is right," Ford said gloomily. "At the time, I didn't even have the information. As far as I knew, you two could have been midgets flying in on kites."

"Did you divulge the information to anyone else?" Camellion looked steadily at O'Connor. He noticed that next to the wall, close to the door between the living room and the kitchen, four cases of empty beer bottles were stacked up. Next to the cases, a black cat lay curled in relaxed sleep.

"Your wife, for instance," cut in McLoughlin, his stare as sharp as the ends of two icepick blades.

O'Connor bristled and thrust out his jaw in anger. "My missus and me are one and the same, we are. We share the same bed and the same secrets. She knows it's a wise head that makes for a still tongue. Her tongue is tight at both ends."

"The fact that the Provos haven't killed you both is proof that she has a locked mouth," Camellion intoned (*unless both of you are Provo or Officials agents!*), "but did you tell anyone else about us?"

"My brother, only my brother." O'Connor's manner changed to one of extreme nervousness. "I can assure you that Harry didn't repeat the rumor. I didn't—"

"Repeat the rumor!" exploded Ford. Leaning forward, he looked as if he might pounce on O'Connor. "You goddam bloody fool! How could you have told him anything? Next you'll be telling us that you confided in him about your work with us!"

"Let me finish," O'Connor said in desperation. He stood up, an anguished expression on his face. "I only told Harry it was a rumor I had heard from someone in the cell I belong to. I told him I couldn't even remember who had told me. Me brother let it go at that."

O'Connor's explanation did not mollify Robert Ford, who was still furious, conveniently ignoring the salient fact that it had been he who had told O'Connor about the two agents from Dublin. Ford looked up and nailed O'Connor with his eyes. "None of that explains why you had to tell your brother

31

in the first place. What else have you told him? But first, why did you tell him at all?"

Crestfallen, O'Connor sat back down, his eyes cast downward. "It was a Saturday afternoon," he said reluctantly. "Harry and his missus came visiting, they did. While the women talked, Harry and me went to the Green Lantern down the street to lift a few pints. We got to talking, me and Harry, about the cells we belong to, and discussing the general situation here in Ulster. Harry he—"

"Your brother belongs to the Ulster Defense Association?" interposed the Death Merchant.

"That he does, and he's also a member of the UVF, just like me," O'Connor said quickly. "He's a good man, a decent man who loves God and does right by his wife and children. That he does."

Convinced that it was the believers, the "spiritual" people, who tend to mistake form for substance, prayers for performance, and worship for practice, the Death Merchant withered O'Connor with a scornful glance and said, "You're a Catholic pretending to be a Protestant, and because you're supposed to be a Protestant, you're in the UDA and the UVF. But you're working for SIS."

Frowning, O'Connor eyed Camellion speculatively. "All that is true, but—I don't understand?"

"How do you know that your brother isn't really a Provo spying on the UDA?" offered Camellion. "When you get right down to the nitty-gritty of it, how in hell do we know that you're not a Provo? It's not unusual for Provos to have agents in the cells of Officials, and vice versa."

"But me and my brother Harry are Officials!" O'Connor insisted, his voice hollow, full of shock. "Hell yes, we send reports to the Officials' Command about UDA and UVF plans and activities." He pointed a bony finger at the furious-faced Ford. "He knows that we report to the Officials' Command. Harry and me are doing it with full knowledge and permission of SIS. I mean that I do."

"Would you say that your brother does not suspect you're in the employ of SIS?" Camellion said, his tone sounding as though he were hinting that O'Connor was some kind of traitor.

Before the Irishman could answer, Ford jumped in. "I asked you a direct question, O'Connor," he said through clenched teeth. "Why did you even mention the two men from Dublin to your brother? I want to know why."

A trapped expression dropped over O'Connor's face. He shifted uneasily on the couch, fumbling for words.

"I can tell you why he bumped his gums," McLoughlin said casually, uncrossing his legs. "He was playing the big shot, bragging to his brother, trying to act important."

"I'm inclined to think you're right," Camellion agreed, his smile amiable. "He reminds me of a stockbroker I once knew, a con artist by the name of Varney Halloway, the biggest bag of hot air I ever met. Say 'Good morning' to him and he'd instantly start telling you about all kinds of nonexistent big deals or else start bragging about what a lady killer he was. He even admitted that 'lying is part of the business.' Some joker finally got wise to him, put the screws to him, and now he's out of business."

"O'Connor, don't sit there like a stray brick looking for a building," Ford said sternly in his clipped British accent. "Are they right? You told your brother in a fit of boasting?"

O'Connor seemed to be having trouble with his tongue.

"I guess you could say that," he finally admitted, his tone one of humble deference. "I guess I drank too much ale and got carried away."

None of it actually adds up, Camellion felt a voice inside his head whisper. *Something, some factor, is missing. But I don't know what it is. . . .* He got up, went over to the couch, and sat down on one end, to the right of O'Connor, who turned and looked at him in alarm.

"Relax," Camellion said sympathetically. "The couch is more comfortable than the chair. If I wanted to do you in, you'd never see it coming." He turned his attention to Ford, who, across from him, was carefully adjusting his tie, all the while looking unhappy and worried. "Listen, O'Connor's admitting that he blabbed because the urge to brag got the best of him doesn't tell us how the gunmen waiting in the Victoria Station knew about us. You didn't give O'Connor any vital information. He didn't pass on anything incriminating to his brother."

Grimacing, Ford leaned forward, put an elbow on his right knee, and cupped his chin in his right hand. "We can't discuss it here."

"Would you lads care for a drink?" Liam O'Connor asked, his voice very conciliatory. "Beer? Tea? Coffee perhaps?"

McLoughlin, who neither smoked nor touched alcohol, shook his head. Camellion and Ford also declined with a quick shake of the head.

"Whoever it was waiting for us in the station knew we were due to arrive on that train," McLoughlin said briskly. "For my money, I think it's going to take a miracle for us to find out."

The Death Merchant gave a waggish chuckle. "Miracles are all over the place. Before there were UFOs there was the Devil. Martin Luther not only reported seeing old Satan, but also throwing a book at him. Now that's what I call a miracle! Personally, I place logic and deductive reasoning ahead of miracles, in spite of what they may believe in Ireland."

The Death Merchant leaned back, looked up, contemplated the dirty ceiling, and said, "O'Connor, can you tell us anything about where Keenan McGuire, Clyde Lynch, and Ruairi Paisley might be hiding?"

O'Connor blinked in confusion at Camellion. "The Provos hate the Officials almost as much as they hate the UDA. How could I even hear worthwhile rumors about the Bomber and his two lieutenants?"

"The Provos don't hate the UVF," Camellion pointed out. "You're a member of the UVF and report to the Officials' Command. How do you know there isn't a Provo agent in the Officials' Command?"

"I don't know," O'Connor argued. "But I don't have any idea where McGuire is. And there's no love lost between the Provos and the UVF."

McLoughlin said, "From the reports I've read, some factions of the Ulster Volunteer Force are even more murderous than the IRA."

"That's true," Ford said acidly. "Like last year, when the UVF blew up a bus full of Catholic school children. That bloody biscuit is the ultimate in cowardly attacks. Thirty families 'celebrated' Christmas after burying their children."

"It wasn't my group that done in them tykes," O'Connor said defensively. "We didn't know about it, me and the other lads in my cell, until the news came over the telly. We still don't know who did it, or we'd bash 'em, we would."

"Not even a hint, eh?" smirked the Death Merchant.

"The UDA, and the UVF within the UDA, operate in cells. Each cell is closed," O'Connor explained in a low, nervous voice. "Only the men and women on the UVF Planning Commission know which UVF cell did the job on them tykes. I swear by the Mother of Christ I'm telling you the truth, I am."

34

"I take it then you have no information about McGuire?" Camellion said drily.

"McGuire is always on the move," O'Connor said sincerely. "Why, I tell you, lads, only a handful of top Provos ever know where he is. The Republic's police are after him. The British want him and the RUCs want to hang him. He could be anywhere—Belfast, Londonderry, or maybe south in Dublin. Who knows?"

The mention of Dublin was the perfect opportunity for McLoughlin, who said to Camellion with a great deal of enthusiasm, "How nice it would be if McGuire were in Dublin and if we could lure him to the safe house on Bynner Street. We could—"

"Damn it! Shut up!" Camellion said savagely, the wrath of hell on his lean face. "All you forgot to mention was the address."

"Sorry, old man," mumbled McLoughlin.

The Death Merchant swung around on the couch to stab O'Connor with a warning stare. "Forget what you just heard. If you tell your brother about that safe house on Bynner Street, even Satan won't be able to protect you. Understand, me boy?"

O'Connor nodded, his face full of fear. "I—I won't tell a living soul. I swear it."

"See that you don't," Camellion said approvingly. "We still want information about McGuire. We don't expect you to put your head on the chopping block. Be damned careful. But we want to know anything you hear about McGuire, any rumor, no matter how slight it is."

"All I ever hear about McGuire is general gossip," O'Connor begged off. "Why, good Lord! Your people hear more than we do, at least as much."

Ford got up and walked over to the old-style telephone on the wall next to the door between the living room and one of the bedrooms. While he put in the call to Sergeant Grenfell, the Death Merchant did some hard thinking. McLoughlin had played his role like a well-trained actor; his "slip" about the safe house in Dublin had been perfect. It would have been too convenient, too obvious, if Chris had let "slip" the street number. There was a safe house on Bynner Street, one that was a joint effort of British SIS and the Irish Republic's secret service. If Liam O'Connor was a double agent and reported the information to the Provos, it would not be too difficult for the

Provos in Dublin to decide which building was the safe house. Bynner Street was only a block long.

There were no guarantees—*the Provos might suspect a trap. If O'Connor is a spy and working against us, the Provos might very well suspect it's a trap. At least they don't know about the safe house on Mervue Street. No, they can't—unless that tall drink of water, Briscoe, is a Provo plant.* . . .

Robert Ford came back to the chair, sat down, and looked at his watch. "We'll wait another ten minutes, then go down to the foyer. He'll pick us up in front of the building." He added, "O'Connor, we'll contact you again in a week. You'll get the usual phone call first. We don't want to pop in while you're entertaining. Don't forget McGuire. Concentrate on him."

O'Connor nodded and swallowed, his Adam's apple going up and down like a yoyo.

While they waited, O'Connor brought up the subject of the old people in Belfast, mentioning that it was they—Catholics and Protestants alike—who were suffering the most. Homes they had lived in for thirty or forty years and longer had been destroyed by fire. Now the government had warehoused the elderly in run-down residential hotels, hotels with mockingly grand names like "The Plaza" and "The Riviera."

"It was President De Gaulle who said that old age is like a shipwreck," commented McLoughlin. "I guess he knew. He navigated it well."

"It's the same with old folks the world over," Camellion said, thankful that he would never experience the miseries of old age. "It's that constant sense of being superfluous, of being useless, that causes so much depression in the frigid years of life—that and the solitude."

"The young also become depressed," McLoughlin said, "and kill themselves."

Camellion agreed with a nod of his head. "Yes, but generally speaking the young can bear solitude better than the old because passion occupies their thoughts. For the elderly, ailments and anxieties have replaced passions as the only avenue of escape from the melancholy that usually accompanies a retrospective cast of mind."

"There is an old Irish saying," Ford said. " 'Old rivers grow wider, old trees grow stronger, but old people just grow more lonesome and more alone.' "

"There isn't any overall answer," McLoughlin said with a shrug.

36

"Oh yes there is," Camellion said. "A realist knows that every human being is born alone and dies alone. So he never loves anyone or lets anyone love him. He remains an observer, but never becomes one of the observed."

McLoughlin smiled cunningly. "A man like that would never reach old age. He'd be like us."

"Precisely—and that's your answer. Make damn sure you don't grow old."

"Let's get down to the foyer," Ford said. He got up and put on his topcoat. As O'Connor ushered them to the door, the Death Merchant spotted a cartoon pasted on the wall to the left of the door. It showed a little man with a gun sitting in a graveyard. Underneath was the caption: *Here I am, the last livin' person in Ireland, and I can't remember if I'm Catholic or Protestant.* . . .

CHAPTER FIVE

After St. Patrick and other men of God brought Christianity into Ireland during the first half of the fifth century, a slow change came over the organization of the Irish Church. Instead of bishoprics, as existed in other Roman Catholic countries, a network of monasteries—each under the rule of its own abbot—was established, this system flourishing until the twelfth century.

One of these ancient monasteries was known as Skellig Michael. Dedicated to the Archangel Michael, the monastery lay on an island known as the Greater Skellig which is in Lough Foyle.

Skellig Michael is a huge, precipitous mass of slate rock that rises 705 feet above the water—two miles north of the coastal village of Ballykelly and sixteen miles northeast of Londonderry.

The monastery is at the top, the church, the monks' cells, the oratory, the refectory, and other buildings built of rock. The cells are laid out on a terrace, not in a monotonous line like a modern housing estate, but in such a way as to offer an unexpected surprise around every corner. The cells and the other buildings are built of numerous small stones placed in a circular fashion and layered on one another in an irregular patchwork, jutting ever inward, creating buildings that resemble beehives. Yet while the buildings are round outside, they are square inside. The simple doorways, with straight sides and flat lintels, lead into a dark interior. Once a visitor's eyes grow accustomed to the gloom, it can be seen how ingeniously the stones were laid to prevent collapse.

But Keenan McGuire and the three men and two women with him in the monk's cell were not the least bit interested in the architecture of the buildings. For the past three years, McGuire and the Provos had used old monasteries and other ruins all over Ireland as meeting and hiding places, excepting those that were tourist attractions. The burned-out ruin of

39

Moore Hall near Ballinrobe in the Republic of Ireland, once the home of novelist George Moore, was a major storage depot. Buried in the basement were ten cases of Czech Skorpion VZ61 submachine guns and forty thousand rounds of 7.65-mm ammo for the deadly little machine pistols. Seven other cases contained Armalite AR18s and 5.56-mm ammunition for the American automatic rifles.

There were other storage depots in Northern Ireland. Five light machine guns, stolen from the British Army, were buried beneath the stones of the ruined Clare Abbey in the meadows outside Larne.

"It's cold in here," Rosemary Keane complained.

"It will be warm soon enough." Keenan McGuire, a big, curly-headed man with a ruddy complexion, turned up the Primus infrared heater, then removed his sheepskin-lined jacket. He knew that with the door tightly closed, the cell would heat up very quickly. Best of all, they didn't have to worry about detection. No one ever came to Skellig Michael. Not even the British Coast Guard bothered with the hunk of useless rock. Even if the British should stop on the coast, the two motorboats were well hidden in a cave, and the three IRA spotters would see them coming in and warn McGuire by walkie-talkie.

"I don't like it," Clyde Lynch, a young man with a short black beard and cunning eyes, said stubbornly. "The Limey Coast Guard cutters are always cruising off Ballycastle, and you know that the Russians don't want to fire on British boats."

Cade O'Brian and Ruairi Paisley, sitting at a table cleaning Heckler and Koch VP70 machine pistols, glanced in annoyance at Lynch, who was sitting on a case of fragmentation grenades, his back against the stones of the wall. Both men were used to Lynch's perpetual pessimism, but held him in high regard for his knowledge of tactics; they knew that this time he was right, but neither was going to say so, not with the ugly mood McGuire was in.

In contrast, Bridget Bowen was not one to keep her thoughts to herself. In her early forties, eleven years the senior of McGuire, Bridget was noted not only for her guerrilla expertise (learned from training with the PLO in the Middle East) but also for her sharp tongue.

"Clyde's right, Keenan," she said in her harsh voice. "We all know how the British patrol the North Channel. And what about their coast guard station on Rathlin Island? I know you haven't forgotten about that!"

"Rosie, open some canned meat and make some tea," McGuire growled at Rosemary Keane. "It's almost 4:30 and we're all hungry."

Rosemary nodded and went over to one of the heavy packs the men had carried up the 840 stone steps that led from the base of the cliff to the level on which the monastery was built.

McGuire gave Lynch a dirty look, then pulled out a chair and sat down at the table, his eyes darting to Bridget Bowen. She reminded him of a woman wearing a steel-belted radial brassiere. But, by God, she wasn't at all bad in bed—even better when the lights were off.

Dressed in brown corduroy pants, a black and red wool plaid shirt, a brown wilderness jacket, and thick-soled walking shoes, Bridget Bowen was a plain-faced woman with big breasts and wide hips, her arms heavy, her hands pudgy. Despite being a fanatical Catholic who wore a rosary around her neck, she didn't let her firm belief in Heaven, Hell, and Purgatory ever interfere when any Provo man who might be hard up wanted to push her into bed.

McGuire said, "All of you are forgetting that right off Ballycastle is the safest place for the Russian sub to come in. Several miles west of Rathlin Island, at three o'clock in the morning, is perfect. The British station is on the other side of the island, and their cutters won't be in the area at that hour of the morning." He banged a big fist on the table, causing O'Brian and Paisley to glance at him in surprise. "We've got to have that bomb. Once we have it hidden in Belfast, we can demand that the British send every single soldier in Northern Ireland back to England or face the results."

"We'd be killing hundreds of our own people if we carried out the threat," Ruairi Paisley said, uncapping a can of oil.

"They would die as martyrs to the cause of nationalism," McGuire said. "Think of the thousands who died before the South was free. There would not be a Republic of Ireland today if it weren't for the IRA. And mark my words, all of you: it will be the IRA that unites Ulster with the rest of Ireland."

"The sub won't have to surface. We have that in our favor," O'Brian said. He shoved the magazine into the butt of the VP70 machine pistol. "Or has that part of the plan been changed?"

McGuire grinned, revealing large tobacco-stained teeth.

41

"The sub will remain submerged. The bomb is only a hundred centimeters long and forty centimeters in diameter—forty inches by fifteen. Once we contact the sub, the Russian bastards will float the bomb to the surface in a container. All we have to do is pull the container on board the boat and head for shore. We'll have three—"

"I've found a few cans of chicken soup," Rosemary Keane called out from one corner of the room. "Anyone want chicken soup? I'll have to heat it first."

"Yeah, some hot chicken soup would go fine." Paisley turned and looked at Rosemary, who was the other half of what he and McGuire and some of the other men in the Provo Command referred to as the "Odd Couple." While Bridget Bowen was unattractive and nymphomaniacal, Rosemary Keane was slim, pretty, and as frigid as the surface of the moon. She did have a figure that could make the juices of any man bubble, but woe to the man who might even hint at bedroom acrobatics. Twenty-eight years old and an ex-nun, Rosemary had very definite ideas about sex. Sex was fine. It was necessary and should be enjoyed, but only within the confines of marriage—and that marriage had better have been performed by a priest. Despite her dogmatic opinion about sex and her fear of mortal sin, Rosemary didn't let any of these scruples interfere with her work for the IRA. One of the worst kind of fanatics, her single goal in life was to unify Northern Ireland with the Irish Republic. It was she who had developed a totally new strategy of terror: putting children in the front ranks of mobs attacking British soldiers, on the theory that the British army units would not fire on children. The practice was discontinued after six children were killed in a Londonderry riot, not because of any compassion on the part of Rosemary Keane or the other high members of the Irish Republican Army. The reason was that the Catholic moderates in both the North and the South were disgusted with such inhuman tactics—and the IRA needed all the support it could get.

"I can't get this new bottle of gas connected to the stove," Rosemary said helplessly.

"God damn it, can't you do anything?" Clyde Lynch said in disgust. He got up from the box of grenades and walked over to where she was trying to attach a propane cylinder to a portable Primus stove resting on an empty crate.

"Don't take the name of the Lord in vain," Rosemary snapped. "It's a mortal sin."

Lynch gave her a disgusted look and took the cylinder out of her hand.

Bridget Bowen finished lighting a British Players cigarette. With her short haircut and full face, she looked more man than woman. "We have three speedboats," she said gruffly. "Should a patrol boat spot us, we can outrun it, or sink it with a missile. What about the shore? We can't fight a British force on land."

"They've got Hublers and Beaverettes in Ballycastle," Lynch called out as he attached one end of the copper tubing to the coupling on the bottle of propane gas. "And the British patrol the shore at all hours, staggering them at different intervals."

"Who the hell gives a damn what the Limeys have in Ballycastle," McGuire said roughly. "We'll hit the shore six miles west of there. The way I have it figured, we can slip in a hundred men and have them scattered along the beach area. We'll have another fifty men, maybe more, scattered along the west road from town, just in case we're spotted by a patrol boat and they radio the Limeys on shore."

Cade O'Brian, a big round man with a friendly baby face, shoved the VP70 machine pistol into a shoulder holster, pushed his leather hat far back on his head, and sucked on a tooth. Finally he intoned solemnly, "I agree with Clyde and Bridget. The pickup is too close to the British Coast Guard Station on Rathlin Island, and when we land on shore, we'll be to damned close to Ballycastle."

"Why can't we move the transfer point fifteen or twenty miles west of Rathlin?" suggested Paisley, glancing sideways at Clyde Lynch, who was coming back from helping Rosemary Keane.

Bridget Bowen jumped in, thinking that she had allies in O'Brian and Paisley, as well as Lynch. "It's a mystery to me why you must persist in attempting this operation so close to British forces!"

Inserted Paisley, "How about the Russians? Those damned nippers won't want to come in that close to the Limey Coast Guard. They're a bunch of no-good atheistic bastards, but they're not noted for being stupid." He stared intently at McGuire, his heavy eyebrows arching. "When do we confirm the location with the Russians at their embassy in Dublin?"

"It's already been confirmed," McGuire said smugly. "A messenger arrived several days ago from Dublin and brought the exact coordinates. The Russians chose the location because of the topography of the North Channel. There's a trench down there that's three kilometers wide and slightly more than fifty-six kilometers long. The sub will creep in along the trench. I couldn't disagree with the location. The Russian devils have the edge. They're giving us the bomb."

"It all makes sense now," Lynch said. He stroked his beard as though it was made of fine silk. "Every time the communist trash gives us a hand, they always make sure that if there's a hooley, they'll be as snug as a bedbug behind a baseboard."

"We can blame them for any trouble," McGuire said with a shrug. "They think they're using us and can move in with their 'advisers' when the time comes."

"We're a long way from the day that all of Ireland will be one land, one nation," Bridget Bowen said bitterly. Exhaling cigarette smoke, she leaned forward and put her elbows on the table. "The Dublin government isn't about to send its troops up here to reclaim the six counties, not unless we can force the UDA into more violence. The regular Irish army isn't any match for an all-out war with the damned Limeys."

"We've got to have a civil war," McGuire said, his voice ringing with determination as solid as steel.

Bridget poked a pudgy finger at him. "I'll tell you another thing, Keenan. "If we threaten the British government with the bomb, and the Limeys call our bluff and we have to explode it, we won't have a friend in the world. A bomb like that would destroy all of Belfast."

"The Arabs would respect us," laughed Ruairi Paisley. "The rest of the world would hate our guts until doomsday."

"Ru, I don't think you're very funny," McGuire said in a low voice, his hard face darkening with anger.

"I'm not trying to be." Paisley held his ground. "I'm saying what the rest of us are saying: the bomb idea is madness. We're all candidates for hanging as it is. We explode that bomb, and there'll be no place on earth where we can hide. Not even the PLO would take us in. Don't try to tell me different."

A man with a hair-trigger temper, McGuire glared ferociously at Paisley and knotted his hands into fists.

Paisley, now regretting that he had spoken his mind, stared right back. A small man, he couldn't win in a fight, and he knew it. But it was better to take a beating than to back down and have the others lose respect for him. He was relieved when Clyde Lynch, behind him, spoke up in a loud, firm voice.

"There's more to it than that damned bomb, Keenan. We and the Council of Seven in Dublin voted you in as Coordinator. Keep acting like a dictator and we'll vote you right out, we will."

Instantly, McGuire jumped to his feet and swung around to face Lynch, knocking the chair to the floor in his haste.

With equal speed, Lynch was on his own feet, his own face filled with dark fury. During that brief moment, the two men measured each other. Both were well muscled, and both weighed in the neighborhood of two-hundred pounds. Both were experienced street fighters.

O'Brian and Paisley froze. Rosemary Keane turned from the Primus stove, where she was frying meat, and stared with some slight amusement.

Bridget Bowen's voice was like the snap of a whip. "Stop this nonsense, both of you! Our difficulties are serious enough without fighting among ourselves. Sit down!"

Slowly the brute savagery and ferocity faded from the faces of McGuire and Lynch, and their muscles relaxed. Still watching McGuire, Lynch sat down on the case of grenades. McGuire stooped, picked up the chair, sat down again at the table, and turned around to look at Rosemary Keane.

"I thought we were going to eat?" he said robustly.

Her golden blonde hair tumbling around her neck and shoulders, Rosemary refused to be intimidated, refused because behind her pretty, almost delicate appearance was a steel toughness that made her more than a match for McGuire in any verbal duel.

"Keenan, don't get smart with me, or you'll get a pan of hot grease in your face." This time her voice didn't have its usual timbre, like that of a good-natured child. Nor had it been sharp, only solid, like a barrel full of hardened concrete.

A calculating smile spread over McGuire's face. He turned, faced the three people at the table and, with an abrupt change of mood, winked at Bridget Bowen, who was putting out her second cigarette.

"Our situation isn't as shaky as all of you might think," McGuire said. "The operation has been worked out to the last detail in my mind."

"I was thinking of what happened back during World War II," Bridget said. "It was during that period that some fool in the IRA command got the stupid idea to help the Nazis by harboring German spies. In return, the Nazis would smuggle them arms by U-boat. The history of what happened is well known. So many leaders of the IRA were hunted down by the De Valera government that the IRA was almost wiped out."

"I remember my father talking about it," Cade O'Brian said. "He said it was the worst mistake the IRA ever made."

"Of course it was," Bridget said. "By 1944 the IRA was in such a terrible state the Belfast leader had to flee the city. He managed to get out of Ireland by joining the Magnet Dance Band as a banjo player. Frank Flynn was the chief of staff in Dublin at the time. He was captured, given a quick trial, and topped."

She stopped talking and gazed solemnly at McGuire, the meaning of her warning clear to everyone: should the IRA detonate a small atomic bomb in Belfast, the explosion might very well mark the beginning of the end of the IRA. The world would not permit such a massacre. The Irishmen in the south would not permit such brutal butchery.

"Time to eat," called out Rosemary Keane.

Cade O'Brian took a big bite out of the hot spam sandwich and started chewing and talking at the same time. "It's the Soviets that worry me, them and their buckshee. The saints preserve us! I'd rather trust the Limeys."

"I wish you wouldn't talk when you're eating," snapped Rosemary Keane. "You sound like some kind of grinding machine."

Continuing to chew, O'Brian did not reply.

McGuire looked genuinely pleased. He had explained his master plan in detail—how to transfer the bomb, get it past the British on the north coast of Ulster, and smuggle the deadly package into Ulster. Finally, he had even succeeded in bringing Bridget Bowen around to his way of thinking, but only after he had explained that they could delay detonating the bomb until they had studied all possible results.

"Who are we going to get to replace O'Faolain? He was a good laddie, he was." Ruairi Paisley wiped his fingers on a handkerchief, then reached for his cigarettes in his jacket pocket.

McGuire moved the mug of tea from his mouth. "We have to find out how the UVF discovered Tomas," he said, his eyes flashing menacingly. "There's a UVF spy in one of our cells. That we know."

"It could take months," Rosemary Keane said. "There are two hundred cells in Ulster, sixty of them in Belfast."

"We will never find out," McGuire said. "It's impossible

46

to check even the men and women in the Belfast cells. It would take years to question all the members."

"The informer might not be in one of the Belfast cells," Clyde Lynch pointed out. "The only thing we can be sure of is that he—or she—is not in our own group."

Thinking of the A-bomb, McGuire didn't reply. He himself was positive of another fact: once the bomb was in Belfast, it would be exploded. To the devil with what the others thought. There was only one way to unite Ireland, and that was to force the issue.

A hundred thousand people going up in a radioactive cloud would do just that. . . .

CHAPTER SIX

The dark night and steady drizzle suited the Death Merchant perfectly. Relaxed in the rear seat of the British Ford (SIS never used the same car twice when approaching the home of an informer), he listened to the weary swish-swish of the windshield wipers and sorted the information that he and Chris McLoughlin had absorbed from reading reports during the previous week.

Chris was right: religious convictions could turn some people into savages and sadists. The men and women—children, too—of North Ireland, both Catholic and Protestant, put even the stone killers of the Mafia to shame. It was the Middle East all over again, only instead of Arabs versus Jews, Allah versus Jehovah, it was Catholic against Protestant—*the reason why the situation here is unique,* mused Camellion. *Both sides are Christians—the damned hypocrites!* Short of the Second Coming of J. Christ, the siege mentality would continue. The fighting would continue for years, riot after riot, death after death. With each new martyrdom, be the victim a "damned Papist" or a "dirty Prot," the determination would be strengthened by blood, for there are no people who place a higher value on martyrdom than the Irish, even if that value is purely emotional. All over Ireland there is hardly a place where some past bloodletting is not marked, either by some kind of plaque or a Celtic cross. Every Sunday there is always some kind of commemoration to this or that long-dead hero or victim of past injustice—going back as far as eight hundred years!

Robert Ford, in the front seat, broke the silence that had lasted almost five minutes. "I still have that uneasy feeling about O'Connor," he said significantly.

"I've had a creepy-crawly feeling ever since we landed at the airport in Dublin," Chris McLoughlin said. He wasn't smiling, and he had not meant the remark as a joke. "At least in Vietnam you had some idea where the battlefield was. Over here, all of Ulster seems to be one big bomb with half a million fuses."

"You did phone O'Connor back," Camellion remarked to Ford, wanting to analyze the response Ford might make. He got what he anticipated.

"Yes, I did," Ford said. "But he didn't sound right. He said all the right words. No company was coming. He managed to work in the word 'sunny,' the key word that everything was all right. But . . ."

"But he didn't sound like he should," Camellion finished casually.

"It could be my imagination. It must be."

"Possibly . . ."

And maybe not. Over the years, Camellion had learned that a truly talented survivor never ignored his instincts, his hunches and intuitive feelings. Right now, they were flashing danger. Here in Belfast, death could come from anywhere, at any time. The IRA and the UVF certainly had the weapons and the methods; especially the IRA, which had techniques that made other terrorists in the world drool with envy. A favorite with the IRA was to drop a V40 mini-grenade into a gas tank, after the pin had been removed and an elastic band was holding the safety lever in place. Gradually the gas would dissolve the elastic band, and then—*blam!* Both sides had special impact grenades with a zero delay mine function—ordinary grenades, with the pins removed and the levers held in place inside glass fruit jars. Homemade thermite—made from iron rust or the hammer scale of pig iron and from aluminum filings or the metallic sparkle additive of paints—would then be poured into the jar around the grenade and the lid screwed on. All one had to do then was throw the jar. . . .

"Two more blocks," Sergeant Grenfell said. "The back or the front?"

"The front," Ford ordered. "I don't feel right about taking the alley tonight. I'll telephone as usual."

"Point seven?"

"Yes. And Sergeant, keep the radio on and turned to 265.5 megahertz. I'm going to take the E-unit with me."

"Let's hope you don't have to use it, sir."

"I hope you're right." Ford opened the glove compartment and took out a device slightly larger than a matchbox. The sole purpose of the transmitter was to broadcast a single signal when activated. The range was 3.219 kilometers, or two miles.

"You chaps back there get set," Ford said. "We'll be there straightaway."

Sergeant Grenfell turned the car onto Mallow Street, but this time he drove past the alley and continued to St. George's Street. Reaching the intersection of Malloway and St. George's Street, he made a left turn and headed for Liam O'Connor's building on the left side of the street.

The Death Merchant's eyes raked the rainy darkness. Everything appeared to be normal. There were half a dozen cars parked on the block, two to the left, four to the right. A man was on the right side of the street. Apparently hurrying home, he was bent down against the rain and walking away from their car.

"Each time we come, I keep thinking that we should have had a tetanus shot first," McLoughlin said in a low voice.

"It isn't exactly a barrel of laughs, is it?" Camellion said.

Grenfell pulled up to the curb in front of O'Connor's building, and Ford, Camellion, and McLoughlin got out, making sure they didn't slam the doors. Grenfell pulled away, and the three men, their hands on pistols in their coat pockets, went across the cracked concrete sidewalk past the rusty iron fence, the gate creaking in protest as Ford pulled it open and closed it. They hurried up the paved walk in the center of the postage stamp-sized yard filled with weeds, walked up the steps, opened the door, and entered the dingy foyer. Everything was in order. The pay phone on the wall. The Early Depression side table. Ahead were the stairs, with their worn, paper-thin carpeting.

The Death Merchant felt like a walking arsenal. Earlier in the day he had sensed danger and had prepared himself. In addition to a 9-mm Hi-Power Browning in each pocket of the trench coat, he carried two "Backpacker" auto mags in shoulder holsters.

Going up the first flight of stairs with Ford and McLoughlin, the Death Merchant was not overly concerned, only extremely cautious. A long, long time ago, he had learned that it was always unrealistic to fight evil with goodness. The trouble with goodness was that it went to bed every night and slept soundly. Evil was an insomniac, forever awake, forever active.

They reached the second floor, the "personality" of the building drifting to them. Fish fried in oil. Tobacco smoke. Garlic. Maybe we got mixed up and are in Italy! And that particular kind of mustiness that emanates from buildings of

51

another era—relics that have outlived their usefulness but are still standing.

They looked up and down the hall, then turned and went up the steps to the third floor, their eyes darting in a St. Vitus' Dance pattern. They paused on the third floor and looked from the left to the right. The hall was empty. Liam O'Connor's door was twenty-five feet to the right, on the north side of the hall.

No sooner had Camellion and the other men stepped into the hall than Camellion noticed O'Connor's door, which opened inward, close very gently. The door had been cracked open only a few inches, just enough to permit someone to look out and see whoever might enter the hall from the mouth of the stairs. Simultaneously, the keen-eyed McLoughlin detected another door—to the left on the south side—being gently pushed shut.

"We've walked into a trap," Camellion said in a low voice. "Someone was looking from O'Connor's door."

"And a door to the left," whispered McLoughlin. "We've stepped into either a snatch and grab job or we're the targets for slugs."

"We'll bloody well be victims if we don't get out of here," remarked Ford, his eyes measuring the distance they had moved from the mouth of the steps, not more than seven feet.

"You two turn around and head back for the stairs," Camellion ordered. "If the IRA's as good as I think it is, there'll be more of them on the second floor—*now!*"

As Ford and McLoughlin spun and pulled their own auto-pistols, Camellion pulled the two Browning automatics from his pocket, moved backward, and spun around. He knew that for the moment he and his two companions were safe. The IRA in O'Connor's apartment wouldn't get wise until there wasn't a knock on the door.

By this time, Robert and Chris were five steps below on the stairs, a Belgian FN auto-loader in Ford's hand, a 9-mm Beretta in each of McLoughlin's. With the Death Merchant watching the top of the stairs and Ford and McLoughlin the bottom, the trio proceeded downward.

They were halfway to the bottom, and Ford had taken out the Emergency-unit and had switched it on, when they saw four young men come out of a room on the second floor and start quickly for the stairs, one of the men carrying a British BSA 9-mm submachine gun loosely in one hand. By the time the first two gunmen looked up and saw the grim threesome on the stairs, it was far too late. One Irish gunman tried to yell a warning. The man with the machine gun didn't even have time to use both hands. Ford's and McLoughlin's pistols started to roar, the loud reports within the confines of the building sounding like grenades exploding.

The man with the chatterbox went down with 9-mm Beretta slugs and FN 7.65-mm projectiles in his chest. The one next to him died at the same time. Caught completely off guard, the two other terrorists attempted to jerk weapons from under their coats. The first two corpses were falling to the floor when McLoughlin triggered another round, the hollow-pointed bullet catching the gunman to the left in the throat. Ford terminated the fourth termite with a well-placed 7.65-mm bullet that hit him high in the chest and kicked him back against the closed door of the apartment the four had just left.

"Oh, sweet sassafras!" McLoughlin said calmly. "Now we're in for it."

They were. There were shouts of alarm from the first floor, three rapid shots from the direction of Liam O'Connor's apartment, then the slamming of three doors on the third floor.

Camellion didn't even take time to tell the other two to watch the steps to the first floor. His long legs working furiously, he raced to the top of the stairs, spun to the left, and started triggering both Brownings as he flung himself to the carpet.

The very last thing the gunmen on the third floor expected was for one of the intended victims to come after them, so it was this unexpected attack that gave Camellion a slight edge and a few seconds lag time. Two men had come out of an apartment on the north side of the hall. A woman had been in an apartment on the south side of the hall. All three had a second to blink disbelievingly before 9-mm by 19 Parabellum projectiles punched into their bodies. Simon Teague got the big stab in the stomach. He cried out and fell backward, as if his feet had been kicked out from under him. Lingus Armagh, who resembled the part of a Polaroid photo you tear off and throw away, squawked like a chicken when a 9-mm swaged slug hit him in the upper lip, cut a bloody ditch through the roof of his mouth and tunneled through the back of his throat. Kathleen Clancy—only eighteen, pretty, with red hair—went down with the horror of her own approaching death etched on her face. The Enfield revolver slipped from her right hand.

A single drop of blood oozed from the blue-black hole an inch above the bridge of her nose, and her life was over.

Her corpse was still sagging to the floor when Camellion rolled over on his back, his head toward the west, his feet and legs slightly northeast. A submachine rattled and two pistols cracked. Dozens of slugs slammed into the floor where he had lain only moments before, pieces of green, yellow, and blue carpeting, ripped up by the projectiles, falling over Camellion. Four bullets—two from a 9-mm Star auto-loader, one from a 9-mm Hungarian Tokagypt pistol, and the last from the French 9-mm MAT submachine gun—tore through his clothes on the right side of his body. Two bullets stabbed harmlessly through his trench coat at the bottom. The third piece of hard lead core cut through coat, sweater, and shirt underneath, and raked along the outside of his biceps, its lightning-like passage feeling like the sting of a whip. The fourth bullet tore through at the shoulder knob—another sting, another graze that drew blood.

A fraction of a second ticked off and both Brownings in the Death Merchant's hands were roaring, each weapon spitting out high-velocity slugs before the three men, who had come out of Liam O'Connor's apartment, could realign their pistols and the submachine gun.

Four loud cracks from the two Brownings! Roger Carrowmore, the terrorist with the MAT, was knocked backward by the impact of the two 9-mm slugs. George Brehon uttered a long "Ohhh," dropped the Star pistol, half spun, and started to go down like a reverse corkscrew, a bullet buried in his belly against the spine. Boyle Ryan got lead-chopped in the chest. He staggered back, pain etched on his face, hate-crazed eyes riveted on Camellion. When it looked as if he might be able to raise the Tokagypt pistol and get off another shot, the Death Merchant fired again. Ryan died instantly, a bullet hole in his forehead, a chunk of lead in his brain. He toppled backward and crashed to the floor like an oak struck by lightning. Camellion got to his feet, looked up and down the hall, and for a moment toyed with the idea of crashing into Liam O'Connor's apartment. No, he'd be leaving Ford and McLoughlin to fight alone. The firing of several machine guns and pistols from the first floor, plus the cracking of Ford and McLoughlin's weapons, definitely made up his mind for him. From the first floor came screaming, the frantic shrieking of women overcome with terror, with the fear of dying.

Camellion ran to the corner of the south wall by the mouth

of the stairs, leaned out, and looked down. All hell had broken loose. Ford and McLoughlin were firing furiously, ducking and dodging and retreating backward up the steps. Below them at the top of the first flight of stairs, gunmen were snapping off shots. Every now and then one of the Irish terrorists would lean around the corner and, not having time to aim, trigger a few rounds. In turn, Ford and McLoughlin would return the fire and take a step upward.

Only by sheer luck and the whim of Fate had none of the enemy slugs hit the two men, although bullets had come very very close. From the amount of blood on Robert Ford's right shoulder, he might have been retreating with his throat cut. A bullet had only nicked his right earlobe. As for McLoughlin, a bullet had zinged through the top of his ragged knit slouch hat and had knocked it to one side on his head. It hung there like a deformed stocking cap.

McLoughlin looked so comical that Camellion almost laughed as he stepped down on the third step from the top and began firing both Hi-Power Brownings to cover Ford and McLoughlin's retreat. They turned and raced for the top of the stairs. Very quickly all three were on the third floor, protected by the corner of the south wall, McLoughlin firing down four more times while Ford and Camellion shoved full magazines into their weapons.

"Is that all of them on this floor?" Ford said, his voice nervous. He looked in disbelief at the six bodies in the hall.

"It has to be or we'd all be dead by now," Camellion said gaily.

"We can't remain here," announced McLoughlin in exasperation. "If we do, we'll end up as cold cuts in the Belfast morgue's ice box. "Let's find the stairs to the roof and hold them off from up there until Grenfell and reinforcements arrive."

Camellion leaned around the corner and triggered four shots. He turned to McLoughlin. "We can't. There aren't any stairs to the roof."

McLoughlin looked astonished. "Are you sure?"

"Positive."

"I told him," Ford remarked and jerked in reflex when there was a blast from a submachine below and a dozen projectiles thudded into the wall above the stairs.

"We'll crash into an apartment and hole up there," Camellion said, his irritation mounting. "It's our only chance."

"Like hell it is!" McLoughlin said scornfully. While Camellion might be boss, Chris considered himself an equal: by no means was he the follow-the-leader type—only one of the reasons the Death Merchant had chosen him. "Once inside, we'll be bottled up. And it will be another ten minutes before Grenfell and the Tommies get here."

"Bottled up—yes," admitted Camellion. "But I've a surprise for them."

Without giving either McLoughlin or Ford a chance to reply, Camellion darted northwest across the open space to the west end of the hall. Having no choice, Ford and McLoughlin first tossed slugs down the stairs, then raced after the Death Merchant, who paused for a moment before an apartment door on the north side, the same apartment that two of the terrorists had used.

The Death Merchant tried to turn the knob. The door was locked. Camellion stepped back and kicked. The door flew inward, the noise triggering screams from a woman in one of the bedrooms. Camellion first, the three men stormed into the room, their eyes raking the small living room and the three doors, leading to the kitchen and two bedrooms.

"Each of you take a bedroom," Camellion growled. "The windows and the fire escape have to be watched. And shut up that damned broad."

"You intend to hold them off by yourself?" McLoughlin stared incredulously at the Death Merchant. "And what's this surprise?"

"They shoot through walls," grinned Camellion. "Get going."

McLoughlin caught on instantly. "The auto mags! I should have known. These old walls might as well be paper. Well, I hope you know what you're doing."

"I do," Camellion said. As McLoughlin rushed into one bedroom and Ford into the other, Camellion went across the room and overturned a large old-fashioned sofa, tilting it so that the back became the front. He got down behind the sofa, took six full magazines of .44 Magnum AMP ammo from one of his pockets, put them on the rug, and pulled both "Backpackers" from their holsters.

There was time. The terrorists on the first and second floors, knowing they were not fighting amateurs, would approach the third floor cautiously.

The screaming in one of the bedrooms stopped. Camellion could barely hear McLoughlin's voice—"You two get under the bed and stay there. And shut up. We're not terrorists. We're with the police."

There were no shots. The sudden silence was almost diabolical. Camellion knew that when the next attack started, it would not be without warning. First, the IRA gunmen would have to find out which apartment Camellion and Company were using.

The seconds slipped by. Waiting, the Death Merchant thought of the many reports he had read about the mess in Northern Ireland. Of all the cities in the world, Belfast was probably the most dangerous. In 1979, British SIS estimated that in Belfast alone there were some eighty-five thousand weapons in private hands, all the way from auto-loaders and revolvers to shotguns, automatic rifles, and submachine guns. Not a single night passed without snipings and bombings, not a single day without bomb scares. Guards at government offices kept street doors locked and checked people in and out like jailers. On downtown streets there were almost as many armored cars as buses.

In November of 1979, the IRA swept through Belfast on vicious murder raids. John Barnhill, a member of Parliament, was machine gunned in his home; the house was then blown up. Thirteen raids were made on the homes of well-to-do Protestants, most of them magistrates or city councillors, and twenty-two people were murdered. A UDA official was wounded, and the husband of Edith Tagger, Ulster's only woman senator, was pistol-whipped.

But the IRA was slowly losing, with many of its best and most experienced men and women either killed or in prison. The new recruits, according to SIS, would never have been allowed in the old IRA. Edward Windrow had told Camellion, "they're letting in criminals, drunks, sex goofs, and out-and-out psychopaths. . . ."

And now they're after us! thought the Death Merchant.

He heard a scream from the eastern end of the hall, from the apartment on the south side—a high-pitched woman's scream of pure fright. The terrorist gunmen had invaded the apartment.

Next they'll look in O'Connor's place and then come this way to look in the apartment across the hall and this one. I should get some sense and retire, like Vallie West. But if I did, the boredom would drive me crazy!

A few more seconds, and the Death Merchant forgot all about boredom. Three shots rang out from the bedroom farthest from Camellion. He could tell from the resounding echoes that Ford was firing down at someone trying to come up the fire escape from the second floor.

Come, come, my children! Come in and die. . . .

After entering the apartment, Camellion had closed the door, but since he had broken the latch, he hadn't been able to relock it. Suddenly the door was kicked inward and two men rushed into the room. The man in front, dressed in a brown, padded jacket, carried a Czech Vz25 submachine gun. The man behind him, clad in a blue car coat, held a U.S. AMT Combat .45 in his right hand. Both men raised their weapons when they saw Camellion, who noticed several other terrorists behind the first two.

It was a simple matter of Camellion's having the edge—not only had he known what to expect, but he was much faster. Both Backpacker auto mags boomed, the big jacketed hollow-point projectiles leaving the muzzles of the AMPs at a velocity of 1,025 feet per second. When man or beast is hit by a Lee Jurras-designed bullet, impelled by 300 grains of powder, the results are very predictable. Both .44 Magnum projectiles struck the men in the chest, flattened out, tore tunnels two inches in diameter through their bodies, and exploded out their backs. No two men ever died faster. The slug that killed Mickey Tully, the gunman with the .45 auto-pistol, struck the taller Michael Dail, who was behind him, low in the chest. The bullet buried itself deeply in Dail's body and slammed him back across the hall to the south wall.

Hugh Dundalk, a big, bloody hole in his chest, dropped the Vz25 machine gun and pitched backward, the .44 projectile that had shot out of his back rocketing straight at Niall Sheridan, who was behind him. However, the bullet never reached Sheridan; instead, one of those stranger-than-fiction accidents occurred. The .44 Magnum bullet tore directly into the muzzle of the .38 BSW revolver in Sheridan's hand, half of the .44 slug wedging itself into the round opening at the end of the barrel. The terrific impact of the .44 bullet, almost tearing the revolver from Sheridan's hand, forced his finger to pull against the trigger. The revolver went off. The .38 slug, stopped by the lead buried in the end of the barrel, did the rest. The revolver exploded in Sheridan's hand, the barrel coming apart like ripped cardboard.

Camellion continued to fire methodically, putting .44 Magnum projectiles through the walls to the left and right of the doorway clogged with bodies—eleven bullets that ripped through the wallpapered, plastered walls the way an ax would chop through a watermelon.

Eight of the dynamite-packed slugs missed human flesh. Three did not. One zipped through the wall in the west end of the hall and, at an angle, struck Arland Finney just below the belt, on the right side, ripping all the way through his colon and taking its exit out his left side. Finney howled pitifully and started to go down as another .44 Magnum slug banged into the left ribcage of Doreen Shannon, a rather pretty twenty-year-old who combined rabble rousing, bomb throwing, and sniping at British soldiers with freelance prostitution. But her terrorist and whoring days were over. They had ended, and so had her useless life. She went to hell in such a hurry, the bullet ripping through her heart, that she did not even have time to shriek. Her dark hair swirling around her woolen ski mask, she collapsed to the rug just as another .44 jumped out of the wall and stabbed an unlucky Paddy Fitz-Gerald in the groin. He was almost to the top of the stairs, with a potassium nitrate bomb in his hands when the slug struck him. With the ten taped-together sticks of gelignite in his hand, FitzGerald fell backward down the stairs, almost crashing into the last four terrorists who had just rushed into the house from St. George's Street.

Behind the couch, a satisfied Richard J. Camellion reloaded the two Backpacker AMPs, then hurried to the doorway, stepped up on the chest of the dead Mickey Tully, and looked out the door. He felt even greater pleasure when he saw the two fresh cold cuts in the hall, the corpses of Finney and Shannon. But he didn't have time to congratulate himself. Two men were almost at the top of the stairs and two more were behind them, the first two trying to jerk to a stop and swing their weapons around when they saw the Death Merchant.

"*Dominus Lucis vobiscum,*" Camellion said softly, and his finger gently squeezed the trigger. The AMPs boomed twice in rapid succession, the tremendous reports drowning out the sounds of sirens that were getting closer and closer.

Conor Pearse, the terrorist closest to Camellion, was trying to bring up his Luigi Franchi LF57 submachine gun when the .44 Magnum bullet hit him in the center of his ski-masked face. There was a sound as though someone had stamped on an orange as Pearse's face and head exploded. While the entire ski mask jumped outward, the rest of Pearse's head, accompanied by chips of bone and gray-white blobs of brain

59

matter, flew north, south, east, and upward. Parts of brain, splashes of blood, and bone fragments splattered over Rudyard Kelly, the man who had been to the right of the now headless Pearse, and down over Dermot Salthill and David Tornley, the two other gunmen on the stairs.

Kelly didn't have time to notice. Pearse's exploding head was still expanding outward like a runaway nova when a .44 projectile zipped into Kelly's chest, ripped away his left lung, tore off a rib, bored through his left side, and thudded into the wall.

Pearse—blood spurting from his neck—and Kelly toppled backward and started to tumble down the stairs while Tornley and Salthill, almost gagging in revulsion against the bits of brain and blood that had splashed over them, did their best to keep ahead of them. Half falling, half stumbling, they rushed down the steps.

"We've got to get out of here," panted Salthill at the bottom of the stairs. "Whoever they are up there, they're straight out of hell."

"Y—Yeah. Everyone's dead but us," mumbled Tornley.

Neither terrorist had a chance to escape. The front door was thrown open, and there stood Sergeant Grenfell and a British soldier, a BSA submachine gun in each man's hands. Behind them were more Tommies. Other soldiers were surrounding the apartment building.

The BSAs chattered and a flood of 9-mm slugs flowed all over Salthill and Tornley, punching holes in their bodies and kicking them back to the steps.

Camellion, Ford, McLoughlin, and several British soldiers cautiously entered Liam O'Connor's apartment. Under Sergeant Grenfell's direction other Tommies checked apartments on all three floors and assured terrified occupants that the gun battle was over.

They found Liam O'Connor lying on the couch, hands tied behind his back, feet on the floor. It was apparent that he had been shot in the chest while sitting on the couch and had toppled sideways. His eyes were blackened, his lips puffed, his cheeks bruised.

A low moan came from his lips.

The Death Merchant bent down and felt of O'Connor's throat pulse.

"He's still alive. Help me place him upright."

60

"We'll get him to hospital," Ford said, trying hard to maintain a cool and breezy front. "We'll—"

"We'll question him right here," Camellion said firmly. "He'll be dead before we get him to the hospital."

Chris McLoughlin hurried out of one of the bedrooms, leaned close to Camellion and whispered, "The wife and a little girl are both dead—shot."

"They had two daughters," Ford said in a low voice as he helped Camellion gently place Liam O'Connor in an upright position on the couch.

A soldier came out of the other bedroom. "Nothing in there." Another came out of the kitchen. "Those bloody bastards even killed the cat!"

O'Connor moaned again, opened his eyes, and stared weakly at the three men bending over him.

"Annie an M—Mary . . . they're d—dead, aren't t—they?" O'Connor said.

The Death Merchant nodded slowly. A dying man deserved the truth.

Slowly, in bits and pieces, O'Connor revealed what had taken place. The terrorists had not been IRA gunmen, but terror squads of the equally vicious Ulster Volunteer Force. For the past seven months the UVF had suspected that it was either Liam O'Connor or Harry O'Connor—or both men since they were brothers—who was betraying them to either the Provos or to the RUC police. Doing some clever detective work, the UVF had found out that both men had been reared Roman Catholics. At once the UVF was convinced that both Liam and Harry O'Connor were Provo agents.

"O—Our other daughter, s—she d—didn't c—come home from . . . from school," O'Connor said in a barely audible voice, blood forming on his lips as he spoke.

Elaine, the older daughter, was an hour overdue when three UVF gunmen came to the apartment and confronted the O'Connors and their other daughter, only five years old, with drawn guns. They gagged Annie O'Connor and the little girl, forced them into the bedroom, and tied them to the bed. The terrorists tied Liam O'Connor's hands behind him, shoved him roughly to the couch, and coldbloodedly informed him that if he didn't talk and confess, they not only would kill his wife and child, but would gouge out the eyes of Elaine, whom they had kidnapped on her way home from school. They had then gagged Liam O'Connor and had beat him with soapjacks—bars of soap slipped into thick socks—to prove they

61

meant business. After the vicious beating, they had removed the gag and had ordered him to talk, or they'd strangle the little girl to death.

"I—I told them . . . w—what I knew they w—wanted to h—hear," O'Connor admitted weakly. "I told them I . . . I w—was a Provo spy. I a—also told them about w—working for SIS. I w—was afraid not to . . . a—afraid for m—my f—family. I told them . . . I said you'd b—be c—coming here t—tonight."

"Now we know why they were waiting for us," McLoughlin said, a deep scowl on his good-looking face.

"T—they wanted to . . . to kidnap the t—three of you . . . or—or else k—kill you." O'Connor said, his voice weaker.

It was only after O'Connor had admitted everything to the UVF gunmen that they told him they had tortured Harry O'Connor during the afternoon—using a blowtorch—and that Harry had admitted he was not only a member of the Officials, but was also an agent for the Provos. Furthermore, he had also admitted to the UVF sadists that Liam had told him about two SIS agents who were supposed to come to Belfast from Dublin.

"They d—didn't know about the two of you at the Vic—toria S—Street station," O'Connor whispered. "They didn't even know y—you were on the train."

In a voice growing constantly weaker—so much so that Ford, Camellion, and McLoughlin had to lean very close to catch his words—O'Connor explained that while the UVF terrorists had waited, they had talked and bragged among themselves. It was then that O'Connor had given up all hope, realizing that if the killers intended him and his wife and child to live, they would not have spoken so openly.

From the conversation of the terrorists, O'Connor had learned that the men at the Great Victoria Street Railway Station had been members of a UVF assassination squad sent to ambush Tomas O'Faolain, a leader of the Provo organization in Dublin. A UVF agent in a Belfast Provo cell had learned when O'Faolain would arrive.

The only thing that still puzzled the UVF was that O'Faolain must have expected trouble. Instead of one bodyguard, three had been with him, and two of them had killed every member of the hit squad!

The Death Merchant and Christopher McLoughlin locked eyes. So that was the explanation. There hadn't been a leak in security. The two men who had walked behind them in the station, just before the fire-fire had begun, the two men who had been wasted—one had been O'Faolain, the other his bodyguard. The gunman by the tea counter who had drawn the .380 Enfield revolver had been after O'Faolain!

And we had to open fire! Camellion told himself. *Well, it was an honest mistake. . . .*

O'Connor was whispering, "I heard t—them mention that UVF agent has learned the location of an i—important Provo base to the n—north. They said that the UVF was not strong enough in the area to a—attack the P—Provos."

O'Connor paused, more blood welling up in his mouth, some of it dripping down to his already bloody shirt. His breathing was deep and rapid, then at times almost absent. The Death Merchant recognized the Cheyne–Stokes type of breathing as a serious prognostic sigh—*he'll be dead within minutes, if not sooner.*

"Please, g—get me a p—priest," the dying man gasped.

"One's on his way," Ford lied, then insisted, "Where man, where? Give us the location of the Provo base."

Weakly O'Connor whispered, "L—Lha-Beul-tinne Castle. It's . . . i—it's . . ." His voice drifted into silence and he floated away into nothingness. His chest did not move. His eyes remained open, sightless.

Reaching down and closing O'Connor's dead eyes, Ford said, "Lah-Beul-tinne Castle is five milse west of Londonderry. It's nothing but a pile of ruins that's never been restored." He became enthusiastic and rubbed the palms of his hands together. "What a catch we'll get when we go fishing up there for Provos . . . maybe even McGuire himself!"

"It's an odd name for a castle," McLoughlin commented, looking down at the dead O'Connor. Ironic! They had suspected the man of being a double agent, but he had been on their side all along. "Lha-Beul-tinne is Old Gaelic and means 'The Day of Baal's Fire.' "

Ford turned and stared at McLoughlin with extreme skepticism. "How do you know? Are you sure?"

McLoughlin, who always did his homework to the nth degree, smiled pleasantly at Ford. Chris was always tolerant of those who might disagree with his facts. After all, they had a right to their ridiculous opinions.

"If I weren't positive, I wouldn't have said it. The term is derived from a druid convocation, at which cattle were driven between two fires to protect them from disease. This ritual was held at the palace of the King of Connaught on May first. Long after the druids went out of business, the first of May was known as Lha-Beul-tinne, the Day of Baal's Fire."

"I've never been there, but I understand the castle is a lonely place," Ford said stolidly, then turned slightly to face Camellion. "We can fly to Londonderry by helicopter by tomorrow afternoon. First we'll have to clear this establishment of all the bodies—and I'll have to radio London."

"Yes, Ulster has more dead heroes," McLoughlin said wearily. "They'll plant them in the ground and say something stupid like 'he's with God,' or 'at peace,' or something equally ridiculous."

Camellion's eyes went to Sergeant Grenfell and a British soldier who were coming into the room from the hall. "What else can you expect? Since all who think about God think of Him as living, they can only form conceptions that are absurd."

"All the terrorists are dead, sir," Sergeant Grenfell reported to Ford. "All the occupants are all right, except for one chap who got a pistol-whipping from one of the terrorists when he protested about their having invaded his apartment." He shook his head bitterly. "How these damned Irish stick together. He called us a bunch of 'heathen bastards' just for being in this building, this cockroach heaven."

The Death Merchant gently tapped Ford on the shoulder. "I suggest we get out of here and start making preparations. Sergeant Grenfell can take care of the cleanup operations. We have a lot of careful planning to do."

"Yes, you're right, Mr. Ringgall." Ford seemed pleased with himself. He cleared his throat, then said to Grenfell, "Don't forget the two terrorists I killed on the fire escape. Search them and the others thoroughly. I doubt if you'll find anything of value. On a raid terrorists always carry false identification."

"Yes sir," Grenfell said. "We'll do our best." He and the other soldier saluted and hurried from the room.

Ford's brows contracted and his expression became thoughtful.

"Perhaps by the time we finish with the IRA at Lha-Beul-tinne, we'll have some answers," he said hopefully.

Camellion smiled slightly—*Or we'll be dead.* . . .

"Maybe so," McLoughlin said. "The trouble with this whole mess in Northern Ireland is that by the time we start learning all the answers, the IRA or the UVF changes the questions."

CHAPTER SEVEN

During the flight to Londonderry in the Royal Air Force Puma HC 1 helicopter, Humphrey Grimes and Robert Ford briefed "Mr. Ringgall" and "Mr. Weaver" on the murderous situation in Londonderry. It was the same as in Belfast, only on a smaller scale.

McLoughlin summed it up succinctly by saying, "Since Londonderry is the second largest city in Northern Ireland, I guess one could say it has the second biggest mess of murder."

Grimes, a man with a firm British face and pleasant manners, laughed good-naturedly. "A rather novel way to describe Londonderry," he said, then grabbed the end of the metal bench as the Puma HC 1 hit an air pocket. "It is, however, an accurate description."

"The first big riot was on January 30th, 1972," Ford said slowly, as if remembering. "It's still known as Bloody Sunday."

Ford explained that it didn't matter to the Catholics or the Protestants that all marches had been banned, that Orange Day, Apprentice Day, and Easter parades had been outlawed by the government. On the day that became Bloody Sunday, the Roman Catholics—many of them IRA—began to march south on Strand Road which, downtown, became Foyle Street and then John Street. The Protestants, moving north, started their march on Bishop Street which, after it turned sharply, became Abercorn Road. British troops, having closed all the other downtown streets, waited behind barbed wire at the square where Abercorn Road and John Street and the west end of Craigavon Bridge, over the River Foyle, met.

The Catholic mob arrived first. In order to get past the British, IRA thugs began to assault the British troops with bricks, bottles, and nail bombs. In the meantime, the Protestants—their ranks filled with members of the Ulster Defense Association and terrorists of the Ulster Volunteer Force—approached the soldiers from the south. The British Tommies were firing rubber bullets and spraying the Catholic mob with

CN gas by the time the Protestants were half a block away on Abercorn Road. At this point, Hubler and Saracen armored cars and troop carriers, loaded with British paratroopers, arrived to reinforce the several hundred soldiers.

It was the two converging mobs that fired the first shots—as General Ian Clark-Masterson, the commander of all the British forces in Northern Ireland, reported to London: "a total of several hundred rounds of ammunition fired indiscriminately in the general direction of the soldiers."

The British returned the fire, not only with rifles but with machine guns in the turrets of the armored cars. The shooting lasted only several minutes. When the firing stopped, 152 men and women were dead. Seven children had been killed. Another 204 of the mobs were wounded. Eighteen died in hospital within a week. Forty-six British soldiers had been killed, nineteen wounded. Five died later.

"The Irish refuse to admit that it was the IRA and the UVF that fired the first shots." Humphrey Grimes collected himself with an effort. "The IRA and the UVF got what they wanted—a massacre. They're still trying to promote a civil war, like the one you Yanks had in the States during the 1860s. A mucky lot, these fanatic paddywhacks."

"A shame really," Ford said. "Londonderry is an armed camp. The Catholics are in the north, the Prots in the south, and—"

"And you British are in the middle," Camellion finished.

"And hated by both sides, as you well know," said Ford.

After the RAF Puma HC 1 set down at the small military airport northwest of Londonderry, the Death Merchant and the other men started the drive to the Agricultural Show Ground in the southern part of the city.

The Agricultural Show Ground, sandwiched between Anne Street and Lone Moor Road, had been taken over by the British who had built on it barracks and other installations. The British had also taken possession of the Brandywell Recreation Ground attached to the north end of the Show Ground. Appropriately enough, across from both grounds on the other side of Lone Moor Road was the Londonderry Cemetery.

Arriving at the Show Ground, Camellion and his three companions went straight to the headquarters and conferred with Colonel Charles Hempstead, a ramrod-straight British officer of the old school, who was in command of the battalion. Colonel Hempstead at once informed Grimes, who was acting as spokesman for SIS, that he could supply only two troop carriers and two armored cars.

More angered than surprised, Grimes almost got up from the low-backed office chair on which he was sitting. "Colonel, didn't you read the order from General Clark-Masterson? It states quite plainly that you are to give your full cooperation. We don't know what we might find at Lha-Beul-tinne Castle! Yet you stand there and tell us that we can have only sixty men and two armored cars! Dash it all, man! That's ridiculous."

Colonel Hempstead agreed without hesitation. In a standing position, he leaned over his desk, bracing himself on his hands. "It's not a matter of cooperation, Mr. Grimes, but of logistics. Come, gentlemen. Permit me to show you the position we're in, here in Londonderry."

A sixtyish man with a flat stomach, Hempstead moved quickly from behind his desk, went to a map on the wall, and picked up a wooden pointer. The other men got up and gathered round him.

"Gentlemen, this is Londonderry," Hempstead said, turning to the map. "Let me show you the trouble spots."

The end of the pointer moved rapidly over the map as Colonel Hempstead explained where Catholics and Protestants were more than likely to try to kill each other and where both warring factions were prone to gang up on the British— St. Eugene's Cathedral, at the corner of Infirmary Road and James Street; the Courthouse; Bishop Gate; Craigavon Bridge; Guildhall; the railroad and bus stations, especially the Mill Street Railroad Station; all the parks—St. Columb's Park, east of the River Foyle, in particular.

Colonel Hemstead turned and faced Camellion and the other men. "The point is, I have 107 armored cars deployed throughout the city. I have no choice. Armored cars keep the peace and protect our men. At all times I must keep ten armored vehicles on standby, here at this base. I now have twelve. You can have two. I can spare only sixty men. I don't dare lower my strength here at headquarters, or pull troops from vital points within the city."

Camellion intoned, "You're the cavalry and the Irish are the Indians."

"I beg your pardon, Mr. Ringgall?" Hempstead blinked coolly at the Death Merchant.

"I am comparing your situation here in Londonderry to that of the U.S. Cavalry, during the days of the Old West in the United States. You and your men are the good guys, here in the fort. The Irish are the Indians."

"Oh! Yes, quite," Hempstead said curtly. "The Wild West in America! Yes indeed, a splendid comparison. We are surrounded by the Irish 'Indians.' "

Humphrey Grimes walked back to a chair and sat down, dejection etched on his face. "We shouldn't go to Lha-Beultinne Castle with only sixty men and two armored cars." His worried eyes moved to Colonel Hempstead, his hard stare demanding. "You are sure that you can't spare more paratroopers?"

"Positive," Hempstead said professionally.

Robert Ford, also fuming, took a more cautious approach. "Colonel, the radio message we gave you from General Clark-Masterson was a B-6 priority. I trust you understand that?"

"Don't tell me about priorities," Colonel Hempstead said indignantly, pausing to give Ford a hard look on the way to his desk. "A B-6 does not cancel a B-4, which gives any commander the right to secure an already established position. I can't take the risk. I will not weaken my forces in Londonderry to give you men to go off on what might prove to be a wild goose chase."

Ford and Grimes glanced at each other, both infuriated by Hempstead's cool self-assurance. The tragedy was that he was absolutely correct. There was no way they could make him release more armor or more paratroopers. The two SIS agents were still trying to form some new method of verbal attack when Richard Camellion intervened, speaking in a pleasant, persuasive tone, "Gentlemen, I don't see why we shouldn't be able to get the job done with sixty men. I've attacked larger places with less."

He got up and walked across the room and looked at the map of Londonderry on the wall.

"By God, I do!" Ford snapped. He jerked around and glared at the Death Merchant's back. "You've seen scale drawings of those ruins. Damn it! You know full well the size of Lha-Beul-tinne Castle!"

"I agree." Grimes was visibly mortified. "Why, there could be a hundred Provos hiding in there!" he said fiercely. "There's more than enough room for them to hide. The castle has two basement levels.

"There could even be more Provos," Ford added quickly. "Don't forget what O'Connor said. The Provos are so strongly entrenched that the UVF in Londonderry won't attack them."

70

Even McLoughlin's analysis forced him to agree with the two Secret Intelligence Service agents.

"Mr. Ringgall, there isn't the slightest bit of cover in the approaches to the ruins," he said calmly. "A few men with light machine guns could cut us down in less than a few minutes."

The Death Merchant turned from the map, a serious expression on his suntanned face. "Wrong. We do have cover—Derryberry Creek. I know that it's nothing more than a wide ditch, but the northern bank is high enough to conceal us when we sneak in."

McLoughlin stroked his short beard. "Good point! But not good enough for my money. To me, it only means that our getting wasted will be delayed, that's all."

Once more Ford and Grimes exchanged worried looks. The biggest trouble with Americans was their proclivity for violence. Ringgall and Weaver were not exceptions, especially Ringgall, who seemed to have a mystical covenant with death.

Grimes said acidly, "Mr. Ringgall, Derryberry Creek is more than one hundred and fifty feet from the front of the castle. Do you propose to make all of us invisible while we cross the area between the creek and the castle?"

Camellion acted as if he hadn't heard Grimes's remark. "Colonel Hempstead, can you supply a helicopter gunship, one equipped with a GAU-2 Minigun?"

Hemstead thought for a moment, leaning back in his swivel chair and putting the tips of his fingers together. "You chaps are in luck," he said at length. I have one, a BV YUH-61A. Besides a brace of thirties in the port and starboard openings, it has a 20-mm M197 electric gun mounted underneath. Will that serve your purpose?"

Headford Road lay behind them, and now the four-vehicle armored column was in the country.

The first vehicle was a Hubler VI armored car. Beside the crew, Captain Ralph Gurney, the British officer in charge of the search operation, rode in the Hubler. Camellion, and McLoughlin, Ford, and Grimes rode in an FV 432-L, a vehicle that was a cross between an armored car and a personnel carrier. The FV 432-L was simply an armored steel box on tracks. On the left front there was a one-man turret and a GP machine gun. On top was a hatch forty inches in diameter, through the opening of which a 61-mm mortar could be fired. A single rear door gave access to the interior, in which ten fully-equipped infantrymen could ride. Side ports permitted the occupants to see out. In front of the Hubler and the FV 432-L were two Harrington K-13 personnel carriers. Thirty British paratroopers of the Royal Green Jackets were in each personnel carrier. On the front of each carrier was mounted a Bren .303 light machine gun.

Lieutenant Jackson Merriweather, a young officer fresh out of Sandhurst, Great Britain's "West Point," rode in the first personnel carrier in line. Sergeant Malcolm Weston, a thirty-year man in the army, was also in the first carrier.

Sergeant Jock Saint-Cluis—another spit-and-polish and by-the-book professional—rode in the FV 432-L, and like the rest of the British force considered the operation a waste of time, vehicles, and manpower.

"We 'ave sent out patrols any number of times, we 'ave," he said in a thick Cockney accent as the column moved deeper into the Irish countryside, " 'oping to give the bloody bastards a good bashing."

"But have any patrols ever inspected the ruins of Lha-Beul-tinne Castle?" insisted Robert Ford, who looked completely out of place in battle fatigues.

The cleaving wrinkles in Saint-Cluis' forehead deepened. "Wot for, mate? Them Provo bastards couldn't 'ide in a pile of old stones."

"Then, Sergeant, it is only pure conjecture on your part that there aren't any Provos at the ruins," Humphrey Grimes said stiffly. "On that basis, we won't actually know until we get there and see for ourselves."

" 'Ave it your way," Sergeant Saint-Cluis said gruffly. "But you'll see that I'm right."

Chris McLoughlin, sitting across from Camellion and looking out the side opening, turned and glanced at the Merchant of Death, a slight smile on one side of his face, as if to say, *Ford and Grimes are wasting their time. They're trying to convince themselves as well as the Sergeant, who has a closed mind.*

Camellion winked, turned on the padded bench, looked through the square opening on his side of the armored vehicle, and thought that convincing a hardheaded Britisher was every bit as tricky as conversing with a typical Irishman—always a haphazard business for literal-minded people of Saxon descent or upbringing in Britain or in the United States, even though the Irish themselves are winningly full of self-criticism. *They're notorious for it! Who has flayed the*

Irish more unmercifully than their own writers and profes-
sional moralists?

The early spring countryside was peaceful and quiet, noth-ing about the budding trees even hinting at the murderous violence stalking the ancient land of Ulster. The column moved past stone farmhouses with thatched roofs, past wrought-iron gates and whitewashed stone pillars typical of the Ulster countryside.

Close to Coppington's Bridge, spanning the narrow Derry-berry Creek, the column passed a small cemetery in which stone tombs were shaped like miniature oratories—tiny pri-vate chapels.

The radio to the right of the driver of the FV 432-L buzzed and its red light flashed. Sergeant Saint-Cluis hurried to the radio, picked up the mike, and pressed the button.

"Yes, *sir*. Sergeant Saint-Cluis, *sir,*" he said with the usual British noncom efficiency.

The crisp voice of Captain Gurney came over the speaker. "Sergeant, please advise the civilians in your vehicle that we are only one quarter of a mile from Point Y. Confirm."

"Yes, *sir*. Confirmed, *sir*. They 'ave 'eard you, *sir*, and un-derstand."

"Very well, Sergeant. Out."

Saint-Cluis hung up the mike and, making his way back to his seat next to Chris McLoughlin, said, "You 'eard 'im, mates. Only a quarter of a mile to Point Y."

Saint-Cluis could have saved his breath. Already Camellion and Humphrey Grimes were sitting beside each other huddled over a topographical grid map of Londonderry County. Point Y was the position where the four vehicles would leave the hard dirt road, turn north, and proceed into an area of gently sloping hills through which meandered Derryberry Creek. They would stop two miles north of the ruins of Grianan of Aileach, originally the sun-palace of Aileach, an ancient king. Later, the spot had been the royal seat and stronghold of the O'Neills, Kings of Ulster, and was perhaps Ulster's best known and most conspicuous antiquity. Set on top of an eight hundred-foot hill, the fort commanded a view of the entire countryside.

The possibility that the Provos might be holed up in Grianan of Aileach had crossed the Death Merchant's mind. The possibility was dispelled when Ford and Grimes informed Camellion that the ruins were a tourist attraction guarded not only by the RUC constabulary but by British soldiers.

In a short time the small caravan of four armored vehicles reached Point Y, an open area two hundred feet east of sail-box farmhouse—a frame dwelling with two stories in front and one behind a roof with a long rear slope.

The Hubler turned off the road and swung north, the three other vehicles following, the wide rubber tires of the Hubler and the tracks of the two carriers and the FV 432-L sinking several inches into the soft, rocky soil. Now the ground was uneven, the ride bumpy, and the Death Merchant and the others in the FV 432-L bounced up and down in their seats as the steel box on tracks crawled its way over craggy terrain.

Finally, however, the plunge to the north was over, and Captain Gurney radioed the drivers of the vehicles to move into the positions that had been agreed on during the master briefing. The Hubler and the FV 432-L stopped side by side fifty feet south of a long hill with gentle, elongated sides. The two troop carriers came to a halt fifty feet behind the Hubler and the FV 432-L. Everyone got out, the paratroopers assembling into squads. Eight of the paratroopers immediately secured the perimeter by running to the edges of the area and taking positions, their .280 EM2 rifles set to fire.

Two hundred feet to the east was the big twisting ditch that was Derryberry Creek. The wide ribbon of water was hidden by the hills, except where it cut north through a hedgerow and turned west to flow in front of the long hill hiding the small British force from whoever might be in the castle.

While Sergeant Saint-Cluis and Weston and Lieutenant Merriweather gave final orders to the assembled paratroopers, Captain Gurney conferred with Camellion, McLoughlin, and the two SIS officers. A man in his mid-thirties with sharp features, Gurney always had a pessimistic tone to his voice even when he spoke optimistic words.

Gurney glanced at his watch: two-thirty. "We are a bit ahead of schedule, a good half hour," he said.

"Fourteen-thirty hours isn't all that great," Camellion said. "What matters now is getting the paratroopers into the creek and having them move around the north bank facing the ruins. We must make sure that each man stays down and doesn't show himself until we're prepared to make the charge."

Inserted McLoughlin, "Yeah, the sooner we do it the sooner we can get our parking tickets validated and go home."

Unfamiliar with American euphemisms, Captain Gurney

glanced in surprise at McLoughlin. No one had told him, but he suspected that both Mr. Ringgall and Mr. Weaver were Americans. He further suspected that the two men were with the American CIA and that Ford and Grimes—obviously British—were SIS operatives.

He was wondering about the stainless steel auto pistols belted around Camellion's waist and was about to mention the Boeing-Vertol helicopter gunship when Lieutenant Merriweather walked up, saluted, and said, "Sir, the men are ready to get into the creek and move into position. The three teams are waiting for the order to move up the hillside. They will be six meters from the top, sir."

"Thank you, Lieutenant," Gurney said. "Send the three teams on their way and have the men move into the creek. As soon as the gunship arrives and begins to pepper the ruins, the teams on the hillside and the mortar in the FV will open fire." He paused as if slightly embarrassed. "Mr. Ringgall will give the actual order for the charge. All contact will be maintained by ML9s. Any questions, Lieutenant Merriweather?"

Astonishment flickered briefly over Merriweather's youthful face. "Sir, Mr. Ringgall is a civilian. It's . . . it's most unusual, isn't it, sir, for a civilian—"

"Yes, yes, I know." Captain Gurney cut him short. "However, this is a very special situation."

"Lieutenant, we are experts in these tactics," tacked on the Death Merchant in a calm but firm voice. "The four of us"— he indicated Ford, Grimes, and McLoughlin with a nod of his helmeted head—"will be going with you and the men, Lieutenant. One more thing: when I give the word to leave the creek, be sure that the paratroopers do not rush in diagonally or in a zigzag fashion. The distance from the creek to the front of the castle is too great, and we can't count all that much on the smoke. Make sure your men move straight in, with a slight dipping motion from side to side. Understand?"

"Yes, sir. I do." Merriweather looked at Captain Gurney. "Permission to speak, sir."

"You have it, Lieutenant."

"Sir, wouldn't it be better to try oral tactics first?"

Gurney smiled indulgently. "Lieutenant, once you've been in Ulster for a while, you will realize that it's impossible to talk any Provos into surrendering. They're fanatics of the worst kind. Carry on, Lieutenant."

"Yes, sir." Merriweather became ramrod straight and sa-

75

luted, the odd British salute in which the palm of the right hand is held outward.

"I'll be in the Hubler at the radio," Gurney said. "It's also banded to the ML9s."

The Death Merchant and the other men nodded, then started to follow Lieutenant Merriweather, who had taken his leave and was returning to the assembled paratroopers. As usual, the Death Merchant was bored. As far as he was concerned, the attack was merely a bit of excitement in an otherwise weary existence. In his own personal philosophy, existing in a three-dimensional continuum (four when one considers time) in a flesh-and-blood-and-bone body was definitely a horse-and-buggy way to travel through the universe.

Robert Ford and Humphrey Grimes were nervous and trying hard not to show it. Being in British SIS was one thing; attacking the IRA in the open countryside with paratroopers was quite another.

Like the Death Merchant, Chris McLoughlin was as calm as the pope praying in his private chapel. His only regret was that, because the mission was top secret, he would never be able to tell his friends at Cobrey International, the anti-terrorist school where he taught karate in his everyday life, how he had actually spent his "vacation."

And if he got wasted? Wasn't death a part of life?

CHAPTER EIGHT

They waited. Crouched against the high, half-muddy bank of the Derryberry Creek, the Death Merchant and the sixty men with him in the big ditch waited for the helicopter gunship to arrive and begin shelling the ruins of Lha-Beul-tinne Castle, which was about a hundred fifty feet to the north. Between the creek and the ruins was a flat, open field, blades of green grass poking up here and there.

Although the ruins were called a "castle," the title was a misnomer. Lha-Beul-tinne had never been a castle, not in the conventional sense. There was no moat. There had never been a drawbridge or a central keep; there had never been a wall with towers from which fighters could shoot arrows at, or drop stones or burning pitch on, an enemy. Lha-Beul-tinne had actually been an enormous stone house—three storeys and 72 rooms, not counting the Grand Hall.

Originally built by Sir Hugh Klinsworthy-Kyle between 1613 and 1638, the house had known violence and bloodshed, not only in local wars but in wars with the hated British. It was Sir John Klinsworthy-Kyle who added the two octagonal towers and enlarged the structure. It was also Sir John who had, from a weird sense of humor, named it Lha-Beul-tinne.

The Death Merchant had not had much time, but from the little he had read about the ancient house he had learned that the "castle" had once been a showplace, with its black basalt masonry and Gothic sandstone decorations. The cut-stone features surrounding and surmounting the main entrance were the oldest part of the structure, which had been burned out in 1922. Since then, the enormous stone shell had been ignored by the British government, and the house had not been restored. Over the years, five adults and two children had died while poking around in the ruins. Stones and timbers, weakened by wind and rain, had fallen and killed the curious explorers. The ruins were a blackened monstrosity, a big, ugly boil on the clear skin of the countryside. Gone were the picturesque bays and wooded escarpments. There were only hundreds of glassless windows staring out over the countryside like empty eye sockets. Since the deaths of the last two people from Londonderry, the ruins had been widely shunned; and of course it was reputed to be haunted. In contrast, the castle demesne, the land surrounding Lha-Beul-tinne, was noted for its fine trees, rhododendrons, and other shrubs.

It did seem unlikely that any Provo terrorists could be hiding in the relic of the past, in any of the scores of rooms, many of which sagged dangerously on their supporting timbers—*unlikely to anyone without imagination!* Unless Liam O'Connor had not heard correctly, the IRA could have established quarters and a supply depot in the two stories below the ground level. When Lha-Beul-tinne was in its prime, the two basements had been used as dungeons, storage areas, and quarters for servants. Solid stone, this vast area would have survived the fire and would be intact—as good now as the day it was built.

The Death Merchant looked up and down the line leaning against the slanting bank. To his right were McLoughlin and Lieutenant Merriweather; to his left Robert Ford and Humphrey Grimes. Sergeant Weston was with the paratroopers, far down the line to the left; Sergeant Saint-Cluis to the right with other soldiers.

Finally, Camellion and the others heard the "flub-flub-flub-flub" of helicopter rotors in the distance. Once the paratroopers had been positioned, the Death Merchant had contacted Captain Gurney on an ML9 walkie-talkie. Gurney had then used the radio in the FV 432-L to contact battalion headquarters at the Agricultural Show Ground in Londonderry. It had taken less than five minutes for the Boeing-Vertol YUH 61A to arrive on the scene. And there it was in the distance, growing larger and larger, until it was clearly discernible as a BV helicopter gunship. At four hundred feet, the gunship swung to the west of the ruins, its four-bladed main rotor and two T700 turboshaft engines making a racket that was almost deafening. The chopper then made a short half turn and, roaring northeast, headed for the ruins of Lha-Beul-tinne, all the while decreasing its altitude.

The chopper opened fire with the M197 Minigun when the gunship was several hundred feet southwest of the ruins and not more than a hundred feet above the relic. A television camera mounted on the underside of the craft made it possible for the copilot, who was firing the weapon, to view the results on a small TV screen set in the control panel.

The rate of fire of the three-barreled electric Minigun was awesome. The M197 began to rake the stone and timbers at the unbelievable rate of 4,560 shells per minute. The 20-mm M197 was known as a CHAG (Compact High-Performance Aerial Gun), and no other weapon that could be carried on a helicopter could match its terrible firepower.

Too fast for counting, thousands of armor-piercing tungsten carbide-cored 20-mm projectiles splattered the ruins of Lha-Beul-tinne, the deluge of projectiles of such ferocious intensity that a cloud of dust started to float upward from the mass of rock and timbers. The deadly rain of projectiles cut through beams and braces and joists. What was left of the roof crashed downward. Entire rooms on the third floor collapsed. Shells ripped into part of a brick chimney and it dissolved into a shower of chips and bits of broken bricks. Small clouds of splinters and black basalt shards flew outward from facings, Gothic trim, and stone quoins. Entire stairways on the second floor dropped to the floor below. Rusted decorative metal-work exploded from the impact of shells. No doubt about it: the top of the ruins was being ripped apart by the projectiles.

"A fly couldn't live in that barrage," McLoughlin said happily. "Using that Minigun is like spraying water out of a hose. It doesn't miss a damn thing."

McLoughlin and Camellion and the others had stood up and were watching the electric Minigun demolish the ruins, each man convinced that he was invincible—for who can imagine his own non-existence?

"Tiger turds," the Death Merchant said. "Those shells aren't even reaching the first floor of the basements. The only value of the gunship is its psychological effect."

"Yes, you're right about that," admitted McLoughlin. "We'll soon know if your theory is right."

"I just hope that the spotter on the other side of the hill doesn't give the wrong coordinates to the mortar crews," Robert Ford said, pulling a British Army gasmask from the kit bag on his hip. "All we need is for a few of those shells to fall among us."

The Death Merchant nodded understandingly. Ford was a good SIS agent, but under combat conditions, he and Grimes weren't even in a Boy Scout league.

"The first three or four rounds will fall short of the castle, but not this far short," Camellion reassured Ford. "We're as safe here as a baby in its crib."

Because the electric Minigun used ammo at such a fantastic rate, the spraying of the ruins lasted only 72 seconds. The helicopter gunship, its ammo exhausted, then rose up and roared off to the south. Expertly the pilot began to sit down behind the two troop carriers.

The three mortar crews on the south side of the hill had set up a periscope on a tripod, the "eye" of the P-scope just above the level top of the rise. Two of the mortars would lob Intense Smoke (I-S) shells. The third stovepipe would fire 81-mm explosive shells. As soon as the 81-mm mortar team had the exact range, they would walkie-talkie the coordinates to the 81-mm mortar team, who would fire from the top opening in the FV 432-L.

The first 81-mm shell from the mortar on the hillside fell forty feet in front of the ruins, exploding with a flash of fire and leaving a small crater. The second shell missed the ruins by thirty feet. The fourth shell exploded on target—right in front of the castle. Several empty window frames and part of the stone wall were flung inward from the force of the explosion. *Uh huh*, thought Camellion. *The paratroopers firing that stovepipe know their business. They're damned good.*

The fifth and sixth shells tore out more of the castle wall, wood, stone, and metal flying away in a flash of fire and smoke. The 81-mm crew on the hillside contacted the crew in the FV 432-L, and soon two mortars were lobbing 81-mm shells at the front of Lha-Beul-tinne Castle. The first shells of the crew in the FV 432-L fell short, since the paratroopers had to compensate for their greater distance from the ruins, a task that was comparatively easy. Two elevating mechanisms, one coarse and one fine, permitted a total range of elevation from 43.5 degrees to 90 degrees. A range scale, calibrated in meters from 0 to 525, was screwed to the left side of the breech ring. A hook-shaped lever, pinned to the rear left-hand side of the cradle, rode along the range scale as the elevation of the mortar was changed, and served as an indicator. The combination leveling and traversing mechanism allowed a total traverse of 30 degrees, 15 in each direction. Center traverse was indicated by an arrow, pointing to a "O" engraved on the rear top of a ball joint about which the cradle traversed.

Altogether, 26 High Explosive (H-E) shells fell directly in front of the ruins. By the time the bombardment was over, part of the main entrance and many of the empty window frames on the first floor had disappeared. Beams and masses of dislodged stones hung precariously in all directions, blue-gray smoke drifting across the face of the wreckage.

The first I-S shell landed sixty feet in front of the ruins, the second a hundred feet to the right of where the first one was already spewing out thick clouds of purple smoke. The second shell gave a pop and began to hiss black smoke. In quick succession, nine more I-S shells landed in the area between Derryberry Creek and the ruins of Lha-Beul-tinne. Within a few minutes a wall of black-purple smoke had formed between the creek and the ruins. Camellion and the other men didn't mind; they were protected by gas masks.

Captain Gurney contacted Camellion on the ML9. "I say, Mr. Ringgall. How is the situation down there? Under control, I presume? Confirm, please."

"Confirmed. I'm waiting for—"

"Waiting for what?' chimed in Sergeant Saint-Cluis. "We 'ave enough smoke to use for cover."

"Sergeant Saint-Cluis, keep off the air. That is an order," Gurney said angrily. "Mr. Ringgall is a tactical expert. He will give the order to advance. Confirm, Sergeant."

"Yes, *sir*. Confirmed."

"Mr. Ringgall, please let me know when you give the order to advance," Captain Gurney said in a more pleasant tone. "Out."

Chris McLoughlin turned to Camellion. "I say, old boy"— he mocked the British—"what are we waiting for? Like old blood-and-guts said, 'We 'ave enough smoke.' "

"We wait," Camellion said firmly, his voice slightly muffled but clear enough through the voicemitter of the gas mask. He switched on the walkie-talkie, held the mike end close to his mouth, and said in a loud voice, "Sergeant Saint-Cluis, Sergeant Weston, make damn sure your men don't have their heads above the bank of the creek."

"I was under the impression that we were supposed to advance?" Sergeant Weston's gruff voice floated back through the ML9.

"We will—when I say so, not before."

Hearing Camellion's words, Ford, Grimes, McLoughlin, and Lieutenant Merriweather quickly pulled their heads down. Although curious about why Camellion was delaying the rush to the ruins, they knew he had a reason and assumed he knew what he was doing as they watched him contact the mortar crews on the hillside.

"Men, this is Ringgall," Camellion said. "Lay four more smoke shells on them. I want the smoke ahead to look as solid as a wall."

"Yes, sir. As you have ordered," one of the paratroopers replied.

The smoke between the creek and the ruins was so thick that the Death Merchant and the others had no way of knowing where the first I-S shell landed. Not that it made much difference. The light machine gun from the ruins began firing while the third smoke shell was arcing from the other side of the long hill. Lines of projectiles streaked across the opening, stabbed over the creek, and buried themselves in the hillside.

"I say! All the firing from the gunship and the IRA is still able to use a machine gun!" exclaimed Humphrey Grimes.

McLoughlin patted Camellion on the shoulder. "Smart thinking, 'Mr. Ringgold.' The IRA can't see us because of the smoke, but they assume we're out there."

"If we weren't here, we'd have been riddled," Lieutenant Merriweather said hollowly, tightly clutching a 9-mm Parabellum Patchett submachine gun as though the weapon gave him special security. "But what made you suspect that the IRA might have a light machine gun and use it against us?"

The Death Merchant's eyes twinkled behind the wideview lenses of the gas mask over his face. "Commonsense, Lieutenant. Wouldn't you open fire if you were in the IRA's place in those ruins?"

Chris McLoughlin's question was more practical. "How do we get from here to there?" he asked significantly. "We can't go up against that thirty-caliber job. Not more than ten of us would reach the castle."

"Wouldn't you say that machine gun is on the first level?" The Death Merchant cocked his head to one side and listened to the loud, cracking bursts.

"Yeah, they're firing from the first floor." McLoughlin stared speculatively at Camellion whose face was hidden for one brief moment by drifting smoke. "They're moving it from side to side, raking the entire area. Why? What have you got in mind?"

"I'll go ahead and put the gun out of commission," Camellion said lazily. "I'll radio back when it's safe for the rest of you to advance."

"The old 'listen and drop' technique," McLoughlin said

quickly. "One-second miscalculation . . ." He sighed. "They could change the firing pattern or open up with a second light job. Very soon they're going to realize that we're waiting for them to let up. They're not hearing any yells—nothing!"

"See here, Ringgall," thrust in Humphrey Grimes with something akin to awe, "if you go out there, you'll be committing suicide"

Camellion pulled the two custom model 200 International auto mags from the holsters low on his hips, then made sure that the ML9 was strapped securely in its case.

"You handle things at this end for me," he said calmly to McLoughlin. "Should Captain Gurney call, tell him that everything is all right. And make damn sure that none of the paratroopers get trigger-happy while I'm making the cross-over."

Camellion cocked his head again and listened to the firing of the light machine gun. From the sound of the weapon, he was almost certain it was a 7.62-mm NATO FAO M59 light machine gun. His trained ear told him that the LMG was situated toward the southeast corner of the house—*I'll have to move along the front of the ruins to get to it. The shorter the length I have to cover in front of the house, the quicker I'll be able to silence the chatterbox.*

"Luck, buddy," murmured McLoughlin. "Watch out for green and pink streetcars."

"Yeah, and falling anvils, too."

Camellion tensed, braced himself by digging his feet into the soft earth, and listened to the snarling of the machine gun. When he was satisfied that the weapon was throwing projectiles straight south, he jumped up, dug his heels into the side of the sloping creek bank, and, reaching level ground, sprinted twenty feet, then dropped to the ground when he detected that the IRA gunner was swinging the barrel to the west. He lay there on his stomach, listening to slugs cut the air several feet above his head and feeling sorry for the young paratroopers and for Ford, Grimes, and Lieutenant Merriweather. They were all so terrified of death, none of them realizing that it was this "life" that was the only real "death." *Once a person learns that life is the transitory illusion*—no matter how real it appears during its duration—*then he has mastered dying. . . .*

Lying on the ground, the thick smoke all around him, Camellion couldn't see more than a few feet. But that was all he needed. Carefully he listened to the roaring of the machine gun to his right, and when the sound of the chattering told him that the barrel had also been turned to the right and that the slugs were nowhere near him, he jumped up and darted slightly northeast.

Unexpectedly, the burst of firing stopped—*either they're putting on a new box of ammo or else they've wised up.*

This time, he covered eighty feet before he decided not to push his luck, dropped to the grass and listened intently. Dead silence. There was only a slight breeze. And because each I-S shell had a fifteen-minute supply of smoke, it seemed that he was in the center of a world composed of nothing but black-purple fog, a world in which there were no directions. Yet his own built-in sense of direction, fixed in his mind, would keep him on course.

He was about to get up and dash the final lap when the machine gun began to snarl again—ten-round bursts—the IRA gunner once more moving the weapon slowly from left to right, from east to west. Once more the Death Merchant could sense high-velocity projectiles punching over his head through the thick smoke. Again, twenty seconds later, he could detect by the sound of the firing that the gunner had swivelled the barrel back toward the east.

I've got them! The Death Merchant leaped up and raced straight toward the ruins. All the time he realized that he was safe from the machine gun, even if the Provo operating the weapon did swing the barrel west. There was a limit to the horizontal swing of the weapon on its mount. Now that he was so close to the ruins, the trajectory of the slugs posed no threat.

His two kit bags buckled to the sides of his legs, the cross-straps cutting into his shoulders, the Death Merchant pumped his long legs and closed in on the front of the castle, over whose wrecked front drifted thick smoke. He quickly reached the ruins—so close that he could almost reach out and touch the old stones, many of which, toward ground level, were covered with a blanket of moss. The front of the castle loomed over him, the tall, empty windows bleak and forlorn, the rooms beyond desolate and as dank and moldy as an ancient crypt.

Staying close to the stones, Camellion moved swiftly toward where he could hear the LMG firing. Occasionally, a fragment of stone or a piece of other debris, loosened by the terrible shelling of the helicopter gunship, would fall from the upper stories. Camellion ignored the risks of falling rubbish, and instead concentrated on the human element. Although convinced that none of the Provos were on the second and third floors, he nevertheless watched the windows of all three floors as he drew closer to the machine gun, moving stealthily past decorations that resembled pillars sunk into stone.

He was only twenty feet from where the light machine gun was chattering when he saw the three figures crouched behind a windowsill. Two men and a woman, all three in their early twenties. They had as much chance against the Death Merchant as a cake of ice would have in a blast furnace. The two men tried to swing up a couple of Spanish Parinco submachine guns. The girl—wide-eyed, her mouth open in surprise—attempted to maneuver a .38 Enfield revolver.

Poor slow-butt fools! The two AMPs in Camellion's hands roared. An M/200 International AMP, actually a handgun for hunting big game, delivers a 137-grain .357 Magnum projectile at 2,150 feet per second. What bigger and deadlier game than Man?

The two .357 jacketed soft-point projectiles struck the two men in their chests at the same time, the terrific impact smashing them back from the window. Crying out in fear, the young woman died a second later. One AMP roared again, the big weapon jerking in the Death Merchant's experienced hand. The blue beret on the girl's head, the top of her head, and its long brown hair went flying upward as the .357 Magnum projectile exploded her skull, scrambled her brains, then went on its way to bury itself deeply in a stone wall.

Camellion didn't take time to holster the AMP and reach for a fragmentation grenade. Keeping low, he dashed toward the machine gun, keenly aware that the thunderous sounds of the Auto Mags had alerted the Provos at the weapon.

The Death Merchant reached a position that put him only eight feet from the side of the light machine gun, whose bipod was resting on the windowsill. Camellion jumped from the side of the wall, all his instincts sharp from the danger facing him. During that microsecond, he saw four angry and confused faces. Four men. One at the machine gun. One man to the left, two to the right. Two with Russian AK47s, two with Polish Radom Wz auto pistols.

Camellion ducked to his right as the skinny-faced creep with one of the Radoms triggered a round, the 9-mm bullet skimming within an inch of his left shoulder. Both AMPs boomed while Camellion flung himself sideways to the right, and a stream of 7.62-mm slugs from one of the AK47 assault rifles burned the air over his body, which was headed for the ground. The terrorist with the other Radom and the dummy who had fired the AK47 were practically picked up off their feet by the impact of the .357 Magnum bullets that smashed into their lower chests.

The Provo who had been firing the machine gun—rum-pot eyes, long, heavy jaw, protruding teeth—got off a single shot with the Radom, the 9-mm coming so close to Camellion's left side—just below the armpit—that it singed the tough cloth of his fatigues. A second more and the Provo was dead, a big, bloody hole in his chest and back from a .357 Magnum slug.

The fourth man, sensing that Death was staring him in the face, squealed like a stuck pig and did his best to get the AK47 into action. In that mini-slice of a moment, Camellion knew that if he shot the man in either the head, gut, or chest, reflex would pull the finger of the corpse against the trigger and the AK47 would spit out a stream of steel-cored 7.62-mm slugs—*and one of them will almost have to get me!* He twisted his body, fired both AMPs, and landed heavily on his back. The two .357 projectiles didn't miss. One struck the man's left hand that was around the seasoned wood of the fore-end, and the second powerful bullet caught the side of the rifle just above the banana-shaped magazine.

The Provo's left hand dissolved into pieces of flesh and bone and torn skin, and the AK47 was knocked to the left. Sheer shock did initiate reflex action which caused the man's finger to squeeze the trigger, but the barrel was pointed away from the Death Merchant. The rifle roared a short burst, but the slugs shot harmlessly into the air.

Camellion fired again. The .357 Magnum bullet bored into the man's chest, ripped out through his back, and knocked him sideways. Eyes wide open in death, he fell to the floor, blood from his back pouring out into the dust on the floor.

The Death Merchant jumped up, raced to the southeast corner of the house, holstered one auto mag and pulled the ML9 from its case. He looked around through the still drifting smoke, then switched on the walkie-talkie.

"Mr. Weaver, I trust you are there?"

"And waiting, Mr. Ringgall."

"Your waiting is over. Advance—fast."

CHAPTER NINE

The British paratroopers closed in on Lha-Beul-tinne like a huge hand tightening on an orange. With amazing speed, the Green Jackets raced across the smoke-filled area and, reaching the objective, fanned out. A third of the force, under Sergeant Saint-Cluis, spread out in several rooms in the southwest corner of the castle. Another third, under Sergeant Weston, secured positions in several rooms in the south-center. The remaining third rushed to the southeast corner, where they made contact with the Death Merchant.

"What took you so long?" Camellion looked at McLoughlin, his eyes glinting with irony. "What did you fellows do, stop to smell the roses along the way?"

"Hell! You should have called on Jesus Christ if you wanted greater speed!" McLoughlin shot back. "We can't work miracles."

"I couldn't call on him. I didn't hear angels singing or the blast of a trumpet in the sky," Camellion replied with spurious thoughtfulness, noticing at once that McLoughlin was the only man who was relaxed. Ford, Grimes and Merriweather seemed as nervous as a cat creeping past a barrel of bumblebees.

"Sure," grinned McLoughlin. "I'll believe that one when the 'saints' of every nation lose all gravitation and float up to the clouds. But since we're here, where do you think the entrance to the basements might be located?"

"Or entrances," Robert Ford interposed.

Lieutenant Merriweather, looking all around, said nervously, "I suggest we close in on the IRA before they retreat and vanish into the countryside."

He stared at the corpses lying around the NATO M59 light machine gun, sickened at the sight of death close up, at the sight of drying blood, of open, sightless eyes. He simply didn't know what to make of Warren Ringgall and George Weaver. Were all Americans so damned calm and cold-blooded? No, of course not. Ringgall and Weaver were kill-specialists and inured to this kind of extreme violence.

Merriweather looked around the rest of the large room on the northeast corner of the castle. One could almost feel the age and the memories, as though they were alive but invisible. He glanced at the paratroopers who were guarding the windows and watching the three doors that opened from the room into the interior of the ruins. At least they were battle-hardened . . . young, yes . . . but accustomed to the violence of Northern Ireland.

The Death Merchant, his thumbs hooked over his gunbelt, said, "The entrance—or entrances—might be anywhere on the first floor, but most probably toward the rear." He gave the worried Merriweather a slight smile. "Don't worry, Lieutenant. The Provos won't escape. They are holed up in the series of cellars below!"

"I know," Merriweather said, his voice tight. "Two levels of cellars."

Thrust in Chris McLoughlin, "And we can be sure the entrance will be guarded, maybe even booby-trapped."

Humphrey Grimes cocked his Sterling submachine gun. "What I find incredible is that we wouldn't be here if these bloody Irish would quit their ceaseless fighting over religion. I have never seen such murderous prejudice as exists in Ulster."

"Bigotry is a world-wide disease," Camellion retorted. He pulled the ML9 from its hard plastic case. "Anti-Semitism leads the list. Why in some sections of the United States even, anti-Semitism is so quietly ruthless that some Jews even change their names."

"Surely you must be joking?" Robert Ford contemplated Camellion with curious eyes. "Why should a Jew anywhere want to change his name in these times, even in Germany?"

"Because the hypocrites and the halfwits of this world make it an advantage not to be a Jew," Camellion said in an admonitory tone, "or not to have a trace of black blood, or whatever, depending on the country you're in."

He switched on the walkie-talkie and held the mike end close to the speaking diaphragm of his gas mask.

After explaining to Captain Gurney that all the Green Jackets had reached the objective, Camellion switched off the walkie-talkie and turned his attention to Lieutenant Merriweather who, so far, had not given a single order. The Death Merchant, who was careful never to step on a man's natural pride, said, "Lieutenant, get out your ML9. I want you to transmit some orders to Sergeant Weston and Sergeant Saint-Cluis."

Jock Saint-Cluis and his men, in the west end of the ruins, proceeded to move north toward the rear, while Malcolm Weston and his Green Jackets moved north through the center area of the first floor. Leading the third group, the Death Merchant moved toward the rear through the empty rooms on the east side. When he and the others reached the northwest corner of the ruins, they turned and crept west, moving through rooms in the rear of the enormous structure.

"Reminds me of a tomb it does," one of the paratroopers whispered. "I keep feeling there's something always looking over my shoulder."

"You're daft, man," another paratrooper said with a nervous little laugh. "It's not the dead we have to worry about, it's them IRA blokes who'll do us in if they get half the chance."

Camellion did not hurry; he knew better. And he had instructed Lieutenant Merriweather to order Weston and Saint-Cluis to use extreme caution in moving toward the rear. There was adequate light, the afternoon sun slanting cheerfully inward from the tall, narrow windows.

The rooms were empty, if one discounted the trash and rubbish. In some rooms the weather had curled decorative wood paneling from the stone walls, and the large squares had fallen to the floor. There they lay, rotted to splinters. In other rooms parts of the ceiling had caved in, and broken beams and shattered edges of flooring ringed the holes above. Everywhere was dampness and mold and the smell of ancient history, of a past that no longer mattered.

A room with any pile of rubble had to be approached with the utmost discretion. The tumbled stones, often resting on broken joists, could be a camouflage for a trapdoor to the first basement below.

Twice, the Death Merchant called a halt and Lieutenant Merriweather contacted the two other groups on the walkie-talkie. Neither group had discovered anything significant, finding only empty, debris-filled rooms. Sergeant Weston reported that his group had moved through the ballroom and had found the grand staircase to the second story. "The bottom half of the stairs is missing," he said. "The top half is just hanging there."

"There has to be a stairway to the cellars—somewhere!" said McLoughlin in a low voice. Walking next to Camellion, he carried a 9-mm Ingram submachine gun. "We couldn't have passed any entrance. They couldn't have disguised it that well."

"The steps are there," Camellion assured him staunchly. "Those Provos I wasted up front were not here all by themselves, or they wouldn't have opened fire. They would have kept out of sight, kept hidden."

"We still have a dozen or more rooms to explore," Humphrey Grimes declared with vehemence. "We'll find them. Hopefully we'll succeed in capturing a few who can give us a lead to Keenan McGuire. I intend to see that sadist swinging from a gallows in London."

As if to sneer at Grimes, a submachine gun roared from one of the rooms far ahead. The echo of the firing was just beginning to bounce back and forth throughout the empty rooms when the cracking of half a dozen British EM automatic rifles cut short the snarling of the chatterbox.

"They've found the bastards!" Merriweather cried excitedly, and made a movement to charge ahead.

Chris McLoughlin's arm shot out and blocked him. "Wait! Contact them first on the ML9. We're not going to charge in like a bull in a tea shop . . . old chap."

Embarrassed over his sudden impulse, which was against all his training, Merriweather checked himself. "Yes, you're right, of course." But he didn't reach for the ML9 on his belt. Crestfallen, he saw that Camellion had already taken out his own walkie-talkie and was contacting the other two groups.

Sergeant Jock Saint-Cluis' bass voice came out of the ML9.

"Sir, we 'ave found 'em, we 'ave. One of those Provo laddies opened a trapdoor and opened fire. Killed one of the boys 'e did. We sent the bloomin' bloody jocko to 'ell in a 'urry we did."

"What is your position, Sergeant?" Camellion asked in a calm voice.

"We're in the second room from the northwest corner of this bloody wreck."

"Secure your position; we'll be there straightaway." The Death Merchant then said to Captain Ralph Gurney, who was keeping an open channel. "You heard that report, Captain?"

"Yes. It's a good show so far," responded. "I'm sorry one of our lads is dead. Keep me informed and good luck to you chaps."

"Out," Camellion said. He switched off the walkie-talkie,

shoved it into the plastic case on his belt and raked the anxious faces around him with keen eyes.

The room, very large, had been a kitchen, as evidenced by the long stone hearth on the south side of the room. The closed trapdoor was toward the center of the room, ancient boards covering the steel square, the boards arranged so that they appeared to have fallen haphazardly.

"We were inspecting that mass of stones over there, when the Provo bloke poked up and opened fire," Sergeant Saint-Cluis explained, pointing to the northwest corner of the room. There half a dozen paratroopers were inspecting a large mass of squared stone blocks that filled the stairway that led below to the cellar. In front of the blocks one could see the first two stone steps and the top section of an iron handrail, part of it crumbling to rust dust when a paratrooper tugged at it.

"The Provo sonofabitch killed Davidson right off," Saint-Cluis said. "Luck was with us. I warned the boys to 'ave eyes in back of their 'eads, I did. Some of 'em were on the other side of the room and saw the damned Provo fire. They killed 'im before 'e 'ad 'alf a chance to do any more damage."

"The trapdoor is closed," Camellion said soberly. "Are you positive there's a trapdoor there?"

Saint-Cluis objected vigorously. "Sir, you think I'm 'aving 'allucinations?" He called out to half a dozen of the paratroopers and told them to "get over 'ere on the double." The six hurried over and Saint-Cluis snapped to one of them, "Fillmore, tell this 'ere gent what you and the others saw and did."

Private Willard Fillmore responded quickly and mechanically. He said that he and five of the other men had been standing twenty feet slightly southwest of the pile of boards which they had suddenly lifted, just enough to permit a man to rear up on steps or a ladder and fire.

"We blew his head off before he even knew we was there," Fillmore said. "He sagged and the trapdoor slammed shut."

Sergeant Weston and his group had arrived in the kitchen at the same time that Camellion and his group had entered. Now, Weston said, "If you ask me, there's going to be a lot of us killed before we get to them Provos below. And—" Noticing disapproval on the face of Lieutenant Merriweather, he stopped, drew himself up straight, and said, "Sorry, sir. I spoke out of turn."

91

It was Camellion who rescued Weston from his embarrassment.

"Sergeant, you merely put into words what the rest of us have been thinking." He shrugged. "Really though, the job is not as difficult as it appears."

"To my way of thinking, it's much worse," chuckled McLoughlin, who had never won any medals for not saying what he thought. "Even with the flash bombs, we're going to have the devil of a time getting down there without the Provos wasting us."

"I daresay we're not going to have a jolly time once we're below," joined in Robert Ford, with humor. "And the way some of the IRA fanatics are, they might damn well decide to blow up this place and us with it, rather than surrender."

"No one can live forever," McLoughlin said jocularly.

"Yes, but by jove I don't know of any man who's anxious to die either," commented Humphrey Grimes.

The Death Merchant got down to business without further preamble. With the others watching, he went over to the pile of lumber, stooped down, and tugged at one end of a one-by-six-inch board, all the while careful not to lean over the pile. The board he tried to move was evidently nailed to the one below it.

"Give me a hand, but don't lean over the mess," he said. "Or you might get a blast of slugs if the trapdoor is wood."

Within five minutes, Camellion, McLoughlin, and the two Green Jacket Sergeants had broken off as many of the longer boards as was possible, and it was evident that the middle sections of four pieces were bolted to the trapdoor; the bolt heads could be seen, and so could the edges of the trapdoor—steel plate painted gray and about thirty inches on all four sides. Together the four men tried to lift the trapdoor. To the surprise of no one, it didn't budge.

"Well, Mr. Ringgall, we either blast or go home," commented McLoughlin. He stood up straight and looked from the boards and the trapdoor to Camellion.

"Have you considered the implication of using explosives?" Lieutenant Merriweather's voice contained more than several notes of apprehension. He looked up at the ceiling which, strangely enough, was coffered, containing ornamental sunken panels. "These ruins are only standing because of luck. Why damn it, man! If we use explosives we could very well bring the building down on us."

The Death Merchant, who had reached into one of his

large gusset shoulder bags and pulled out a one-pound block of COMP-4 (a stable plastic explosive composed largely of cyclonite), glanced at Merriweather, but didn't smile. "Lieutenant, this so-called castle is made of stone, and it and its foundation are as solid as bedrock. Concussion might make loose rubble and other material fall a bit from the upper floors, but there's no danger of the entire structure collapsing."

"The blast won't be all that big, sir," added Sergeant Weston, who was familiar with explosives.

"Certainly hope you are correct, Sergeant," Merriweather said stiffly. Turning away, he looked down at Camellion who, squatting down, was carefully stuffing the putty-like COMP-4 into a four-inch length of the half-inch-wide crack by the second hinge. He put the same amount in the crack—between the edge of the trapdoor and the stones—behind the second hinge, molding some of the plastic explosive into a tiny hill. He next stuffed the front crack with a five-inch length of COMP-4. Humming a portion of Berlioz's *Symphonie fantastique*, he then took three electronic detonator-timers from his shoulder bag and gingerly pushed the prongs of the devices into the hilly sections of the three lengths of explosives. The detonators could either be triggered by turning the small timing knobs or by remote control from a central station.

By now many of the paratroopers were glancing nervously at the walls and the coffered ceiling, as if trying to decide the damage the COMP-4 would do. Ford, Grimes, Merriweather, and Saint-Cluis didn't appear exactly happy. Only Sergeant Weston and Chris McLoughlin seemed at ease and unburdened by anxiety—and, of course, Camellion.

Not for a moment did Ford and Grimes believe that "Warren Ringgall" and "George Weaver" were the genuine names of the two Americans. "Weaver" was cold-blooded enough, but "Ringgall" was even worse—and more private! Both Ford and Grimes suspected who "Ringgall" might really be; yet they had not voiced their suspicions even to each other. They had heard too many rumors about people who got in the way of the Death Merchant. They met with accidents. They became ill. They died. Hell itself seemed to be on the side of the Death Merchant. Ford and Grimes didn't believe in rocking any boats. The sea was calm. Why make waves?

"All right, chaps. Let's move into another room," Camellion announced cheerfully. "Line up with your faces toward the walls. That way you'll be safe from junk falling from the ceiling."

He didn't have to repeat the order; the men were only too happy to put some distance between themselves and the COMP-4. Once all the men were in the room to the east of the kitchen and in position, Camellion took a small, black oblong box from one of his shoulder bags, flipped open the lid, and watched the tiny red light come on. "Here we go," he said and pressed the black button.

The COMP-4 exploded with a hollow boom, the sound only half as loud as most of the men expected it to be, because much of the sound had been directed downward.

There was a loud clanging sound as the steel-plate trapdoor, thrown eight feet upward, came back down and fell flat on the stone floor, a dozen feet northwest of the smoking opening. This noise was accompanied by the clatter of chunks of stone, torn loose from around the trapdoor, falling to the floor. *Plunk!* The last jagged piece hit the floor. Then a strange silence and the bitter smell of burnt COMP-4.

Camellion held up a hand, indicating that every man should stay where he was. He then turned to McLoughlin. "Cover me, Mr. Weaver."

"As good as done, old chap," McLoughlin said pleasantly.

Slowly the two men started advancing into the room, McLoughlin to the right of Camellion, who had drawn both M/200 International auto mags.

Behind them, Ford whispered, "I say, why are they moving so slowly?"

Even Lieutenant Merriweather, whose only battle experience had so far been in a textbook, could answer that question. "They suspect that some of the Provos might rear up on something and fire, or toss a grenade," he said.

No one fired at Camellion and McLoughlin. No one tossed a grenade. While McLoughlin stood seven feet from the cavity in the floor, the barrel of his Ingram trained on the opening, the Death Merchant crept closer to where the trapdoor had been. In blowing off the trapdoor, the explosion had enlarged the mouth, so that now it was easily forty inches on all four sides.

Camellion could see that he had been right in more than one aspect: the floor—the bottom side of which was the ceiling of the area below—was two feet thick. Camellion's eyes narrowed—*Solid stone. There has to be a lot of support on both bottom levels to hold all that weight.*

94

He got down on his knees, and from one of his bags took a fishline wound on a large wooden spool. At every twelve inches a tiny lead weight was fastened to the linen line. Camellion unwound part of the line, tossed one weighted end into the opening, and began lowering the line to the floor below. When the weighted end reached the floor and the line slackened, he tightened up gently, took up the slack, and looked closely at the tab on the weight at the edge of the square opening— *almost ten feet. Too far to jump. I could do it and so could Chris. Some of the others might get a broken leg, a severely sprained ankle at minimum.*

Eight of the paratroopers had each carried a one-foot-length section of the aluminum mountain-climbing ladder that curved at the top so that the two ends could be fastened to the floor. Very quickly a six-foot section was bolted together and, with half a dozen paratroopers ringing the square opening, lowered into the darkness below. One of the paratroopers pushed down on the handle at each curved end of the ladder; the diaphragms expanded, suction holding the ladder firmly to the stone floor.

Camellion, McLoughlin and the rest of the men then took Q-beam headlights from their bags and clipped them to the front of their helmets. Each light was powered by a 6-volt battery in a belt power pack and could be adjusted from spotlight/searchlight to a wide-area walking or worklight.

The Death Merchant addressed the force. "Mr. Weaver and I will do down first. The rest of you will follow as soon as we give you the word, but keep those lights off. I think the IRA is in the second basement. I could be wrong." He smiled at McLoughlin. "Should we do it, Mr. Weaver?"

"I think we should, Mr. Ringgall," responded McLoughlin, taking a tear gas grenade from one of his bags.

Camellion and McLoughlin first lobbed two tear gas grenades into the opening, then followed with several flash "bombs"—plastic canisters filled with concentrated barium nitrate, aluminum powder, and potassium perchlorate—photoflash powder. Although considered a pyrotechnic, flash powder is actually an explosive. The two grenades exploded like two large firecrackers and with a blinding flash, some of the intense brightness shooting up through the square opening in the floor and momentarily lighting up the room. Any Provos in the basement below would have been blinded for several minutes.

An instant after the dazzling flash, the Death Merchant was on the ladder and stepping downward on the rungs into the darkness below, an auto mag in his right hand. During those seconds, he was helpless. On the ladder and unable to see into the darkness, Camellion couldn't have prevented a thirteen-year-old boy from picking him off. He was dropping the few feet to the floor by the time McLoughlin was halfway down the ladder.

"Over here," whispered Camellion. He moved to the right, got down on one knee, and took a Night Sight infrared scope from one of his gusset bags. He switched on the power, held the scope to his eyes, and looked through the duel eyepieces. Instantly the blackness changed to medium twilight.

McLoughlin moved beside Camellion, took out his own night scope, turned it on and, like the Death Merchant, looked from the left to the right. The view was depressing. On either side, for a distance of sixty to seventy feet, there was an open area, except for the enormous stone pillars, the columns usually extending downward from the curved areas of the intersecting vaults of the ceiling. Beyond, at each end of the open space, were narrow doorways to rooms or halls, some with rotting wooden doors. Except for dust, the stone floor was free of litter.

McLoughlin said decisively, "It's times like this that make me feel I should have chosen another line of work."

The Death Merchant lowered the Night Sight device and returned it to the bag. "Years ago I toyed with the idea of becoming a preacher, but I changed my mind. I don't like blank verse."

Knowing that Camellion was leading up to something built around his brand of macabre humor, McLoughlin played along. "So what does blank verse have to do with being a preacher?"

"The entire Bible is written in blank verse." Camellion looked for a moment at the square of dim light on the floor, made by light reflecting from the room above, then he called to the men upstairs, "Come on down. It's clear."

They used delayed L-Flares to explore the first level. All Sergeants Weston and Saint-Cluis had to do was pull out the 8-inch-long flares, twist off the tabs, and toss the flares ahead. Ten seconds later the end of the flare would burst into flame and burn with a blue-white radiance, giving off more than enough light for Camellion and his force to see their surroundings and the area ahead. But they didn't see a single terrorist on the first level, which was one-fourth the size of a city block. They didn't find anything but empty rooms, dust, stale time, and an eerie too-quiet silence.

Toward the center of the first basement level, they found wide stone steps that led downward to the second basement. At the bottom of the steps was a landing the size of a large pantry. Across the landing, there was a door in the stone wall. By the light of an L-Flare, Camellion and the others saw that the door was made of thick, rough wood—and far from ancient.

"Either the Provos are down there or they aren't," said Robert Ford, glancing nervously at Camellion for reassurance.

"This is like buying pantyhose and finding the egg empty!" McLoughlin said soberly. "Only I don't think the egg below is empty."

Camellion studied the bottom of the stairs, the landing beyond, and the far wall with the door in the center. The back wall was about ten feet long, the walls on each side seven feet, indicating that there was a two-foot-thick, seven-foot overhang.

"We blow the door and charge in," McLoughlin said, "and they'll cut us to pieces when we come in."

"We'll have to make more entrances, won't we, Mr. Weaver?" said Camellion, smiling slightly.

"Yes, I think so, Mr. Ringgall. I should say at least two more."

CHAPTER TEN

Even Sergeant Weston, trained as he was in demolition, considered the Death Merchant's plan a kind of Russian roulette—only instead of a bullet it was COMP-4.

Lieutenant Merriweather was blunt in his opinion of the scheme. "See here, Ringgall. I'm responsible for the safety of my command. Why, damn it! What you propose to do will bring the ceiling down on us!"

"No, Lieutenant. The ceiling will not fall," Camellion said softly but very firmly. "Some of the ceiling will come down, the sections between the pillars, but that is all."

"Nonsense! How can you be positive?" Equally adamant in his conviction, Merriweather looked as angry as a wildcat missing her kittens.

"I am positive, and that's enough," Camellion said quietly—*and if I told you why I am positive—because only a small number of your men have no auras, showing them to be closer to death than to life—you would think I was insane, or a liar. Probably both!*

Camellion didn't wait for an answer, any more than he intended to have a prolonged debate with a fool. Motioning to McLoughlin, he started walking to the left of the steps that led to the second basement level.

It took Camellion and McLoughlin only thirteen minutes to place and ready the three packages of COMP-4. The first five pounds were placed on the dusty stone floor and centered between four pillars that extended downward from an intersecting vault, seventy-five feet west of the steps. The second package was fifty feet east of the steps. Three pounds of COMP-4 were placed against the thick oak door at the bottom of the steps.

The entire force hurried to rooms on the south side of the stale-smelling level and stood against the south wall while the Death Merchant made a final mental run-down, then pressed the button in the remote control device, holding his finger down.

Although the entire area was vast in width and length, it was still confining, in that the vibration of concussion would have a difficult time escaping. For that reason, Camellion had set the electric battery-powered timers to explode within ten seconds of each other.

BERROOOMMM! The first blast, to the west, made Camellion and the rest of the men feel that they were in the center of an enormous clap of thunder, the terrific blast followed by stones crashing to the floor of the second level from the ceiling of the first level. Stones were still falling when the COMP-4 to the east exploded, this explosion twice as loud. The third boom was slightly muffled and not quite so torturing; yet it too was followed by the sound of falling stones, while the floor and ceiling shook and shuddered, as if a slight earthquake were in progress. Gradually the sounds of falling stones ceased and the shuddering of the stones subsided.

"Let's move our butts," Camellion said mockingly. He unslung the Model 10 9-mm Ingram submachine gun from his back and shot hard glances at Lieutenant Merriweather, Sergeant Weston, and Sergeant Saint-Cluis. "The roof didn't collapse. Neither did the floor. And all of you know what to do."

With McLoughlin beside him, the Death Merchant moved through the wide arch of the room. More than half the force had been in two rooms on each side of the main room. These men came into the big room through doorways in the side wall and followed the Death Merchant and his group. Once the men were in the area that could contain the entire force, they quickly formed into three groups, then split up and proceeded with the task ahead.

While Camellion and his men raced toward the steps, Sergeant Saint-Cluis and his group hurried in a westerly direction. Sergeant Weston and his men ran north, toward where the package of explosive had been placed east of the steps.

The Death Merchant was proved correct. The three explosions had not brought the roof tumbling down and the floor caving in, except in the vicinity of the explosions. Where the COMP-4 had been centered between the pillars, there was now a cavity eight feet in diameter in the two-foot-thick stone floor, some of the stones at the edge loose and hanging in various positions, looking as if they were being held in place by invisible wires. The holes in the ceiling were smaller, but also ringed with loose stones that threatened to come down at any moment. Piles of stones littered the floor under the holes. Throughout the entire area, drifting dust was almost thick enough to shoot at.

The two forces that had gone to the sites of the explosions to the west and east not only kept their distance from the holes in the floors, but also were careful to keep the muzzles of their EM .280 automatic rifles pointed downward, their fingers on the triggers. If so much as a flea had flown within the large circle, he would have had his head shot off. Sergeants Weston and Saint-Cluis impatiently waited for the order from Camellion. It was the waiting that bothered Weston and Saint-Cluis and the Green Jackets, the waiting and the uncertainty.

McLoughlin and the other men waited, standing back and covering the stairway opening from the east and west sides. On his hands and knees, the Death Merchant started crawling to the southwest corner of the stairway gap, edging along very slowly, very carefully testing each stone with his hands, most of the stones being 25 inches wide and 35 inches long. It wasn't until he reached the corner that he found a stone that was loose and unstable. Even so, it was wedged tight enough to support his left knee and the weight on the knee as he leaned forward and looked over the edge. *What a mess!*

The three pounds of COMP-4 had done their work with slightly more efficiency than Camellion had expected. There was no trace of the door. Three feet of the wall on either side of the door had also disappeared, and so had some of the floor where the explosive had been placed. Now there was nothing but a hole five feet in diameter, around which were strewn chunks of rock of all sizes and masses of gray-white clay. Rocks were also on the steps. For all practical purposes, the entire back wall had been demolished, leaving only a foot or so of jagged stone at the east and west edges. Beyond, where the rear wall had stood, was darkness, a blackness that was threatening. Staring down at the destruction, Camellion felt a dirty thought skid into his mind—suppose the IRA isn't there? Suppose the dummies I wasted earlier were all there was?

He edged back from the corner and, twenty feet from the edge, stood up and hurried to the west side of the stairway slot. Robert Ford and Humphrey Grimes stared impatiently at Camellion. On the east side of the steps, Lieutenant Merriweather and his group of Green Jackets waited nervously.

McLoughlin asked, "As we expected?"

"And then some," Camellion said. "The whole wall is gone and there's a small crater in the floor. But we can leap across it with ease."

Hmm . . . well, well . . ." McLoughlin was perceptibly cool. "The IRA could hold off an army—if they're down there. And if the grenades and other stuff don't work, the Provos could send us straight to hell at full speed."

"We can't go charging down there!" protested Ford, astonishment in his voice. "We'd be committing suicide!"

Camellion turned his gas-masked covered face to McLoughlin. "Mr. Weaver, are you with me?"

"To be sure, Mr. Ringgall," McLoughlin said mockingly. "I want to get ahead in the world."

The Death Merchant, smiling, turned to Willard Fillmore, who was in charge of the Green Jackets on the west side of the steps. "You know what you and the others have to do. Get set."

Fillmore nodded and turned to the men. The Death Merchant looked across the steps at Lieutenant Merriweather, who was forty feet away, and raised his right arm above his head. Merriweather said something to one of the paratroopers, and immediately six of the men from the group detached themselves from the main body and hurried to a position that placed them twenty feet to the south of the stair slot. In a line, they got down on their hands and knees and began to crawl slowly to the south end of the opening. At the same time the two groups on either side of the rectangular-shaped opening moved toward the north end, where the steps began. Included in the group on the west side were Camellion and McLoughlin.

Only five of the paratroopers were able to reach the south end of the stairway opening. The sixth man could not reach the top of the overhang because of a large loose stone in the southwest corner. The other five took out a variety of grenades and canisters from their equipment bags. Finally, one raised his hand and looked at the Death Merchant, who was standing with the ML9 transceiver in his left hand. Camellion said, *"Now—do it!"* into the mike-end. He raised his right arm and brought it down in a chopping motion.

The five Green Jackets went to work. First they lobbed in flash grenades, tossing them down and inward so that the white canisters would sail inward into the "wall" of darkness. With practiced speed, the five paratroopers followed with tear gas canisters and anti-personnel British K31 grenades—deadly

102

little bombs whose main bursting charge was 12.6 ounces of TNT and whose walls were filled with thousands of slivers of metal. To be caught in the spray of an exploding K31 grenade was like trying to take a bath with a sandblaster. After the grenades and the tear gas came half a dozen L-flares.

Simultaneously, Sergeants Saint-Cluis and Weston and some of their men attacked the two blasted openings in the floor of the east and the west ends, tossing tear gas, K31 grenades, and two incendiaries into each hold. L-flares came last.

Grenades were still thundering into life all over the second level—the explosions mixed with screams of agony—and the ceiling and the floor of the first level were vibrating from concussion when a dozen Green Jackets from the east and the west groups merged at the top of the steps and opened fire with EM automatic rifles. More than three hundred high-powered .280 caliber boat-tailed projectiles zinged through the space where the south wall had stood, many of the slugs glancing off the stone floor with screaming whines. The four thermite incendiaries and the L-flares had killed the darkness, so that the area beyond the blasted opening at the bottom of the stairs glowed with a flickering blue-white glow.

The deep echoes of the K31 grenades and the EM rifles were still rumbling back and forth, sideways, and up and down as Camellion and McLoughlin raced around from the northwest corner of the slot and started down the steps, each man carrying an Ingram submachine gun with an extra-long magazine, each clip filled with 56 special 9-mm cartridges whose projectiles would explode on impact.

Careful not to slip on any loose rock rubble on the steps, Camellion and McLoughlin were almost to the bottom step when the huge stone block, the one that was part of the floor and the overhang in the southwest corner, fell with a loud crash, one end of it sinking into the crater where the door had been. The stone, however, didn't deter Camellion and McLoughlin, both of whom leaped over the crater and stormed into the second basement level.

A scene from the anteroom of hell confronted them. It was apparent that there were any number of rooms on all four sides of the second basement, all of them built around what would have been a rectangular courtyard on the surface. The ceiling was not vaulted. Instead, it was perfectly flat and supported by massive square stone pillars, some of which had very modern light sockets attached to them, although the bulbs had been shattered by concussion. Looking completely out of

103

place were electric wires stretched between the pillars and running to one of the rooms on the south side.

The Death Merchant and McLoughlin each darted to separate pillars, reaching momentary safety a split second before automatic weapons opened fire, scores of slugs zinging off the west side of the pillars.

The Death Merchant felt he knew what had happened. The Provos must have been spread out all over the place, their weapons trained on the one and only entrance. *The three COMP-4 explosions must have shaken the begorrah out of them. Afraid that the ceiling was going to cave in on them they fled to the safety of rooms to the west and the southwest. That's where the firing is coming from. Why not rooms to the east? Later the grenades and the thermite kept them penned up.*

Safe for the moment behind a pillar, Camellion glanced ten feet to his right at McLoughlin, feeling that he knew what Chris was thinking: from the sounds of the firing there were scores of Provos. Furthermore, they had not heard anyone coughing, in spite of tear gas clouds.

The Provos are wearing gas masks—damn them!

Camellion put down the Ingram, reached into one of his shoulder bags, took out a K31 grenade, pointed to it and looked at McLoughlin, who nodded in understanding and reached into one of his own bags. Only then did Camellion pull the pin and throw the grenade around the side of the massive pillar.

For the next three minutes, the Death Merchant and McLoughlin lobbed grenades toward the southwest, not that they expected the grenades to do more than keep the Provos down. The distance was too great. Grenade after grenade roared off, the thousands and thousands of slivers of steel digging thousands and thousands of tiny pits into the ceiling, the wall, and the floor. There were three or four horrible shrieks of agony from Provos who had exposed themselves at the wrong moment.

As soon as the last grenade exploded, the first of the Green Jacket paratroopers, led by Sergeant Jock Saint-Cluis, charged into the area and quickly took cover behind pillars that were large enough to protect three men. Very swiftly, British EM automatic rifles and two Ingram submachine guns were throwing .280 caliber slugs and 9-mm explosive projectiles (each having a recessed impact fuse, with the explosive charge under the fuse) at the various doorways of rooms in which the Provos were hiding.

Over the firing the Death Merchant heard the loud buzzing of the ML9 on his belt. He took out the walkie-talkie and switched it on. The contactee on the other end was Lieutenant Merriweather.

"What is the situation?" Merriweather wanted to know, his tone that of a man who felt insulted. "You were supposed to let me know when the rest of us were to come down."

Camellion almost had to yell to make himself heard above the roaring of weapons. "Give us three minutes, then come down. The Provos are holed up in the west and the southwest. And Merriweather, have three men remain by the hole in the west end on top."

"Why?"

"I'll tell you later. Do as I tell you. Make sure one of them has an open channel on his ML9." Camellion paused. "Sergeant Saint-Cluis, are you listening?"

"I'm 'ere."

"Wait one minute, then you and your men move forward. Before you go, each of you throw a grenade ahead. Got it?"

"Righto. We'll give them blokes 'ell, we will."

"Out to both of you." Camellion switched off the walkie-talkie, shoved it back into its case, picked up the Ingram, and reloaded the weapon with a full magazine. By the time he was finished, he heard Sergeant Saint-Cluis blowing his signal whistle.

They moved west—the paratroopers racing from pillar to pillar, the first men firing while the second group caught up. One para went down with slugs in his chest; then another Green Jacket was iced by terrorist bullets.

Projectiles of various calibers zipped all around the Death Merchant and Chris McLoughlin, some even cutting through their fatigues. But you never count the misses, just as you never consider the projectiles that almost blow your skull apart. "Almost" is never enough.

By the time the charge forward ended, Camellion and Company had gained fifty feet and were safely behind pillars pitted by steel needle shrapnel from K31 grenades. Behind them, Lieutenant Merriweather, Robert Ford, Humphrey Grimes, Sergeant Weston, and Green Jacket paratroopers poured into the bottom level.

Camellion looked around through the dust and the blue-gray smoke of exploded cartridges, then pulled out the ML9 and switched it on. He waited for a few moments, listening to the firing of the paratroopers and the roaring of the weapons of the Provos as they answered.

"Saint-Cluis. Weston. Answer, please."

"I'm 'ere" —Saint-Cluis.

"Weston here, sir."

"Good. I want you to listen in while I contact the men upstairs."

"I left ten up above," interrupted Merriweather.

"Thank you, Lieutenant. The para with the ML9, standing near the west end hole in the floor—answer please."

"I'm Private Marion Davis, sir. What do you want us to do?"

"When I tell you to, I want you to lob a dozen grenades, but not until I give the word. Confirm."

"It's confirmed, sir."

Camellion said to Weston and Saint-Cluis, "Signal your men to cease firing and keep well behind the pillars until the twelfth grenade has exploded. We'll then charge the rest of the way. Confirm, please."

"Confirmed," both noncoms said together.

The Death Merchant did not speak until he heard two whistles give the signal—one long blast followed by two short ones. Only then did he say, "Private Davis—do it. Exactly twelve grenades, two at a time. No more than twelve. Repeat the number, please."

"No more than twelve grenades, sir. Confirmed, sir."

The first two K31s, dropped from the west end, went off with roars that anticipation seemed to make twice as loud—and killed thirteen Provos and wounded seven others with steel slivers.

The IRA terrorists had made a fatal mistake in judgment: knowing the British were closing in on them, the Provos, thinking they were taking advantage of the lull in the firing, had decided to race to rooms on the northwest corner and on the north side, where for a month they had lived, waiting for word from Keenan McGuire. The word had come—and so had the damned, bloody British.

The first Provos to rush forward had raced right into the first grenades and had died instantly, except for the seven who lay wounded and screaming. They didn't scream for long. Two by two the next ten grenades exploded and splattered floor, ceiling, and the sides of pillars with thousands and thousands of steel slivers.

The instant the twelfth grenade exploded, two loud whistles cut through the rumbling echoes and the British force charged the remaining distance to the rooms in the west and southwest, keeping the desperate Provos pinned down with short bursts of fire. In less than two minutes, the British force was closing in on the IRA terrorists, rifles cracking. Right in the front ranks were Richard Camellion and Christopher McLoughlin. Experienced in close-in combat, the Death Merchant and McLoughlin darted through a wide doorway, each man going in as close to the sides of the opening as possible, their Ingrams chattering. Dozens of explosive slugs popped all over crude furniture, crates of canned goods, and seven Provos, two of whom were women.

A 9-mm explosive slug does not a pretty sight make. . . .

The exploding projectiles erupted all over the five men and two women. Gas masks and clothes were shredded, flesh and bone torn apart, the entire mangled mess creating distorted clouds of hideousness before falling to the floor. Several of the corpses crashing to the stone floor appeared even more gruesome as they lay with eyes and mouths open while tomato juice, from one of the shot-apart cases on the shelf, cascaded over their faces . . . especially bizarre in the flickering blue-white glow of the L-flares the paratroopers had tossed ahead.

By now, the paratroopers and the Provos were practically eyeball to eyeball, shooting point-blank at each other and grappling hand to hand.

With yells and the sound of firing all around them, Camellion and McLoughlin darted between stacked cases of B-rations—stolen from the British Army—put down their Ingrams, and pulled sidearms. McLoughlin muttering, "My dear 'Mr. Ringgall,' if you ever do this again, count me out."

McLoughlin then slipped a ring-razor on the middle finger of his right hand, a terrible instrument with an inch-long blade that protruded one fourth of an inch from the top of the ring and lay horizontal along the length of the finger. Each side of the chrome steel blade was as sharp as a brand-new straight razor.

The Death Merchant, who had just finished attaching a pair of Armament Systems Products "toe-stabbers" to his boots, laughed mockingly. "Who's kidding whom? You're like me, Chris. Without excitement to spice up your life, you'd end up in a rubber room. Anyhow, you've developed the habit of eating regularly, and the thousands of bucks you are getting for this little chore will buy a lot of groceries."

"Sure they will," laughed McLoughlin. "If I live to spend it!"

They left the crates and stormed into the next room to the west, a large one that, hundreds of years before, had been used for storage, but now was filled with struggling men—and half a dozen fanatical IRA women who were doing their best to kill the British Green Jackets.

The Death Merchant's long-barrelled M/200 International auto mags roaring in tune with McLoughlin's Browning DA auto-loaders, the two kill-experts charged into the thick of the fighting. Each time an AMP boomed or a Browning DA cracked, a Provo went to hell from either a .357 JSP Magnum slug or a .45 silvertip hollow-point projectile. All the while, Camellion and McLoughlin darted and ducked, weaved and never stayed in the same spot for more than a shave of a second. Yet, in spite of the deadly accuracy of Camellion and McLoughlin (who was called the "Silent Cobra" by some Green Beret Special Services men who had seen him in action in 'Nam), the IRA gradually closed in around the two experts in violence, simply because there were more IRAs than British in the room. On the credit side of Camellion and McLoughlin, the majority of Provos had not had time to reload their weapons; those who had succeeded in doing so were already dead or about to die—including Doreen Roscaberry, a dumpy IRA broad, who was about to get off a round at one of the paratroopers. She was within a split second of pulling the trigger of her Enfield revolver when Camellion put a .357 Magnum slug between her melon-like breasts and made them do a two-second rhumba. With a bullet hole in her red turtleneck sweater, she stumbled backward, her feet trying to keep up with the rest of her. The same para she had been aiming at then put an FN Browning 9-mm into a mean-faced Provo about to bear down, with a Polish P64 SL pistol, on McLoughlin who, beside the Death Merchant, was in the process of wasting the closest Provos trying to surround them.

McLoughlin had exhausted the ammo in the right Browning and had shoved it into a holster. He now used the last 9-mm Parabellum cartridge in the Browning in his left hand to put a hole in the blue jacket of Desmond Ryan, who had been convinced that he could kill the mustached, short-bearded "Silent Cobra." McLoughlin's .45 projectile changed Ryan's mind. The hollow-pointed bullet, designed for maximum upset, also exploded Ryan's heart, blew apart one of his thoracic vertebrae and bored its way through his back. Dead on his feet, Ryan sagged to the left of Chris, falling against Earl Shannon, who was undecided whether to go for Camellion or McLoughlin. The Death Merchant made up Shannon's mind for him. He used the last bullet in his left auto mag to explode Shannon's head and send blobs of his think machine rocketing in all directions.

A few seconds more and Camellion and McLoughlin were forced to rely on their knowledge of, and experience in, hand-to-hand combat. In this area of survival, both men could have given lessons to experts. While in the Green Berets, McLoughlin had even written a book, *Personal Defense*, on the vital subject of staying alive.

Wearing gas masks, three IRAs rushed the Death Merchant. One man had a bayonet; the other two carried short lengths of pipe. Eirann Tone shoved the bayonet forward in an attempt to pierce Camellion's stomach, while Michael Vaughan swung an eighteen-inch pipe at his head. Not to be outdone by his brother crackpots, John Millington tried to get behind the Death Merchant, none of the Provos realizing that they were trying to kill a man who had a working relationship with the Cosmic Lord of Death.

Lightning quick, Camellion ducked, jerked his body to the right, and let the blade of the bayonet slide by his left side, and the pipe swish above his head. At the same time, he slammed the stainless steel barrel of the auto mag down on Tone's right wrist and struck Vaughan in the throat with an expertly delivered *Shito–Ryu Yubi Basami* knuckle/fingertip strike, thumb and finger closing like a vice on the Adam's apple.

The Death Merchant dropped the AMP, raised his left leg slightly to break its fall, sidestepped to the left, reached up with both hands, and grabbed John Millington's right arm that was coming down at him, the length of steel pipe aimed at the back of his head. Before Millington knew what was happening to him. Camellion, while retaining his hold on the man's wrist with his left hand, jerked the man in close and slammed him in the solar plexus with a right-elbow *Hiji* strike. The breath jumped from Millington and he gagged in fear and agony, never realizing that Camellion had half turned. 1—2—3—4! A *Hiji* slam to the point of Millington's chin. Another to the bridge of his nose, along with a left foot heel stamp to the instep of Millington's right foot. And when the man doubled over, his entire body exploding in agony, Camellion slammed his right elbow into the back of his neck.

Camellion spun as the unconscious Millington started to sink to the floor and caught Eirann Tone bending down in an effort to pick up the bayonet with his left hand. Tone couldn't have picked a worse time, although the Death Merchant gave him a big "E" for effort. Tone's right wrist might be broken, but the man had never stopped trying—*even if he does have the intelligence of a retarded frog!* Camellion kicked the man not too hard with his right foot, the three-inch double-edged blade of the "toe-stabber" ripping into the Provo's throat. Just as rapidly the Death Merchant withdrew his foot to keep blood from gushing all over it. Bubbling blood, the terrorist crumpled like a wet paper bag and dropped beside Michael Vaughan, who was lying on his back choking to death, his body jerking, his frantic fingers clawing desperately at his throat.

The IRA terrorists who had attacked Chris McLoughlin were suddenly of the opinion that they had attacked a giant buzz saw. With one leaping, coordinated motion, McLoughlin took out three men simultaneously.

Percy Wicklow—one of the IRA's "Black Geese"—caught a left-handed *Shuto* sword-hand chop that broke his nose and upper jaw and made half a dozen Star Wars explode in his head.

As part of the same three-part motion, McLoughlin presented Henry Wilson with a short left-legged front snap kick that tied his stomach in a double bow around his spine and ruptured the abdominal aorta.

The third part of the attack was a vicious right cross to the face of Richard Parnell, who screamed like a woman being raped as the ring-razor sliced off skin to the jawbone. The poor fool might just as well have stuck his face into an electric meat slicer.

A very fast right-handed *Shuto* chop to the bottom of Wicklow's neck broke his collarbone and forced a sharp portion of it into the top of his left lung. A *Ka-soku-tei* kick to Parnell's groin sent the bleeding man flying backward with the speed of a slow-moving cannonball. Parnell, blood streaming from his face, from which hung a flap of skin the size of a man's hand, crashed into Peadar O'Donnell, another Provo who had been trying to pick up a Colt .45 pistol that Corporal Gerald Eversmith had knocked out of his hand. Eversmith used his EM .280 automatic rifle the way a Thai *Krabi-krabong* expert uses a wooden staff. The barrel of the EM stabbed into O'Donnell's temple, crushing his skull. Eversmith then reversed the weapon in his hand and slammed the butt down on Parnell's skull, ending the man's misery.

The Death Merchant stooped, picked up the AMP he had let fall from his hand and, with McLoughlin and a dozen Green Jackets, looked around the area. Seventeen Provos and four paratroopers lay on the floor. Only a few were moaning; the others were dead. No one had to be told that this particular area was secure, but firing was still going on in the next room to the west, and there were shouts and screams.

McLoughlin strode over to the Death Merchant, who was reloading his auto mags. "I wonder how the others have made out?" Chris asked, glancing quizzically at Camellion.

"We'll know soon enough," Camellion replied in a low undertone and started after the paratroopers, who were cautiously approaching the next room. Just before the first paratroopers reached the door to the room on the west, an EM cracked off a full clip. With the firing came very short screams of agony, then silence.

Camellion, McLoughlin and the paratroopers soon learned what had happened. Lieutenant Merriweather had somehow succeeded in reloading an EM rifle and had gunned down six Provos. The remaining two, a man and a woman, had instantly surrendered. They stood like wooden statues, their arms raised high above their heads.

"I—I've never killed anyone before!" Merriweather said hesitantly when Camellion and McLoughlin walked up to him.

"Easy, isn't it?" McLoughlin said, and cocked his head a little to one side like a dog scenting distant game.

Sergeant Jock Saint-Cluis, accompanied by three paras, came through a doorway to the west. Spotting Camellion, he walked toward him and called out, "We got them all, we did, killed most of them."

"The dead communicate only with each other, Sergeant," Camellion said. "Are there any prisoners?"

"We 'ave a dozen," Saint-Cluis said in a pleased tone. "Sergeant Weston and them two blokes who came with you 'ave 'em all snug in one of them big rooms on the west side."

Twelve paratroopers had been killed and seven wounded. Sixty-four Provos were corpses, nine severely wounded, and thirteen had been taken prisoners. While some Green Jackets took care of the wounded, others spread out and inspected all the rooms of the underground level. They soon discovered why the IRA had not split up and placed half the force in the

111

east rooms, a move that would have enabled them to catch the British in a cross-fire. Some of the east rooms were filled with cases of gelignite and boxes of home-made anti-armor grenades. Other rooms were filled with crates of Russian equipment—Russian RGD5 anti-personnel grenades and portable rocket launchers with grenades to fit. A shoot-out in the east section could have blown the ruins sky high!

The IRA had used weapons from all nations and of all calibers. There were two 7.62-mm Russian RPD light machine guns; British 9-mm Stens; numerous Ak47s; a dozen French Brescias; Uzi 9-mm machine guns; rifles of all descriptions—American M16s and .30 caliber carbines, Czech XZ52s, and G3 Mauser bolt-actions.

In reporting what he and some of the men had found in the east rooms. Sergeant Weston said, "We were lucky. There thermite burned itself out only ten feet from one of the rooms with the gelignite. I'll bet the Provos almost doodled in their pants when they saw how close the thermite was to those explosives."

Lieutenant Merriweather nodded in understanding. He had recovered from his first experience at dispensing death and felt rather good about it. He spoke briskly, with a new authority. "Very well, Sergeant. Our concern now must be for the wounded. I've reported to Captain Gurney and he has radioed for helicopters. They are on the way. Of course, we'll take the prisoners to Londonderry for proper interrogation."

"We'll question the IRA trash right now!" the Death Merchant said in a sharp voice. "We're not going to waste time with a lot of red tape, or take time out to drink tea!"

Merriweather's eyes widened in shock. Manifestly annoyed by Camellion's attitude, he couldn't understand what was happening. Under ordinary circumstances,, he was not rigid in his views, and when circumstances warranted it, he was capable of rapid changes of tack. But this was not one of those times. Nominally he was in charge, and—damn it!—Ringgall was, after all, a civilian.

"Now see here, Ringgall," he began, his face reddening slightly. "I am in—"

"*Mr.* Ringgall to you, Lieutenant!" growled the Death Merchant.

"I am in command here, *Mister* Ringgall!" Merriweather announced fiercely, feeling confident that his authority would prevail. Who did Ringgall think he was, anyway? The man wasn't even British. "You, sir, are a civilian! It is not up to you to say how and where the prisoners will be questioned."

"Ford, get on the ML9 and have Captain Gurney tell our young friend what the score is," Camellion said, his cold blue eyes punching holes in Merriweather's face.

Without a word, Robert Ford pulled out a transceiver, contacted Captain Gurney and briefly explained the situation: that "Mr. Ringgall" wanted to question the IRA prisoners on the spot, but Lieutenant Merriweather was of a different opinion. Added Ford in a firm voice, "Captain Gurney, I need not remind you that a certain department in Whitehall is responsible for this operation and has special A-priority from London."

"Let me speak to Lieutenant Merriweather," Gurney said promptly.

Ford handed the ML9 hand-held set to Merriweather, across whose face spasms of emotion were flickering.

"Yes sir, this is Lieutenant Merriweather. His voice was uncertain.

"Lieutenant Merriweather, you will obey each and every order of Mr. Ford or Mr. Grimes," Gurney said mechanically. "Is that clear?"

"Yes, sir." A deep crimson flush began spreading over Merriweather's face and he lowered his voice as though communing with himself. "Is there anything else, sir?"

"Do as they tell you, Lieutenant—out."

His hand shaking, Merriweather switched off the walkie-talkie and handed it back to Ford, who said pleasantly enough, "The prisoners will remain behind with us. We'll bring them to the surface when we're through questioning them."

"Leave Sergeant Saint-Cluis and ten Green Jackets with us," Camellion said with satisfaction.

Merriweather glanced at Ford, an unmistakable expression of misgiving on his face.

"You heard him, Lieutenant," Ford said.

The thirteen IRA captives, nine men and four women, sat on the floor. All had been thoroughly searched, including the women, one of whom had a cut and swollen lip. Rose Mac-Bride had resisted the soldiers and one had smashed her in the face with his fist. All thirteen sat with their backs against the wall, their hands on top of their heads, every one contemplating either long years of imprisonment or internment. All preferred imprisonment, which meant a definite sentence. Internment could mean being locked up for a week, a year, or forever.

The tear gas had cleared and the terrorists, Camellion, and the remaining British force no longer wore gas masks. Sergeant Saint-Cluis looked at the sullen prisoners, whose eyes were filled with hate and determination, and at the six Green Jacket paratroopers guarding them.

"They're a treacherous lot, they are," Saint-Cluis said to Camellion. He motioned with his FN Browning toward the captives. "They never accept imprisonment. They're always trying to escape."

Robert Ford said, "We're not going to get any information out of them, either." His eyes skipped from captive to captive, none of whom was over thirty years old. "We never do, except when we use extreme methods."

Chris McLoughlin smiled like a naughty boy who had just successfully stolen the whole damn cookie jar. "We'll get answers. You can bet on it."

The Death Merchant walked closer to the line of prisoners, looking at them with his curious corn-flower blue eyes. Seven feet in front of the line of captives he stopped, unzipped the front of his fatigues, reached underneath on the left side, and pulled a .22 long-rifle High Standard Sports-King auto pistol from a shoulder holster. Thirteen pairs of eyes watched his every movement. Ford, Grimes, Saint-Cluis, and the paratrooprs knew he wasn't going to shoot birds.

Chris McLoughlin, who had moved to stand alongside Camellion, took the weapon from Camellion's hand and studied it. "Nice," Chris commented. "One of the best small-caliber jobs around." He sighted down the barrel at one of the captives, lining up the sights on the tip of the man's nose. The IRA terrorist didn't flinch.

McLoughlin handed the .22 back to the Death Merchant. "I've always been amazed at the damage a .22 can do to the human body. Its velocity is greater than a bullet of heavier caliber. Once it gets inside a person, a .22 tumbles all over the place, chopping up a man's insides."

"Or a woman's!" Camellion said. He stepped closer to the prisoners and looked down at a man to his left, a baby-faced killer with innocent brown eyes and symmetrical facial features. The man had a thin red scarf knotted around his neck.

"Tell me, my fine leprechaun," Camellion said softly, "Do you feel like talking? Or am I wasting my precious time."

Eoin O'Duffy thrust out his chin in defiance. "Oh, sure'n I

114

could tell you a'plenty," he sneered, "but ye can go to hell."

"Too bad," Camellion said mildly. He dropped the barrel of the Sports-King and pulled the trigger. The High Standard barked, the report bouncing back and forth off the stone walls. The .22 hollow pointed long rifle slug sliced into the belly of O'Duffy who screamed, his body jumping. With loud "Oh—oh—ohs!" pouring out of his mouth, the terrorist flopped over on his left side, his arms and legs jerking in agony.

"I'll bet he doesn't last five minutes," McLoughlin said merrily. "The bullet probably bounced into his inferior vena cava."

"Or the abdominal aorta," Camellion said. "He's bleeding to death right now. We still have twelve of the dear darlings, just bubbling over with eagerness to tell us what we want to know."

While Ford and Grimes and the paras were surprised at the Death Merchant's sudden brutal action, the Provos were terrified, although they tried not to show it. The British had never treated captured IRA terrorists with kid gloves. There were beatings, deprivation of sleep, the "Cells of Noise," and other tortures. Electric cattle prods were a part of every session of questioning. Troublemakers were often isolated for months and months in small cells, thick leather hoods over their heads, hands cuffed behind their backs. Not infrequently they went mad. But this tall man with a pistol! He didn't offer any hope.

The shooting of O'Duffy was more than Paul Kiely could take.

"Murdering bastard!" His hatred overcoming commonsense, he removed his hands from his head and shook his fists at Camellion, screaming, "British pigs—all of you! But we'll have our day. The day will come when not one of ye British will be in Ulster. We'll kill every one of you damned Johnny Bulls. We'll—"

The Sports-King cracked twice. Kiely howled, jumped, and started to make noises like a chicken being plucked alive. Camellion had shot him twice, putting a slug in each kneecap.

Saint-Cluis guffawed. "Well, that's one bucko we don't 'ave to worry about. 'e won't be tryin' to escape. 'e'll be walkin' with canes the rest of 'is life, 'e will."

Humphrey Grimes cleared his throat and shifted uncomfortably from foot to foot. "I say Mr. Ringgall, your method does seem to be a bit extreme."

115

"One does not defend oneself against a snake by throwing rose petals at it," Camellion remarked, coolly searching the faces of the other Provos. They stared back with hate and fear. "Against sadists who murder innocent women and children, one can only use methods they understand."

McLoughlin nodded vigorously in agreement. "Especially true of fanatics who pray to God on Sunday but burn, bomb, and murder the rest of the week."

The Death Merchant's eyes settled on a Provo whose wedge-shaped face mirrored pure hate and deep fear.

"What is your name, my fine piece of murderous trash?"

"Go ta hell!" Mick O'Neill spit out. "If you think you can bully me inta tellin' you anything, you have another think comin.' Shoot and be damned ta hell with the rest of the Protestant scum."

Camellion turned to Sergeant Saint-Cluis. "Have him tied to a pillar."

Giving Camellion a curious look, Saint-Cluis motioned to two of the paras who went over to O'Neill, yanked him to his feet, and dragged him to a pillar. They handcuffed his hands behind his back and used a length of belt from one of the dead Provos to fasten the handcuffs to a large iron ring on the pillar.

Camellion sauntered over to O'Neill. No longer was he wearing that half-crooked smile on his mouth. "An IRA base of this size would have to have contact with Keenan McGuire. Where is he? Where is McGuire?"

"Fuck you and your queen, ye Limey son of a bitch!"

His expression remaining calm, the Death Merchant reached into one of his shoulder bags and took out one of the last L-flares he had. He looked again at the nervous O'Neill.

"Last chance to change your mind, old chap?"

"Go to hell." Fear was etched into O'Neill's face, but he did not have a choice. He could not give in.

Camellion shrugged. "We all will, sooner or later." He reached out, opened the man's jacket and shoved the rounded red cylinder of the L-flare down underneath the man's belt, in such a way that the end which would ignite was shoved into the man's stomach. He pulled the tab.

The sight was not pleasant. Within seconds the L-flare burst into a bright blue-white flame and began to burn into O'Neill's clothes and flesh. Screaming hideously, O'Neill jumped and twisted and struggled against the handcuffs and the belt securing him to the ring, his every movement one of

116

frantic desperation—like a trapped grasshopper being roasted on a red-hot griddle. In no time at all, he was blazing from belt to head, his shrieks of agony ringing throughout the underground rooms, the stink of burning cloth, flesh, and leather heavy in the smoky air. The stench of his woolly pullover, mingled with the fetid odor of fried flesh, was particularly nauseating. Even worse, for those watching—and no one was able to tear his (and her) eyes away from the horrible sight— was how O'Neill's face first turned red, then the skin, shrivelling like bacon, turned brown, then black. Finally he sagged, a blackened, stinking, mushy, unrecognizable mess. . . .

Two of the paratroopers hurried off to one side and vomited. A few of the IRAs also heaved up their insides.

The Death Merchant faced the remaining IRA captives, who now drew back, naked terror on their faces, fear they could neither hide nor disguise. The Provos were at a loss. Confronting them was a man who was more than their equal in violence.

Camellion's eyes settled on a man to his left, a brawny young man with curly brown hair, a short brown beard, long sideburns, and a slack mouth. He reminded Camellion of a man too lazy to work but too frightened to steal.

Camellion motioned to the two paratroopers. "Take him."

"Wait!" yelled Conor MacMassey. He tried to scoot back on his rear end as though trying to push himself through the stone wall. "Why me?" he screamed. "O'Riondan is the messenger. He's the one who can tell you about 'The Bomber!' "

Half a dozen of the terrorists began cursing MacMassey and screaming insults at him.

"Shut up, you damned traitor!" shouted Jane Kissale. "Die like a man, like a true patriot of Ulster. Be man enough to—"

The High Standard auto-loader in Camellion's hand cracked. Jane Kissale fell back, her mouth wide open, her eyes staring. A bullet hole was in her forehead, an inch above the bridge of her nose.

"Which one is O'Riondan?" Camellion looked again at MacMassey. When the terrorist hesitated, as if Kissale's words were making him have second thoughts, Camellion used deadly accuracy to shoot off the tip of his left earlobe, snarling, "Keep stalling, stupid, and you'll end up tied to a pillar and looking like a piece of burnt French toast."

"Him! He's Ian O'Riondan!" MacMassey pointed at a man toward the end of the line to his left, a man with bushy brown hair, eyebrows, and mustache. "He can tell you where

McGuire is. He can also tell you about the Soviet submarine. . . ."

It was an hour later that the Death Merchant, McLoughlin, and the others emerged from the two basement levels of Lha-Beul-tinne. There was only one IRA captive in custody—Ian O'Riondan, who had refused to talk until he had been stripped naked, tied to a pillar, and an L-flare taped to his left ankle.

"It will take you hours to die . . . all alone down here," the Death Merchant had told him.

Only then did O'Riondan crack, but with a stipulation: that all the other Provos be killed. "Or they'll be pointin' me out as a traitor! I wouldn't live with that over me. I wouldn't live a day in prison, I wouldn't."

"Kill 'em," Camellion had said to one of the paratroopers. When the man had hesitated, the Death Merchant gently took the automatic rifle from his hand and had calmly terminated the terrified IRA captives, many of whom screamed in fear and panic when the slugs hit them.

Camellion had then turned back to O'Riondan and had gripped the tab of the L-flare with thumb and forefinger.

"Now—talk."

With the stink of the half-cremated O'Neill fresh in his nostrils, Ian O'Riondan was only too anxious to comply with Camellion's order.

They were close to the center of the ruins and were just entering the grand ballroom when they saw the man coming down the stairs. He had just reached the first step and was moving slowly downward, acting as though he didn't know the bottom portion of the stairs was missing.

The man, in his forties, wore clothes that belonged to another century, to the 1700s—shoes with large brass buckles, blue satin knee-breeches, white hose, and a waistcoat with long split tails and wide lapels. Above his ruffled shirt was a large, folded bow tie. He wore a powdered white wig.

"Blimey!" muttered Sergeant Saunt-Cluis. "That bloke don't 'ave no business here. Where does he think he's going?"

"I don't believe it!" Robert Ford said almost inaudibly, goggling at the strange figure. "I can't believe it!"

"I think a better question might be what is he," said McLoughlin, who sensed that the figure, who by now was in

118

the center of the top half of the steps, was strangely out of context, out of time, out of place.

"He looks real enough," Humphrey Grimes said.

"But where will he go when he reaches the end of the stairs?" one of the Green Jacket paras said. "He can't walk on air."

The Death Merchant studied the figure coming down the stairs, his expression one of faint ennui. *There is only one way to convince them!* "Sergeant, order him to stop." Camellion's tone was equally bored. "If he doesn't"—*And he won't!*—"open fire."

"You there," shouted Saint-Cluis. "I order you to 'alt and identify yourself."

The figure on the steps didn't turn its head or respond in any way, but continued to descend the stairs. Saint-Cluis raised his automatic rifle but didn't fire, sheer shock preventing him from pulling the trigger. A moment before Saint-Cluis' finger would have pulled the trigger, the figure reached the last step of the dangling upper section—and continued to walk downward, seemingly walking on air! Yet from the movement of the man's legs and the motion of the rest of his body, he was walking on steps that were there, at least to him—that had been there when he was alive.

There were loud gasps of astonishment from the paratroopers.

"A bloody damned ghost!" said one man in awe.

"Jesus, Mary, and Joseph!" croaked Ian O'Riondan, who would have crossed himself if his hands hadn't been tied behind his back.

"A collective hallucination," Humphrey Grimes said with passionate intensity, the corners of his mouth twitching. "We are experiencing a collective hallucination."

"In one respect you're partially correct," Camellion said. "An hallucination is strictly one form of consciousness, as good and true a sensation as if there were a real object there. Only the object is not there. The figure we are seeing is not there. What we are seeing is one form of an apparition, that's all."

"But the bloke looks as solid as we do!" whispered Saint-Cluis. "Look! What is he doing?"

The phantom, having reached the bottom of the invisible stairs, walked across the room and began going through the motions of opening a door that wasn't there.

119

"We're seeing a memory pattern," Camellion said. "We are seeing electromagnetic waves that somehow impinged themselves on the surroundings. Our friend is opening a door, a door that existed and was in that spot when he was alive."

The ghost continued on its way. It walked straight ahead for another twenty feet, went straight through a wall, and was gone.

No one spoke. The men stood there, staring at the place in the wall where the specter had vanished.

"We saw a memory from the past," Camellion explained. "It didn't even know it was there. In short, it didn't know it was a 'ghost.'"

Robert Ford looked curiously at Camellion. "You said only one form of apparition. What's the other kind?"

"A genuine apparition, the spirit of a dead person, a spirit with personal awareness, memory, purpose, and a full realization of who and what he is. The second kind is very rare."

Ford and Grimes regarded Camellion dubiously. As far as they were concerned, he might as well have told them that he knew the exact location of Santa Claus' toy factory at the North Pole.

"It all has to do with time and the brain," said McLoughlin who has also studied parapsychology. He looked around the enormous ballroom, whose stone walls were partially covered with moss and creeping vines. The Irish jigs and reels and ballads that must have been played in this room! He could almost hear the hand-clapping and foot-pounding, with men and women energized by the sprightly piping, fiddling, and flute-playing, and by the flashing feet of scores of stepdancers. And just maybe they were still there . . . dancing and singing in their own private world of the dead.

"Mr. Weaver is correct," Camellion said to an intrigued Ford and Grimes and Saint-Cluis. "You see, the brain does not generate consciousness. Rather it serves as a detector, selector, amplifier, and what might be termed a two-way transmitter of consciousness; and consciousness, like time, is relative. There are all kinds of theories about time. The truth is that time does not rush over a static history at a certain rate of speed. There is no fixed 'fate.' History is only what is left behind after time has passed."

"But you can't change a time dimension into a space dimension," Grimes said. "Or didn't that apparition exist in time and space?"

"It existed outside of space and time, outside of our time

and space, both of which are relative in our continuum." Camellion abruptly changed the subject, his voice cool and even. "The dead might be all around us in another continuum, but they're not going to help us get that Soviet sub."

The small group moved through the ruins. Overhead they could hear helicopters coming in to ferry the wounded to a hospital in Londonderry.

They were leaving the ruins and were in the late afternoon air when Humphrey Grimes said to Camellion, "We're going to be cutting it close. Ballycastle isn't all that distant, but there is a matter of organization to be considered."

The Death Merchant did not reply. He had never liked working with the British. They always had a nasty streak of morality that complicated things. *Only the Israelis know how to deal with terrorists!* Camellion thought. *They kill everyone they get their hands on. . . .*

CHAPTER ELEVEN

Colonel Terrance Wyck-Mason, the commander of the British force in Ballycastle would have liked to have told the four men to go to hell. He carefully flicked a piece of lint from the top of his peaked uniform cap, which rested on one side of the desk, and privately conceded that he had no choice but to cooperate with the men sitting in front of his desk. The order from General Ralph Clark-Masterson, confirmed by radio, left no room for doubt. Damn SIS. Those cloak-and-dagger paper-pushers were always sticking their suspicious noses into the business of the Military and blathering about "special missions." And now, here were these four who had arrived just after dark, with talk of a Soviet submarine that was to deliver a mysterious something to Keenan McGuire. The trouble with SIS was that its people watched too many spy thrillers on the telly.

"Very well, gentlemen. My force is at your disposal," Wyck-Mason said pleasantly, neither his tone nor expression betraying his disbelief and annoyance. "Please understand that I can supply only a portion of my men. Ballycastle is a pot full of both IRA and UDA alike. We are the only deterrent against mass anarchy."

"We understand, Colonel." Humphrey Grimes crossed his legs and gazed steadily at the gray-haired, narrow-shouldered man who strove to radiate an aura of brisk efficiency. "Remember that at all times this operation demands the utmost discretion. How many men and vehicles can you supply for tomorrow night's operation?"

"How many regulars and vehicles will you need?"

Grimes turned to Camellion, who was sitting to his right. "What is your estimation, Mr. Ringgall?"

The Death Merchant replied promptly, all the while looking at Wyck-Mason. "Based on what Ian O'Riondan told us, I should say we'll require 125 men, not counting the crews of the armor. We'll need three scout cars, several helicopters, and five armored cars, preferably Boarhounds."

Wyck-Mason opened a blue folder on his desk, removed several sheets of paper and studied them for several minutes. Another sore point with Wyck-Mason was this chap called "Ringgall." He certainly wasn't British. Neither was the other one—"Mr. Weaver." Americans? CIA? If they were, it was almost a certainty they would botch up the operation. No one in his right mind trusted the Americans, mainly because of their President and his State Department. Both seemed to be committed to appeasement wherever possible, from Rhodesia to the PLO, from Teheran to Taiwan. All the President could do was call on the World Court, a body famous only for its do-nothingism. What bloody nonsense! Asking powerless people to ask terrorists not to be naughty! The Soviet Union? More stupidity! Like bashing the Russians with the cobwebs of fishing restrictions

"I can let you have 90 regulars, one helicopter, two scout cars, three Hublers, and one Boarhound," Wyck-Mason said, still looking at the papers. "And of course three Harrington troop carriers. Any more ordnance is not possible."

Putting the papers back into the folder, Wyck-Mason was mildly surprised when none of his guests protested.

Camellion said, "I understand, Colonel Wyck-Mason, that your force is equipped with Atchisson 12-gauge assault shotguns. Could you spare a dozen?"

"More if you want them," Wyck-Mason said, feeling pleased with himself and certain that SIS would forward a good report of his full cooperation to General Clark-Masterson in Belfast. "But how is this operation on land to be coordinated with Her Majesty's Navy?" He gave a polite laugh. "I have no jurisdiction over the Navy."

"The Navy is not to be involved in the operation," said Robert Ford with an air of finality.

Wyck-Mason sat up straight with a new alertness. "But I was under the impression that the Soviet submarine. . . ." He shrugged and left the sentence unfinished, not wanting to appear to be prying. Anyhow, Ford had given him the answer by admitting that the navy would not be involved. SIS did not want to stop the Soviet underseas boat. SIS wanted the delivery to be made.

As if reading Wyck-Mason's mind, the Death Merchant said, "O'Riondan doesn't know where the U-boat will surface. No one does except Keenan McGuire and his close associates.

124

Should a lot of navy patrol boats start crisscrossing the North Channel in a pattern search, all we would accomplish would be to scare the sub away."

"But you are convinced there will be trouble in Ballycastle?" Wyck-Mason bent forward confidentially.

"Affirmative. Either tomorrow night or early in the morning of the next day," Camellion said. "In Ballycastle and in Londonderry, as part of a diversionary tactic."

"But that's about all we know," Humphrey Grimes interjected. "Except that McGuire will be short a lot of IRA personnel. Half the force at the castle ruins was to be used to stir up trouble in Londonderry. The other half was to link up with McGuire's force on the northern coast, six miles west of Ballycastle."

"I presume that section of the coast will be your target area," Wyck-Mason said, a trifle impatiently. "But how will you know the time to move in?"

The Death Merchant smiled half-heartedly. "We don't. We only know that the sub is due to show up between midnight and dawn. We'll have to depend on the helicopter and slip in scouts to watch the area." He terminated the explanation with a wave of his hand. "As things stand, we might scare off McGuire and his killers. But I don't think so." *I don't think so because we're not going to use a chopper and scouts. We're going to depend on the ten USDTs we planted in the area before coming here. But why tell you about it?*

"Your prospects for success are not very good," said Wyck-Mason, with the firm assurance of a weather forecaster predicting heavy showers. "McGuire has spies everywhere. Right now he knows about your success at Lha-Beul-tinne. He may have already decided not to go through with the pickup. He's not noted for taking desperate chances."

"The possibility has crossed our minds," Camellion conceded.

"We're counting on McGuire not being able to contact the Russians in time to cancel out," ventured McLoughlin, cracking the knuckles of his left hand. "We know the Ruskies. They wouldn't be dealing if they hadn't set the time and weren't calling the shots. McGuire will have to dance to the tune they're playing."

"Wherever McGuire is, he's not hiding out in this immediate area," Wyck-Mason said professionally, "although I suppose it is possible that he could be holed up somewhere in Ballycastle. I doubt it."

Humphrey Grimes appeared to be troubled. "Colonel, what about deserted buildings, ruins and the like in this area?"

"Negative, with the exception of Dunaney Castle and Burncourt House," Wyck-Mason said. Dunaney stands on a cliff about three miles south of town. It was built about 1510 by the MacDonnell family and was the inspiration for naming the town—Baile and Chaistil, which means 'Town of the Castle.' McGuire and his men aren't hiding in those ruins. I've had men posted there for the last seven months. In fact, we're using the ruins as an outpost."

"And Burncourt House?" Camellion asked.

"It's east of town, several miles or so. There isn't anything there but a shell, a lot of walls and rubble. It was built in 1641 and was considered one of the most perfect examples of an English fortified Tudor mansion in Ireland. McGurie isn't there. We send patrols there twice a day."

"McGuire could be hiding in or around Londonderry," Ford offered. "For all we know, he could have been within a few miles of us."

"Or south or east of Ballycastle," suggested McLoughlin with an emphatic nod of his head. "He could be anywhere in Ulster. He could have been in the Republic of Ireland. I say 'have been' because he has to be close enough to meet the submarine tomorrow night, or, to be technical, the day after tomorrow."

"At this stage of the game, it's purely academic," the Death Merchant said. He stood up and looked at Colonel Wyck-Mason. "Colonel, we'd appreciate your having the men and the armor ready tomorrow by 18.00 hours."

Wyck-Mason pushed back his chair and got to his feet, as did the other men.

"The men and the armor will be ready." Wyck-Mason nodded congenially. "But permit me to say that I think you're chasing a ghost. I seriously doubt if McGuire keeps his appointment with the Russians."

He pulled at the bottom of his uniform coat, straightening it, and looked startled when the four men on the other side of the desk smiled broadly, as though they might be enjoying a private joke, or a special secret, among themselves.

"You find my remark amusing?"

"Sorry, Colonel," Camellion apologized. "It wasn't anything you said. "We were only thinking of another ghost. . . ."

126

CHAPTER TWELVE

The death of the General must be investigated.

The one-line coded message from Courtland Grojean, the director of the CIA's covert section, had arrived at the American Embassy in Dublin, Ireland, at two o'clock in the afternoon. It was five P.M. by the time the Company station at the embassy tracked Camellion to British Army Headquarters in Ballycastle and radioed the message to him. The station sent the original message in the special code that only Camellion and Grojean could decipher.

The Death Merchant was still thinking of the serious implications of the message at two-fifteen the next morning as the armored column moved through the deserted street of Ballycastle, a coastal port that was divided into two parts, each of which was almost a separate community and wore its own distinctive air of individuality.

Old Upper Town (almost all Protestant) was dignified and spacious, and was linked to the busy Lower Town (Roman Catholic) by a terrace of Victorian houses. The fine buildings of the Lower Town were grouped around the harbor and softened by a grove of mature trees.

Led by a huge Conqueror tank, with its 120-mm gun and infrared searchlight, the other nine vehicles rolled over the cobblestones of Old Upper Town without incident. The tank would stop at the edge of town and return to British Army headquarters half a mile east of Ballycastle. After the tank came the two Snapper TR70 scout cars, four-wheeled vehicles, the tops enclosed in light armor. Two rectangular ports were in the metal windshield. There was independent drive to all four wheels, and entry was through a door in the rear. The rear top could also be opened into one large door that was made in two sections, each section folding accordion-like on either side of the top of the car.

Behind the two scout cars was a Hubler armored car. Next in line was the Boarhound, a 24-ton, 8-wheeled armored car

127

that was virtually a wheeled tank. Carrying a crew of five, the Boarhound had a top speed of fifty MPH, a 50-mm gun in the turret, and two .30 caliber Browning machine guns in the front hull.

Another Hubler was behind the Boarhound. Then came the three Harrington MK7 troop carriers. Last in line was the third Hubler. The tank commander and the gunner stood in the turret of the Conqueror, studying the buildings on each side of the street, each man using an infrared Night Sight scope, one man taking the right side, the other the left. A man was in each open turret of the Hublers; they, too, surveyed the area through infrared scopes.

Captain Thomas Kipp, Lieutenant Arthur George, and Robert Ford rode in the first scout car, with Camellion, McLoughlin, and Grimes in the second, all dressed in British commando fatigues.

McLoughlin consulted his wristwatch. "We're on schedule and should reach the coastal area in plenty of time, even if we do meet resistance on the road."

"Just so we get McGuire," Grimes said savagely, "hopefully alive. "I'm going to enjoy seeing a rope snap his neck."

The Death Merchant remained silent. The hens had just started to sit, and it was too early to count the eggs. Anyhow, there were a lot of IRA weasels around the hen house. On the other hand, there wasn't any point in knocking success. Chris was correct. They were on schedule, and so far everything was working out as planned. At 01.45 hours four of the Ultra-Sound Distance Transmitters (USDTs) had begun to pick up activity along the beach area, eight and a half kilometers west of town, the sounds of vehicles that were transmitted from the USDTs to the central receiving station housed in a metal attache case.

At about the same time, the spotter posted on Fair Head, an enormous talus of rock on the coast, 636 feet high and just west of town, reported that five trucks and seven cars had entered the area and had stopped several hundred feet from the beach, not far from a grove of trees.

The soldier doing the actual spotting was using a B77 Recon Infrared Scope that had a magnification of 40 times 150, with light amplifying power of 200 times that of the human eye. The B77 was so powerful that one could identify a vehicle at seven miles, aircraft at twenty-five miles, and the kind of weapon someone was carrying at five miles.

Excitedly the spotter had reported that the Provos had unloaded motorboats from three of the trucks—small two-seater jobs—and were carrying them to the water. Estimated number of Provos—at least a hundred.

The Death Merchant and the other men had been running toward their own armored vehicles by the time the Provos had set the motorboats in the water.

His eyes on the legs of the soldier standing on the turret platform, Camellion reassured himself that all was in order. A radio watch was on in each vehicle. The British base was relaying messages from the spotter on Fair Head to Captain Kipp in the first scout car. If anything important developed along the beach, Kipp would contact Camellion on a walkie-talkie.

The Conqueror rumbled into Lower Town, its heavy tracks clanking on the cobblestones. Captain Kipp got on the radio and instructed the spotters in the tank and in the turrets of the Hublers to be especially alert. "These Romanists hate every hair on your heads," he said. "Study every roof, every window, every doorway. Don't take chances."

"He seems like a good man," Humphrey Grimes said to Kipp. "Poor chap. Did you see the expression on his face when Wyck-Mason told him that while he would be officially in charge, he'd take final orders from us, since we're 'tactical experts?' "

The Death Merchant moved his eyes toward the driver, then looked at Grimes and shook his head, Signaling for silence. Grimes nodded in understanding.

"Yeah," McLoughlin said with a slight laugh. "Let's not tell anyone what kind of 'tactical experts' we really are. Martian Space Patrol! That's us!"

The soldier standing in the left hatch of the turret leaned down and called out. "We're entering the Diamond. If the bloody damned Provos have planned an ambush, it should be along here."

The Diamond was the business square of Lower Town. On three sides of the Diamond were business houses, none over four stories tall. On the fourth side was a block of Georgian buildings that stood on the site once occupied by Hugh Boyd's fortified manor. Nothing happened. Not a shot was fired. The armored column rolled through the Diamond and headed west on Ardboe Street. Seven more blocks and the column would enter Harpwire Road, which led to the outskirts and the beach area.

When the tank and the nine other vehicles were three

blocks into Ardboe Street, Captain Kipp's voice came over the radio, firm and steady. "Full stop, all vehicles. Full alert all personnel. One of the men in the Conqueror has seen something suspicious on the roof of a building to our left. The building is brick. Front painted white. A greengrocery fronting the street on the bottom floor."

Another voice broke in over the radio. "This is Wilson in H2. Activity on the second floor of the building across from us, to the left. Movement behind drapes on a second floor window. We think"—Wilson's voice then rang with alarm. "They're opening the window. They—"

Wilson's frantic voice was cut short by the rattle and the roar of a submachine gun firing from the second floor of the building to the left of the second Hubler. Several other submachine guns opened fire from the building directly across from the tank—to the right.

The soldiers had already dropped inside the turrets and the hatches had clanged shut by the time the Death Merchant had grabbed the mike of the TC-radio and was barking out orders.

"Attention, men in all vehicles. The turret-mounted Brownings can't be tilted high enough to reach the roofs. Some of you get outside the vehicles and use your submachine guns. Rake every window and the edges of the roofs. Watch out for grenades and incendiaries."

Already the soldier who had been spotting from the half-turret in Camellion's scout car was raking the left side of the street with a .30 caliber Browning, firing from inside the turret, his vision limited to a rounded 4-by-23-inch slot in the armor above the weapon. But even when the weapon was at maximum tilt upward, the stream of metal-jacketed projectiles could not reach past the second floor.

Camellion had to shout to make himself heard above the roaring of the Browning and the chattering of the machine guns of Grimes and McLoughlin, both of whom had left the scout car through the rear door.

"Tank driver!" yelled the Death Merchant. "Your vehicle is too large to maneuver in the street. Turn your gun around and crash into the greengrocer's on the first floor and remain there. If possible, get off some shells into the buildings on the other side of the street."

He tapped the driver of the scout car on the shoulder. "Grab a Patchett and come with me." Camellion turned and, as the driver started to get out of the seat, grabbed a Sterling submachine gun and moved through the oval-shaped hatch-way in the rear.

The soldiers were members of the Forty-sixth Royal Fusil-liers—the "Hell-Devil" Division—and were well-trained. Hell-Devils were behind each vehicle, crouched down and raking the windows on both sides of the street with devastating streams of Sterling and Patchett 9-mm projectiles. While plate glass windows of store fronts exploded and a billion pieces of glass fell from hundreds of upper-story windows, the huge Conqueror tank spun on its tracks and headed for the front of the greengrocery. At the same time the turret revolved so that the barrel of the 120-mm cannon would be stretched out over the rear of the vehicle.

The Conqueror charged across the cobblestones and came to the high curb, the heavy tracks crumbling much of the raised concrete. The front of the tank crashed through the middle of the shop, the mudguards, the front towing hook, and the thick glacis plate ripping through glass, bricks, and wood. Parts of the ceiling and much of the side walls fell in-ward on the tank as the expert driver moved the tons of steel fully inside the building. The floor crumbled like wet tissue paper, and the tank settled three feet to the hard earth below. At once, the commander of the tank began to turn the turret from starboard to port, to keep the barrel of the gun free of the rubble that was still falling.

"Try to sight in on some of the buildings to the southeast," he ordered the gunner.

Apparently the Provos, not counting on being detected, had been taken by surprise, before they could get off their barrage of hand grenades and Molotov cocktails. To make matters worse for them, some of the Hell-Devils had grenade launch-ers attached to their EM rifles and were shooting heat gren-ades through the windows on both sides of the street. There were brief, bright flashes of fire, followed by ear-pounding ex-plosions and thousands of pieces of broken bricks falling to the sidewalks. Provos were firing from windows and rooftops along the entire length of the block where the armored col-umn was strung out. Hell-Devils were behind each vehicle, firing at the upper stories and the roofs of buildings on both sides of Ardboe Street. Within minutes every window in the block was shot out and the bricks were pitted from hundreds of slugs. Now and then one of the spotters in the Hublers would see figures darting about in a room on one of the upper floors and would get off a round with their 37-mm cannon. Wherever the shell struck and exploded, a portion of the wall would disappear, leaving a gaping hole.

Regardless of the wall of steel projectiles that the Hell-Devils were throwing at the Provos, the terrorists continued to fight with fanatical fury. Some even managed to toss grenades and Molotov cocktails through the blasted windows and holes in the walls. The trouble was that, because of the furious firing, none of them could get close enough to a window or a hole to effect a long-distance pitch; so the grenades exploded harmlessly below, although some of them did shower the vehicles with metal fragments, wounding several soldiers who did not duck fast enough. The Molotov cocktails exploded on the sidewalk, a few falling so close to the blasted store-fronts that they started fires in the interior.

It took less than four minutes for the gunner of the Conqueror to fire the first 120-mm shell, which whined over the other vehicles and struck the second story of a building ten feet behind, and to the left of, the last Hubler armored car. The shell exploded with a roar that must have been heard all the way to Belfast. Almost all of the front wall of one building vanished in a flash of red and orange fire and a giant puff of smoke and dust. Tons of broken bricks collapsed inward and outward, dropping to the floor and the ground, many of the chunks striking the tops and left sides of the last Hubler and the last troop carrier in line. A dozen Hell-Devils yelled in pain when chunks of bricks struck them about the shoulders and arms, bouncing harmlessly off their steel helmets.

Humphrey Grimes and Private Lawrence Ogilvie, the driver of the scout car, fired at buildings on the right side of the street. The soldier in the small turret kept revolving the metal cylinder, raking rooms on both side of the street with .30 caliber Browning slugs, while Camellion and McLoughlin "worked" the left side of the road.

Both more enraged than a hornet with the hiccups, Camellion and McLoughlin fired with precision, never wasting ammo. Damn the Provos! The IRA was forcing the British not only to waste ammo but to lose time. The Death Merchant had expected the "treasure" to become the "hunter," but not to this extent.

"If you ask me, the 'Rose of Tralee' is an old bitch!" shouted McLoughlin, who then shoved a full magazine of 9-mm cartridges into his Sterling.

"Let us not complain about the complexities of life," joked

132

Camellion. "Only through suffering, me boy, will we reach the Kingdom of Heaven!"

He spotted figures on the third floor of a building to his right. The provos were behind a window of a room whose front wall had been partially destroyed by a 37-mm shell from one of the Hubler turret guns. As the Death Merchant raised the Sterling and gently touched the trigger, he found something ridiculously grotesque about the ballet of Provo forms whose speed was increased by fear and fanaticism . . . fathers and husbands . . . mothers' sons . . . all doomed to die. And die they did when Camellion's 9-mm projectiles tore into their flesh and ripped away the fabric of their lives.

Blam! Camellion and McLoughlin both fell back when a grenade exploded not far before them, pieces of shrapnel pinging against their helmets and face shields. Half a dozen bits of jagged metal sliced through the fatigues over Camellion's chest, but the pieces of shrapnel were stopped by the Mermex flak "vest" he wore. All the members of the British force wore Mermex flak vests as protection against far-flung shrapnel and small arms fire, the Mermex material covering their chests, stomachs, groins, and backs. However, the material would not stop a machine gun or automatic rifle bullet.

McLoughlin had also taken pieces of shrapnel, but he too was unharmed, except for his dignity. None of the shrapnel had reached Grimes and Private Ogilvie.

The Death Merchant was acutely conscious of the rapidly passing minutes that were eating like a cancer into the schedule. He looked around. During the day the sky had been a deep blue, with only a few scattered clouds. The sunset had been beautiful, an orange-yellow that had faded into deep red, then gradually into maroon, then purple. Then the twilight tiptoed into darkness. But this block of Ardboe Street was far from dark, although every street light had been shot out. With buildings on both sides of the street burning fiercely, the sky was alive with red dancing fire and burning embers that soared starward on the updraft, the forever-hungry flames giving birth to shadows that floated across the IRA corpses that had fallen from the upper stories.

The Conqueror got off another shell from its 120-mm gun, and the entire second-story wall of a building vanished. With it dissolved the room above, as well as a twenty-foot length of stone facade and a portion of the roof. The whole mess fell inward and outward, the loud noise of the crash mingled with the crazed shrieks of IRA men and women who went tumbling toward the street below with the rest of the rubbish. And when the bricks and debris stopped falling, much of it was only several feet to the left of the last Hubler and the last two troop carriers.

There were seven more explosions, all of them running together—four to the left side of the street, three to the right. To the right, three of the Provos still alive had been trying to toss Molotov cocktails. Their plan went to pot when machine gun bullets riddled them and popped the bottles of gasoline and oil; the lighted wicks did the rest. *Blooie! Blooie! Blooie!* The quart bottles exploded, bathing the dead men with liquid fire. Three of the explosions to the left were from Hubler armored car shells that blew up more sections of the front walls; the fourth was a Molotov cocktail held in the hand of a female terrorist. Her chest was torn apart by several .30 caliber Browning projectiles just as the bottle exploded and doused her falling body with crawling fire.

Braced on one foot and a knee, the Death Merchant looked up and down the line of armored vehicles and studied both sides of the street. The firings had slacked off almost completely. The Provos who hadn't fled to the rear of the buildings and escaped by way of the alleys had either been wasted by bullets or roasted to death by the flames.

"We're losing too much time," he said, turning to McLoughlin. "We've got to get out of here."

The Silent Cobra nodded. "Yeah, they were thicker than ants on a picnic sandwich, but it would appear that we've just about polished off those who haven't fled out the back."

The Death Merchant made his way past Grimes and Ogilvie and, hunched over, moved to the rear of the first scout cab. Even before he joined Captain Kipp, Lieutenant George, Robert Ford, and the driver of the car, he saw that the scout car would have to be left behind. A grenade had exploded close to one corner of the vehicle and had blown away half of the solid-rubber tire on the right front wheel.

The four Britishers looked expectantly at Camellion, who snuggled down among them.

"Captain, we must get rolling," Camellion said, grimness clinging to his voice. "We've lost too much time already, and when some of the larger buildings start to collapse, we stand a good chance of getting blocked." He paused and looked at the rolling smoke across the road. "Order your men to pull out. The tank can follow us and blow the living hell out of both sides of the street. Or don't you concur with that procedure?"

A giant of a man, with blue-green eyes and a weather-beaten face, Thomas Kipp instantly changed his opinion of Mr. Ringgall, whom he had previously judged to be an American namby-pamby. Yet here he was, calmly saying that the Conqueror should destroy both sides of the street. What Camellion was suggesting was pure music to his ears; he hated the Irish in general and despised Roman Catholics in particular.

Camellion continued, "And it might be a good idea to have the first two Hublers go ahead of us and blast the buildings on both sides in the next blocks. It's best not to take any chances."

"Excellent suggestions, Mr. Ringgall," Kipp said heartily. "I'll get on the radio straightaway and give the necessary orders."

Holding a half-empty Sterling, Kipp turned and moved toward the open door at the back of the first scout car.

"Ten minutes lost off the schedule," Ford said, looking around at the flames and smoke.

"We'll have to ride with you and your chaps," Lieutenant George said huskily. He was a slim young officer with a tanned face and pleasant features. "I guess you noticed our front tire?"

"Yes, I did," Camellion replied. "Come along. We'll get aboard. By the time we're settled in, the Captain will have given the necessary orders."

Five minutes later, the eight vehicles began to move from the blasted block of burning buildings, the block whose sidewalks were covered with rubble, IRA corpses, and burning material still falling from upper floors.

Two Hubler armored cars went ahead first and drove around the wrecked scout car whose radio Captain Kipp had destroyed, to keep it from falling into the hands of the IRA. The Death Merchant's scout car followed the last Hubler, the Boarhound close behind. The three troop carriers and the third Hubler were next in line, the Browning of the Hubler and the Brens of the carriers tossing .30 and .303 caliber projectiles at both sides of the street. As soon as the third Hubler had driven around the wrecked scout car, the Conqueror burst forth from the wreckage of the greengrocery, the barrel of its 120-mm gun poking through the smoky air like a giant penis. The tank clanked to the middle of the street, jerked to a halt, half turned on its tracks, and started to move toward the west. All the while its turret revolved. The tank was moving forward when the gunner got off a round, the shell exploding in the second story of a building to the left. Bricks flew outward. The long Boyle Apothecary sign hanging over the first floor was turned into a million splinters, and the entire front wall of the three-story building sagged downward in a cloud of dust and smoke.

In the crowded scout car, Richard Camellion sat cursing Time and thinking about the message he had received from Courtland Grojean. At least the risks were worth the money. Ironic though! When it came to pure espionage, an individual would be better off working for the Soviet Union. The Soviets would go to great lengths to break their agents out of foreign prisons. The Soviets would kidnap innocent tourists and trade them for you, to get you out of jail. But not the Americans, who would let an agent rot forever rather than admit that Uncle Sam practiced espionage.

Damn Grojean!

CHAPTER THIRTEEN

They were seemingly in the center of a universe of darkness, a universe of silence, wind, and water. The wind was force 4 on the Beaufort scale, a moderate breeze, with the waves moving at a speed of 11 to 16 knots. Ideal weather for the task at hand.

In the front seat of the motorboat, Ruairi Paisley scanned the area, moving his infrared night scope in a complete circle. A quarter of a mile to the north was the second boat. A fifth of a mile northeast was the third.

In the rear seat, Keenan McGuire and three Russian frogmen were securing the watertight cylindrical tube to the boat. The cylinder was four feet two inches long and two feet in diameter and, with its deadly contents, weighed less than three hundred pounds. As the Russians and McGuire had it figured, in relation to the weight of the cylinder in the boat the total would equal the weight of two men, and small men at that. There wasn't any problem, the hull sinking less than three inches.

Georgi Zuvsko finished bolting the cable to the eye-ring sticking up from the rim of the hull while the other two frogmen and McGuire tested the other cables on the rings. They were secure, tight, and well-bolted.

Zuvsko said in broken English, looking at McGuire, "The cargo will ride—like you say—good. Comrade, the wrenches you have to unfasten the cables most quick?"

"Don't worry; I have the wrenches," McGuire said. He was barely able to contain his excitement and exultation. At last he had it, the A-bomb that would make the British pigs in Ulster look like fools. "And thank the Captain of the submarine and the people in Moscow for us. We of the IRA appreciate the help of the great Soviet Union."

"*Da,* I tell them," Zuvsko said. "We go now. *Dosvidanya,* Irishman." He rattled off a stream of Russian to the other two Soviet frogmen. All three then put the ends of the air tubes in their mouths, tested the air from the tanks on their backs, made sure their nostrils were properly pinched off, and pulled down their face masks. Three splashes in the water and they were gone, beneath the dark water and on their way back to the deep-dive exploration craft moored at the end of a cable, twenty fathoms down. The other end of the steel cable was attached to a nuclear submarine lying quietly in a "ditch" at three hundred fathoms, or eighteen hundred feet, below the surface. Because of the tremendous pressure, the three Soviet frogmen had used the exploration craft to bring the bomb from the submarine to a level that would permit them to leave the enclosed exploration craft and float the tube to the surface.

The cold wind blowing around his woollen Watch cap and leather jacket, McGuire climbed into the front seat of the motorboat and Paisley started the engine. Very quickly the craft was underway, its sharp prow cutting the water, tossing up a V-spray that the wind changed instantly into vapor.

Paisley called out to McGuire, who was turning on a stolen ML9 walkie-talkie, "We should have used signal jammers on the beach to foul up British transmissions."

"You damn fool!" McGuire shouted back. "The jammers work both ways. We would also be without communications."

McGuire soon had a report from Rosemary Keane, who was with the group of Provos on the beach, and learned that the force in Ballycastle had been virtually wiped out. "Only ten of our people escaped," Rosemary said frantically. "The damage they did to the British was almost nil. Only one vehicle damaged, and it was just a scout car."

Angry and surprised, McGuire snapped, "None of the fire bombs worked?"

"Our people were spotted before they got a chance to use them effectively. And only minutes ago, I received a report that the column has pulled out and that the tank is shelling the entire block. Keenan, the British have gone crazy! They are behaving like savages. I'm convinced it's part of a plan worked out by those two strange men our spies told us about."

"Are they with the British force?"

"I don't know. It doesn't matter. Did you get the package?"

"Aye, we have it. Is everything in readiness on Harpwire Road?"

"Yes, our people are in position and waiting."

McGuire's heavy voice rang with notes of victory. "There is

no need for worry. By the time the British get past the end of the road, they'll have been cut to pieces. They'll have to turn back. Even if they don't, we'll still have had time to unload the package and be on our way to Teamhair na Riogh."

"How long until you reach the beach?" Rosemary's voice was very nervous.

"In a short while. Listen for our engines."

McGuire switched off the walkie-talkie and placed it in his lap, convinced that the liberation of Ulster was near. Yet the two men with the British bothered him. Who were they? Americans? Germans? Who? Whoever they were, they fought like maniacs and had the luck of Satan himself. Damn them to hell! It was they who had wrecked the trap set at Liam O'Connor's apartment. And from all reports, they were also responsible for the defeat at Lha-Beul-tinne. The loss of the fighters at the castle ruins had been a severe setback. But now it didn't matter. He had the bomb. . . .

CHAPTER FOURTEEN

It was the last mile of Harpwire Road that the Death Merchant feared. A straight, pebbly stretch, the last mile was perfect for land mines that could be detonated by remote control. At the end of the road was more barren, God-forsaken land, the ground slightly rolling, the surface mostly rocky, clumps of trees standing stark and silent, tiny oases of loneliness in a landscape that was desolate and forbidding.

Camellion didn't dare take the chance. Because of that last mile, he ordered Captain Kipp to halt the column, quietly explaining his reason. With some reluctance, the British officer gave the order over the radio. Camellion was already studying a map by the time the vehicles came to a dead stop. Earlier he had gone over every tiny detail of the same map. But he had to be positive, absolutely certain. Now he was.

"Well, we have stopped," Kipp said coldly. "I know we're not merely going to sit here."

"Captain, have the Conqueror shell the last mile in front of us," Camellion said. "Instruct the gunner to drop a shell every fifty feet for the first five hundred feet, starting at the end of the road. The concussions from 120-mm shells should touch off anything that's buried, except hard-pressure mines."

Kipp's weather-wasted face became tight with disapproval. In the dim light of the scout car, Camellion could see the other men looking at him with curious, expectant expressions.

"Isn't shelling the road a bit drastic?" Kipp asked in a steady voice. "Should there not be any mines, we'll be destroying a perfectly good road and will have a devil of a time driving around the craters made by the explosions."

Camellion looked up from the map and stared at Kipp. "Captain, please give the order—*now*."

Kipp didn't argue. He squeezed his way through the men, reached the radio, and contacted the commander of the Conqueror. With the aid of a penlight, Camellion continued to scan the map. Clearly the entire region was as bleak and uninviting as a cesspool in Hong Kong, every bit of it lonely and isolated, the general terrain composed of gentle slopes that were useless to God and man. Not far from the end of Harpwire road was Brodigdone Hill—a fifth of a mile to the southwest. Brodigdone Hill was a hundred-foot-high mound that was said to be one of the abodes of Pan, the licentious god of forests and mountains. On top of the hill were the remains of an Iron Age camp and the sinister Brodigdone Stone, which centuries before had reportedly been used as an altar for human sacrifice. The citizens of Ballycastle avoided the entire area after dark, especially Brodigdone Hill, feeling that the mound was a weird and suggestive place, where those without strong nerves could easily imagine that strange otherworldly beings were on the prowl.

The hell with things that go bump in the night. The zones on each side of the road were something else. Both sections were slightly hilly, with small mounds and patches of rocks and trees. But there weren't any natural barriers that would prevent the vehicles from getting through to the beach. *Once on the beach, we'll have only four miles to go. . . .*

The Conqueror began the shelling, each exploding 120-mm shell a crashing wall of sound. It was the smashing concussion of the third shell that triggered the first land mine buried in the road. It too went off with a loud roar, a microsecond after the explosion of the tank shell.

The men in the scout car, including Captain Kipp, looked at the Death Merchant with new respect as he turned off the penlight, folded the map and put both into the right chest pocket of his fatigues.

"As soon as the shelling stops, we'll leave the road and move to the left," Camellion said. "Unless the map is out of whack, the left side is smoother than the right. We'll have a bumpy ride for a mile or so, but we'll reach the beach in good shape." He smiled with satisfaction as another land mind exploded.

Lieutenant Arthur George said quickly, "There'll be IRAs on both sides of the road, waiting to finish us off."

"The real danger is from incendiaries," Camellion said. He looked at Kipp. "We had better have some of the Regulars leave the carriers when we move off the road. Have half of them use grenades with launchers. The Provos might have assault trucks hidden. This is ideal territory for such vehicles."

"Jolly good thinking," Kipp agreed. "I'll give the orders as soon as the shelling stops."

For another five minutes the tank shelled the road ahead, during which time a dozen land mines were exploded by the violent concussions. The purpose of the IRA was very clear: to wait until the vehicles were stretched out over the road and over the mines, then detonate the mines simultaneously by remote control. A beautiful plan, except that it had failed.

By radio, Captain Kipp explained the new plan to the men and instructed Sergeant-Major Glenn Terrybow and Sergeant Lucas Mahan to take ten men each from the first two troop carriers and use them as countermeasures against any Provos who might appear, in assault trucks or on foot.

The Death Merchant said to Corporal Burke, "Corporal, open the swing-back door in the top. We'll need the open space when we fire."

"And in case we have to scramble out of this can in a hurry," McLoughlin said seriously.

"That, too, Mr. Weaver," Camellion said, a faint smile appearing on his mouth.

Led by the first two Hubler armored cars, whose turret searchlights probed the darkness, the column left the gravel road and started down the slight incline. The twenty Hell-Devils were spread out on both sides of the three Harrington troop carriers. Five on each side had grenade launchers attached to their .280 EM assault rifles.

All nine vehicles had successfully maneuvered off the road and had just begun to move forward, some on level ground, the others on the slopes of small mounds, when the lookout in the turret of the first Hubler spotted three IRA assault trucks approaching from the southwest, all three roaring down the long slope of Brodigdone Hill. A moment later, the gruff voice of Sergeant-Major Terrybow came over the radios of the vehicles. Calmly, he reported that three more assault trucks had come across the road from the north side and were moving in fast. To compound the danger, there were dozens of Provos running behind the trucks to the left.

Almost immediately the sound of moving vehicles was drowned out by the firing of automatic rifles and short bursts from the submachine guns of the Provos.

Camellion, Ford, McLoughlin, and Captain Kipp stood up in the top opening. Standing straight and bracing themselves by holding tightly to handholds fastened to the inside of the roof, they found that their waists were even with the rim of the large, square opening. They quickly lowered themselves so that only their heads protruded, and looked over the situation.

There was moonlight, and they could see the outlines of the three assault trucks coming toward them from the southwest, as well as the three trucks from the northwest. All six trucks were similar in appearance-large pickups with four-wheel drive, oversized tires, and armor-plate for windshields, the drivers seeing ahead through rectangular openings cut in the steel.

Each truck was equipped with sideswiper cutters, screw-cone log splitters protruding from the hub of each rear wheel—for shredding tires—and a fork lift in front for window ramming and traction denial. Mounted on the roof of each cab was a Bren light machine gun, the gunner, standing in the bed, protected by armor plate bolted to the cab on each side of the weapon.

"Down!" yelled Camellion. "Those Brens will open up any moment."

He and the others ducked just in time. The Bren guns on the six pickup trucks began to chatter just as the 37-mm cannons in the turrets of the first two Hublers started lobbing shells at the three assault trucks to the left and the Boarhound and the third Hubler began blasting away at the three assault trucks to the right. Fortune, however, was with the Provos. The six trucks were moving too fast for the gunners in the Hublers and the Boarhound to sight accurately, so the British gunners overshot the targets. But the luck of the Irish lasted for only a very short time. The ten Hell-Devils with grenade launchers had much more freedom of movement than the turret gunners, who had to turn altazimuth wheels and consume precious time by opening and closing the breeches of cannon. Three of the regular Hell-Devils had already been killed by either .303 Bren slugs or projectiles from weapons in the hands of the Provos to the southwest; but three others had taken their places and, with the 17 other men, were firing from behind the large eight-wheeled troop carriers.

Heat anti-tank rifle grenades stabbed into two of the attacking trucks to the right and exploded. Twin flashes of fire and smoke, double explosions, and the two assault trucks dissolved into useless junk. The roofs of the cabs, the Bren light machine guns, and the bodies of terrorists shot upward in a splash of fire. Just as quickly the mangled corpses and twisted pieces of smoking metal fell back to earth, three of the bodies on fire.

Next a Heat grenade found one of the pickup trucks to the left. Scratch one truck and three Provos. . . .

144

The drivers of the first two Hublers then swung to the left to meet the charge of the two trucks coming at them at a sharp angle, so they missed the trap in the immediate area forward. While the remaining assault truck to the right raced in on an angle that would bring it to the right side of the Boarhound, the two to the left corrected their course and headed for the left side of the second Hubler. At the same time, the scout car moved straight ahead—right into the first loop of concertina wire draped loosely across the area in a series of coils. It all happened in a few seconds. By the time the first series of loops had wound themselves around the scout car, it plunged into the second barrier of barbed wire, which also entangled itself around the car, several strands even stretching tightly across the rear top opening.

The scout car was useless. With barbed wire wedged between the ends of the axials and the wheels, as well as covering the top and sides like some eerie spicer web, the torque of the car was thrown off, and the drag became intolerable. There wasn't anything the driver could do but jam down on the brake and cut the motor.

The Death Merchant glanced up wearily at the barbed wire stretching across the top opening—*why, good Lord, do these things have to happen to me?*

"Everyone out the rear hatch," he ordered, then grabbed both a BSA sub-gun and an Atchisson automatic assault shotgun with a 20-round drum-magazine. "Grab all your weapons. You won't get a second chance. Weaver and I will go first."

The battle-tough Britishers, despite their preoccupation with speed, couldn't help but wonder about Weaver and Ringgall, when McLoughlin said with phony sincerity, "Why do we always have to go first?" and Camellion answered, "Because we have so damned little to lose."

Captain Kipp and the other men didn't wonder for long. The Death Merchant unlatched the door, pushed it outward with his left foot, then crawled through the oval-shaped opening. His feet had not yet touched the ground when the two assault trucks to the left struck the side of the second Hubler. The forklift of one truck was raised high enough to smash against the turret and imprison it like a rounded piece of meat between two tines of a fork. The forks on the lift of the second truck were lowered all the way, and they stabbed underneath the left side of the driver's compartment. At once, the driver of the second truck started to lift the huge prongs, while the driver who had imprisoned the turret began to push. Both drivers hoped that with one lifting and the other pushing, they might be able to turn the Hubler over on its right side. It was a suicide attack, but these Provos were Irish kamikazes and were more than willing to die if they could stop the British.

The gunner in the turret of the first Hubler was helpless. He swung the 37-mm turret gun around, but couldn't fire. Not only was the truck too close to the second Hubler, but the gunner in the first armored car couldn't depress the cannon enough to do the job.

The driver of the Boarhound—almost three times the size of a Hubler—had driven his vehicle to a position that would have permitted the gunner to fire a round. But he didn't fire, afraid that he might miss and hit the rear of the second Hubler or the rear of the scout car. And even if he didn't miss, what would such a large concussion do to the crew inside the second Hubler?

Nor did the gunners in the Hubler and the Boarhound have time to swing their guns toward the remaining assault truck streaking in from the northwest, the Provo behind the cab raking the sides of the Boarhound and the three carriers with the Bren light machine gun, the .303 projectiles glancing off the steel with loud, singing whines. Two of the Hell-Devils went down, riddled and spurting blood. As the truck drew closer to the Boarhound three Provos, braced against the railing bolted to the right side of the truck bed, prepared to throw their cola cans of thermite against the top and right side of the large armored car. Using cigarettes, the three men lighted the long wicks. They might have succeeded if Richard Camellion had stayed home in Texas and not poked his nose into IRA business.

Going through the rear hatch of the scout car, Camellion heard the two trucks slam against the side of the Hubler and guessed what had happened. He also spotted the pickup truck tearing in toward the Boarhound at almost forty MPH. The Boarhound was fifteen feet to the left of, and thirty feet behind, the scout car.

The only things that counted now were speed, experience, and luck. Camellion instantly dropped the BSA submachine gun that had been in his left hand, raised the Atchisson to his right shoulder, and started to aim, only a minimoment after the driver of the assault truck had turned sharply to rocket in between the rear of the scout car and the first troop carrier fifty feet behind the car.

At close range, an Atchisson Assault Automatic Shotgun is the most terrible man-to-man weapon on earth. It shoots equally well all 12-gauge magnum shells containing 1.5 ounces of shot or 1-ounce shotgun slugs. All submissiles can be fired in four seconds at a cyclic rate of 360 rounds per minute, a rate of fire that can be matched only by belt-fed machine guns.

The assault truck that was headed for the Boarhound was only twenty-five feet behind the Death Merchant, its entire right side exposed to the deadly Atchisson. His finger was only half a hair from the trigger when James Raftery, the Provo sitting next to the driver attempted to poke the barrel of a Star submachine gun through the window of the door, and Rose Ann Murphy, the young woman who had been firing the Bren gun on the roof of the cab, tried to get off a shot at Camellion with a Walther P38 pistol.

Camellion pulled the trigger. *Bambambambambam!* The automatic shotgun roared, the run-together explosions as loud as exploding auto mags. The no. 4 buckshot blew away Raftery's face, some of the pellets popping past him and striking the cheek, arms, and right shoulder of the driver, who screamed in pain and released the steering wheel. The .24 caliber, 21-grain shot erased Rose Ann Murphy's features, and carried pieces of her thick coat into her breasts and chest, the shot taking the material right along with it. She wilted faster than a rubber band, fell back between the left railing and the top of the bed, and tumbled to the ground. The three Provos standing by the right railing died on the spot, the 6.1-mm shot exploding their chests, the wind blowing their blood into a fine spray. The corpses dropped the cola cans with the sputtering fuses and sagged to the floor, with the cans rolling around in the bed.

During the next few seconds, the half-conscious driver lost all control of the rushing truck and the vehicle, careening wildly from side to side, started to veer to the left. Its course changed abruptly when its left front wheel struck a fairly large rock and the truck started to turn over and spill out the bodies sloshing around in the bed in their blood. A moment later the three cola cans of thermite whooshed into life and bathed the entire truck in bright blue-white fire as it rolled over on its right side.

The Death Merchant didn't wait to see the wrecked truck blossom into flame. Neither did McLoughlin, who was living up to his nickname of "Silent Cobra," a hypocorism he considered ridiculous.

Camellion, ignoring Captain Kipp and the others crawling through the hatch, got down by the left rear corner of the scout car. Simultaneously, McLoughlin raced around the right side of the vehicle and dashed across the short distance to the right side of the Hubler being tortured by the two assault trucks—all to the accompaniment of EM automatic rifles cracking and anti-tank grenades exploding to the left. The Hell-Devils around the troop carriers were taking out the Provos to the southwest, many of whom were trying to retreat to the west side of Brodigdone Hill. None succeeded. Four were cut to pieces by EM slugs. Ten more were flung high into the air by three grenades that exploded among them.

The Death Merchant looked around the end of the wire-imprisoned scout car, saw that the left side of the Hubler was half a foot off the ground, and jerked back behind the car just in time to avoid a stream of submachine gun slugs fired by one of the Provos who had been manning the Bren light machine gun on one of the assault trucks. Only now the gunner was lying across the bed, triggering a Danish Madsen chatterbox. The man next to the driver fired a shot with a French Manurhin PPK pistol.

A dozen 9-mm Parabellum projectiles buzzed toward Camellion. Some of the projectiles ricocheted off the armor plate of the scout car. The remainder zipped into the ground and sent up tiny geysers of dirt and rocks. The 7.45-mm projectile from the PPK missed. It went on its way, struck the crash-bumper of one of the troop carriers, and zinged off into space.

"Can't we use a regular fragmentation grenade?" asked Lieutenant George, who was next to Camellion, snuggled up to the rear of the vehicle.

Camellion looked to the right. Ford and Kipp were covering McLoughlin, and the regular Hell-Devils were watching both flanks.

"Sure we can, but not the way you think," Camellion said.

He took a fragmentation grenade from his kit bag, mentally measured the distance to the truck, then pitched the grenade over the top of the scout car. A moment later he heard it clank against the side of the door.

"But you didn't pull the pin!" Lieutenant George said in astonishment.

"I forgot!" Camellion very quickly picked up the full automatic shotgun and leaned around the corner of the truck.

Wondering if the drivers of the trucks had spotted him, McLoughlin crept to the right wheel of the Hubler. He was

148

almost positive that the drivers hadn't seen him, because their field of vision was limited by the small slots in the metal windshields of their trucks. Either way, he knew he was risking his life in more ways than one, for already the left-side tires of the Hubler were almost a foot off the ground, and the vehicle was tilting to the right. That was all he needed! To be crushed to death by an armored car in Northern Ireland!

Duck-walking, the Atchisson on safety, McLoughlin waddled around to the front of the vehicle and moved toward the left front wheel. He stopped and gritted his teeth in frustration when some of the barbs of the wire sticking out snagged his fatigues by the left elbow. He jerked his arm free, took several more steps, stopped, and listened to the racket on the other side of the Hubler—the two prongs of the fork lift grinding and groaning against the underside of the Hubler, the roaring of engines straining to make the fork lifts do work they were not intended to do.

McLoughlin knew he couldn't move forward without taking a chance that the driver might see him, or more likely the joker at the Bren gun, provided he was looking down toward the front of the truck. McLoughlin made up his mind. It was now or never. *Go to work!* He switched off the safety, jumped up, and raised the Atchisson.

It's a sucker's trick that always works! The Death Merchant grinned. Just as he had figured, the Provos in the truck had heard the grenade hit and, thinking it was about to explode, had snuggled down. By the time they realized nothing was happening and stood up again, the Death Merchant was ready for them. Neither the dumb cluck with the Madsen nor the loony with the PPK had time to do anything but die.

Bambambambambambam! Two charges of no. 4 buckshot caught the terrorist with the Madsen and blew off his head, neck, and sent pieces of his breastbone and spine to the other side of the truck bed. A Vesuvius of spurting blood, the headless corpse dropped in rhythm with the man who had the PPK, whose head exploded from another double charge of shot. Two more loads of shot splattered the skull and brains and part of the right arm of the driver all over the inside of the cab, which was dripping with blood and gore and tiny pieces of cloth torn from the corpses.

The Death Merchant's last shot was followed by McLoughlin's shotgun booming—ten shells, the sounds of the explosions all tripping into each other. The Silent Cobra first wasted the driver, a woman whose blonde head was wrapped in a green, red, and yellow scarf. The top of her skull and most of the scarf actually hit the inside roof of the cab, the rest of the shot scattering her gray matter all over the inside of the front and back windshields. The Provo next to the woman was dusted next, three charges of .24 caliber shot popping him in the left side of his head and shoulder. Head, neck, and shoulder exploded into a pulpy mass of flesh, blood, and bone, his Adam's apple jumping out of his torn-apart throat and hitting the inside of the metal windshield like a bloody ping-pong ball.

The Irish idiot in the truck bed was as unlucky as his terrorist pals in the cab. He was attempting to lean around the side of the cab and get a Soviet PPsh41 submachine gun into action, but he didn't even get off to a good start. His head and chest exploded as if a grenade had gone off inside his torso, blood, pieces of rib bones, chunks of heart and lungs flying into the spring wind.

The combat-experienced McLoughlin wasn't about to risk getting blasted into oblivion by his own side. He darted back to the front of the Hubler, raced up the right side, dashed across the space between the armored car and the scout vehicle, and soon was telling Camellion that he had iced the men in the assault truck that had been trying to lift the left side of the Hubler.

The Death Merchant laughed softly. "I heard. Of course, I assumed you weren't shooting at yumac birds." He smiled again when he saw Lieutenant George's eyes widen, then grow puzzled. "Don't worry, Lieutenant. All we have to do now is shut off the motors."

"We'll have to push the truck that has its forklift around the turret," McLoughlin said. "We can't get into the cab, or we'll look like we took a bath in blood. Half a dozen men on each side should do it. Man, they're some deals, cutters and everything."

Captain Kipp, who had just surveyed the entire area, said to Camellion, "I'm going to one of the carriers and report to headquarters. I'll send a dozen men to push away the truck from the Hubler."

"Captain, instruct headquarters to send the helicopter," Camellion said, pulling the M/200 International auto mags from their belt holsters. "It can hover until we reach the open beach area. Then contact the spotters on Fair Head. By this time, they should have more to report."

"Righto." Kipp touched his hand to his helmet and started

off toward the troop carriers. He noticed Sergeant-Major Terry-bow trotting toward him.

The Death Merchant and McLoughlin moved to within six feet of the first truck and its bloody cargo of shot apart corpses. With Chris riding shotgun with the Atchisson, just in case, Camellion put five .350 Magnum slugs through the hood. The engine stopped running. The wheels of both trucks had ceased to turn when the drivers had died and their feet had moved from the gas pedals. All that moved now were thick streams of blood that slid under the bottom edge of the door on the right side.

"I've seen less in a slaughterhouse," Camellion commented.

"I've seen far more in 'Nam and other places," McLoughlin said.

Camellion walked to the left side of the second assault truck and repeated his performance. This time it took only four .350s to kill the engine. Immediately the prongs of the fork lift dropped from underneath the Hubler, and the armored car settled down heavily to the left.

The driver of the Hubler threw open the forward hatch and pushed himself up. He looked at Camellion and McLoughlin and shook his head.

"I didn't dare start the engine," he said, wiping sweat from his face. "Any movement of the wheels and the bloody bastards would have tipped us over."

The commander of the Hubler stood tall in the turret hatch, looked from left to right at the prongs on each side of the turret, cursed, then called down to Camellion in a rich English midlands voice. "We can't move ahead until those goddam forks have been moved from the turret. You understand that?"

"Patience, old chap,' Camellion called back. "Captain Kipp is sending some men to push the truck away."

Robert Ford and Humphrey Grimes joined Camellion and McLoughlin, and they regarded the two trucks with that kind of horror that comes to most men only once in a lifetime, that many men have felt only on a battlefield during a war. The grotesquely butchered bodies and the blood and gore in the cabs and in the beds of the trucks seemed especially hideous in the flickering glow of the burning truck that had turned over.

"Those automatic shotguns are terrible weapons," Ford said in a nervous voice. "The Provos look as if they've been chopped apart with axes."

"They get the job done with a minimum of time and a maximum of effectiveness," Camellion said, a twinkle in his eyes. "After all, the idea is kill-power. We're not in the Salvation Army."

"The Regulars are coming," McLoughlin said. "It shouldn't take more than ten minutes to move the trucks."

The Silent Cobra was wrong. Moving the trucks from the Hubler required all of thirteen minutes.

By the time Camellion, McLoughlin, and the others made their way back to Captain Kipp, who was standing twenty feet to the right of one of the troop carriers, Lieutenant George and the two noncoms—barking orders by walkie-talkie—had regrouped the column. This time the tank would lead the parade of armor. The Boarhound, the three troop carriers, and the three Hublers would follow, in that order.

"The helicopter is on its way," Kipp said when Camellion walked up to him. "It will contact us when it reaches these coordinates. But we have another serious problem."

"Does it have to do with the spotters on top Fair Head?" asked the Death Merchant.

"No. But the report from the men on Fair Head isn't good. They reported to Sergeant-Major Terrybow. He was closest to the radio operator at the time. I called back for reaffirmation. The speed boats returned to the beach during the time that you and Weaver were giving the Provos in the trucks a bloody time. The spotter said that the IRA unloaded a cylinder from one of the boats. They put the cylinder into one of the trucks. Then all the trucks and cars moved west."

"What kind of cylinder?"

"Metal. Short. A bit over a meter long, and half as thick. It isn't at all logical. A cylinder that size can't hold many arms. Therefore it has to contain something else."

McLoughlin removed his helmet to let the wind blow through his hair. "We won't know until we catch up with McGuire. He has to have an ace or two up his sleeve. He knows that between us and the forces in Londonderry, we can pincer him. He knows we can keep track of him and his convoy from the air, even before he reaches Bushmills. It's the nearest town and almost fifteen miles west of us."

"McGuire won't go near Bushmills." The flickering light from the still burning truck revealed that Ford was deeply concerned. "The RUCs would spot the column in an instant."

"Yes, and the same applies if he heads south," Grimes said in guarded tones. "Should he turn back east, he knows he'll run into us. The IRA always has a spotter around in case of failure. By now, the spotter will have reported the failure of the assault trucks to stop us. McGuire is too sharp a chap to believe that the trucks could do any real damage. What happened here was only a delaying tactic."

"It's the cylinder that bothers me." Ford looked from Camellion to Captain Kipp. "McGuire wouldn't go to all these elaborate measures if the cylinder didn't contain something of great value. Why, it must have taken months to filter in all the necessary personnel to this northern area.

"Try on a small atomic bomb for size," the Death Merchant said nonchalantly.

Captain Kipp fixed a cold stare on him. "Ridiculous!" he said testily. "The Soviets wouldn't dare give a small A-bomb to a lunatic like McGuire."

"The pig farmers in Mama Russia would give grenades to three-year-old babies, if it suited their purpose!" lashed out Camellion. "And it makes sense, too; McGuire's going west."

"Suppose you let us in on the secret," Grimes suggested in a tight voice, grimacing.

"Let's get into one of the carriers and start rolling," Camellion said. "We're wasting time here, and I don't like standing in the open. I'll tell you while we head for the beach."

Kipp held up a hand. "Hold on. I told you we have a problem. Eight men were killed. There isn't room for them in the carriers, not with the lot of us as extra passengers. We can't put them in the armored cars, either."

Camellion was plainspoken. "We leave them. They can be picked up later."

Kipp stared at Camellion with all the caution of a bomb-disposal expert approaching a field filled with land-mines. "Mr. Ringgall! We never leave our dead. To do so is quite impossible!"

"This is not a time to stand on custom," Camellion said flatly. "We'll leave them because we have to, because we have to catch McGuire, and because I'm giving the orders—or have you forgotten Colonel Wyck-Mason's directive?"

He fixed his eyes on the startled British officer, waiting for the man to reply. Then with the others he glanced toward Lieutenant George, who was coming over from the second carrier.

Reaching the group, George saluted and said to Captain Kipp, "The helicopter called. It's only five minutes away."

"Very well. Let's get in and start moving," Kipp said evenly.

Lieutenant George looked startled. "Sir, what do we do with the dead? We—"

"We leave them," snapped Kipp. Without looking at the others, he turned and started toward the second carrier.

The rest of the group started after Kipp, the Death Merchant noticing that Lieutenant George was giving him curious sideways glances. At length, George said, "Mr. Ringgall, a short time ago you mentioned yumac birds. You see, I'm curious. Ornithology is a hobby of mine. Frankly, I have never heard of such a bird, and I rather suspect you were joking, were you not?"

The Death Merchant smiled; McLoughlin chuckled.

"Let's say that the yumac bird lives in Brazil," Camellion said. "In the jungle. It perches on a limb, and whenever anyone passes by, it calls out, 'Is that you, Mac? Is that you, Mac?'"

CHAPTER FIFTEEN

Its two Tubomeca Turmo turboshaft engines shaking the dark sky with their racket, the Super Puma helicopter flew west by northwest, its infrared television camera on the underside of the nose constantly scanning, the wide-vision lens probing for activity on the Tuathail Road, the coastal route taken by the IRA truck and car convoy, two thousand feet below.

An all-purpose craft, the Super Puma could be used as an attack craft, a troop carrier, or a supply ship. Now it was a carrier and a gunship. Normally it could carry twenty fully equipped troops. On this night it carried the Death Merchant, the Silent Cobra, Lieutenant George, Sergeant Lucas Mahan, and ten Hell-Devils—all that could be spared from the main group, which had reached the Beach area and was also moving west on Tuathail Road. Eight Hell-Devils had been killed. Eleven had been wounded, not only from the last battle, but from the attack of the IRA in Ballycastle. Only sixty-one Regulars were left with the column, excluding the crews of the tank, the Boarhound, and the Hublers.

"You had better be right, Mr. Ringgall." Sitting next to the Death Merchant, McLoughlin slyly emphasized the "Mr. Ringgall," paused slightly, and added, "Your theory seems logical, but personally I don't believe that McGuire or any of his crazies will hole up for even an hour at—what's its name again?"

"Teamhair na Riogh," Camellion said slowly, his thoughts at the moment centered around *The death of the General must be investigated.* Fantastic! Well, World War II had generated more than one mind-boggling event that the world at large would never know about. Or could it be only a rumor? Was it possible that Grojean and his spooks had been psychologically tricked, had forgotten to realize one important factor about their trade: that the more incredible the lie, the more readily it will be believed. Inversely, the more incredible the truth, the less it will be believed. Truly one of the flaws of the human mind was that it always preferred a lie to the truth. *Only wise men seek the truth*, Camellion told himself, *just as wise men never seek to return to the past and take the risk of excavating forgotten pain while looking for remembered happiness.*

Keenan McGuire and his killers? There was always an X-factor. Yet one first had to use simple deduction. The Provos couldn't go very far south or east or west. That left only the north. That left only the North Channel—to the northeast—or the Atlantic Ocean—to the northwest.

Conclusion: McGuire was going to escape by water. This meant he had to have several cabin cruisers waiting for him and his people. Either they were in readiness or else the boats would come for him and the Provos. It was not likely that the crafts were near the shore. They wouldn't want to risk British patrol boats—*and if they were waiting, McGuire wouldn't have returned in the motorboat to shore. The boats are still far out, no doubt in the Atlantic. The North Channel is too well patrolled. There is probably a freighter waiting outside the legal limit. Where else could McGuire and his people go?* There was another conclusion: *the boats would not come close to shore until McGuire gave them the word, until he was positive it would be safe for them to do so.*

Some of the trucks and cars, with only the drivers, would act as decoys. It would not be too difficult for the drivers to abandon their vehicles when the British were close and lose themselves in the desolate region of rocks, woods, and scrubland. *But you don't lose fifty to a hundred men and a metal cylinder so easily!* Camellion had concluded some twenty minutes earlier. McGuire and the people with him would have to hole up—but where? A close survey of the map revealed the only place possible in the area—Teamhair na Riogh, an ancient pagan site that was supposed to have belonged to the druids. Situated on a low hill overlooking a meadow, the site was abandoned in 1021. Most of the ancient settlement was nothing but crumbled rocks, walls half destroyed by erosion, and small mounds of rubble. The only solid structure that remained within the *Rath na Riogh*—the "Royal Enclosure"—was the *Dumha na Giall*, the "Mound of the Hostages." Made of large stones neatly fitted together, it was covered with earth and measured two hundred feet long and seventy-five feet wide. At its highest point it was sixty feet high. The Royal Enclosure itself was an oval, nine hundred eighty feet long and eight hundred feet across.

The mound was not solid. While its walls and top were twelve-feet thick, there was room inside to hold twice the number of men McGuire had with him—*and that's where he's hiding. He'll wait until he thinks we've passed him by. He'll wait until we go after the trucks, then head for the coast, only three miles north of the Royal Enclosure. There isn't any other logical answer. . . .*

Camellion looked around the helicopter. The men, sitting on long metal benches bolted to the fuselage, were mostly silent. There were large cargo doors at both port and starboard. Just inside the port door was a brace of L7A1 heavy machine guns that fired 7.62-mm NATO ammunition, the weapons mounted on a bar that could be swung out to the cargo door opening. There was a similar arrangement for the two L7A1s on the starboard side. On each side of the fuselage was a rocket pod filled with five 36-mm rockets, the Emerson TAT system enabling the pilot to fire each rocket singly, in pairs, or both pods simultaneously.

After consulting his wristwatch, McLoughlin said, "We've been in the air twelve minutes. We should be spotting something, assuming your theory is correct."

"I'm inclined to agree," Camellion replied. "We should have come to the Mound of the Hostages by now. There isn't much chance that the wide-angle lens of the TV camera could have missed any activity below."

"But the copilot reading the television screen could," McLoughlin pointed out with his usual pessimism.

The copilot hadn't. A few minutes later, a buzzer sounded loudly in the cargo section of the helicopter, and a voice from the cockpit floated over the speaker. "Lieutenant George and Mr. Ringgall to the cockpit, please. Caution. We're going to swing around."

McLoughlin's grin was from ear to ear. "Damn, you were right," he said to Camellion.

The Death Merchant and Lieutenant George waited until the pilot had swung the Super Puma in a wide circle and was headed back in the opposite direction; then they got up and staggered to the door of the cockpit, opened it, and squeezed into the small compartment.

"We passed over the mound several minutes ago," the pilot called out over his shoulder, "just in time to see three trucks and several autos pulling away from the enclosure and start-

157

ing to go down the north slope of the hill. Brace yourself, laddies. I'm going to bank and take us back to the hill."

"Caution. We are going to bank again." The copilot spoke into the mike around his neck that was plugged into the helicopter's intercom.

Hanging onto bars overhead, Camellion and Lieutenant George stared at the eight-inch square television screen in front of the copilot. The screen could either be hooked to a camera monitor or to a mini-gun firing system.

The screen showed the ground passing by, two thousand feet below the craft. With the infrared camera, the panorama below appeared to be cloaked in medium twilight. The pilot had completed the turn and the gravity of the momentum had eased, when they saw the three canvas-covered trucks and the two cars. The five vehicles had driven down the long slope and were just turning onto the road a short distance from the bottom of the hill.

The Death Merchant felt triumph soar within him. It was almost a certainty that Keenan McGuire and his lieutenants were only several thousand feet away. And just maybe . . . an atomic bomb was with them.

"We can't be at all positive that McGuire and his people are inside the mound," Lieutenant George said in an undertone. "We won't know until we have a look."

"Copilot, radio Captain Kipp that we've found McGuire," Camellion said. "Tell him that Mr. Ringgall said to bring the column to the Mound of the Hostages as quickly as possible, but to be very cautious. It's possible that the Provos have set more mines on the road." Then he said to the pilot, "Drop down to five hundred feet and hover. But before you do, have the gunners open the cargo doors and get those heavies ready for action."

"Sure thing. It's your party," the pilot said cheerfully. A career pilot in the Royal Air Force, he was a gloomy-faced man with a long mustache and hair that curled down around his ears and neck.

As the pilot spoke into the mike, Camellion said to Lieutenant George, "Look through the door and let me know when the gunners are ready."

Although Lieutenant George didn't like being treated like a lowly Private, he nevertheless opened the door and watched the two gunners attach safety lines to their wide belts, then slide back the cargo doors and swing out the L7A1 machine guns on their mounts. The two gunners checked their weapons and made sure they were ready to spit out thirteen hundred rounds per minute, after which one gunner turned and gave Lieutenant George the "OK" sign.

"The gunners are ready," Lieutenant George said, and there was more than a touch of the professional British Army officer in his tone as he added bluntly, "I hope to the Almighty that you know what you're doing, Ringgall."

The Death Merchant swallowed George's sullen remark without difficulty. After all, George was only voicing his deeply felt convictions. No one could resent a British Army officer if he minded being ordered about by a civilian—and a non-British civilian at that. Camellion actually admired Lieutenant George and Captain Kipp, too, for their self-discipline and tact.

"We're over the hill," the pilot said. "Now what?"

"Take her down to five hundred feet," Camellion said.

Slowly the Super Puma began to lose altitude.

The Death Merchant studied the television screen. Nothing moved within the Royal Enclosure on top of the hill. The Mound of the Hostages, in the center of the oval fort, also seemed to be devoid of life. Around the giant mound of earth were the remains of walls. There were tiny piles of rubble and stone floors where structures had once stood. The Death Merchant had seen graveyards that had looked more inviting.

"It would be a terrible risk to land on top of the mound," declared Lieutenant George. "We could become victims of an ambush."

"How would you attack, Lieutenant?" Camellion asked gently.

George was taken aback; then he appeared pleased. "I would blast both ends of the mound with rockets," George quickly offered. "I would then position the helicopter over the center of the mound. In that position the port and starboard guns would be able to cover both ends, in case the Provos tried to fire at us. The pilot could lower us to within a few feet of the top. We could jump out and attack one end, after we throw in grenades and tear gas."

"Not bad, Lieutenant," commented the Death Merchant. "I had it figured the same way, but with one exception. After using the rockets to open an entrance in the east and the west ends of the mound, I'd come down with the chopper close to either the east or the west end. By being toward one end with the chopper, one of the gunners could not only take out an enemy that might pop up from the opposite end, but he could

159

also cut to pieces anyone who might come out the main entrance, which is in the center on the north side."

Lieutenant George's face fell. "I forgot the entrance," he admitted. "Sorry. . . ."

The pilot turned around in his seat and looked at Camellion.

"We blast both ends with the rockets?"

"Yes, but you had better drop flares first."

"You're behind the times." The pilot laughed lightly, turned and flipped a switch on the control panel. Instantly the picture on the TV screem jumped to the area ahead of the chopper. The pilot turned and grinned boyishly at Camellion and George. "We live in the latter half of the twentieth century. Why drop flares when all we have to do is switch the screen and camera to the TAT system?"

After alerting the Hell-Devils to hang on, the pilot went to work, handling the stick and cyclic controls with an expertise that Camellion appreciated. The pilot banked widely to the south and headed east for a mile. He then banked north, headed west, and turned the controls over to the copilot, who also served as the gunner and who had adjusted the automatic radar rangefinder and Emerson sight.

Just as expertly as the pilot, the copilot guided the Super Puma toward the east end of the mound, all the while losing altitude. At a distance of five hundred feet to the east and three hundred feet altitude, all five 36-mm rockets whooshed from the port-side pod, streaked toward the target, hit, and exploded simultaneously. A wall of red-yellow fire expanded across the east end of the mound and shot up seventy-five feet into the air. With the fire went soil, bushes, small trees, and fragmented stones, the terrible concussion pushing against the chopper that was soaring upward, its rotor blades *thomp-thomping*. This time the copilot flew straight west for two and a half miles before swinging around, taking the Super Puma back east, and lining it up with the west end of the mound.

An identical performance. Only this time the rockets shot from the starboard pod and exploded with a deafening roar that left the men's ears ringing.

"If McGuire and his people are in there, they must be plenty shaken up," Lieutenant George said through clenched teeth. "They will still be dazed by the time we get to them." He paused. "But suppose they make a run for it, say through the front entrance?"

"They won't," Camellion said coldly. "They're too afraid of the chopper's machine guns."

Once more the controls were in the hands of the pilot, who asked, "Which end? And give me definite instructions."

"How far past the hill are we?" Camellion inquired.

"A bit past three k."

"The east end. Low enough for us to jump out. We'll all go down the south side of the mound. We can't go in from the top. The blasted hole is too large. The drop would be too far. We'll have to storm in from hilltop level."

"And we fly off into the moonlight?"

The Death Merchant laughed. "After all of us are on the hilltop, you take the chopper a hundred feet in front of the entrance on the north side and have one of the gunners pepper the doors with slugs, but no longer than two minutes. Then fly to the west and have the other gunner rake the hole. But be damned careful."

"You got it, Mac," the pilot said.

Lieutenant George smiled and looked at Camellion. "Another yumac bird, eh, Ringgall?"

"Let's get the others ready to go out and die," Camellion said, a hint of a smile on his own lips. "And maybe we'll go to hell with those who do. . . ."

Turning, he pushed open the door.

Once more the pilot banked and headed west. Only this time, when the Super Puma was several hundred feet east of the mound, he turned the chopper so that its nose was pointed north and called to the gunners to be ready. With the port side facing the mound, the helicopter closed in. Taking no chances, the port side gunner sent a stream of 7.62-mm projectiles into the hole as the craft passed over.

Gently the pilot lowered the big blue and white bird until its wheels were only four feet above the dead grass of the mound, sixty feet west of the top edge of the giant rent torn by the rockets into the sloping east side of the ancient burial structure.

Camellion, McLoughlin, and four of the Hell-Devils jumped to the ground from the starboard side of the chopper. Lieutenant George, Sergeant Mahan, and six Regulars left the Super Puma from the left side, carrying EM assault rifles, their faces covered with gas masks, their bodies weighed down with shoulder bags of spare magazines, thermite and tear gas canisters, and fragmentation grenades.

The instant the last man was on the ground, the port-side

gunner signalled the pilot. The helicopter lifted fifty feet, then moved forward, its Tubomeca Turmo turboshaft engines roaring. When the chopper was a hundred and fifty feet north of the mound, the pilot turned the craft and ordered the starboard gunner to open fire—". . . until I tell you to stop."

A second later, the L7A1 machine guns were roaring and two streams of 7.62-mm projectiles were sizzling through the muzzles by the hundreds, their force dissolving the short but wide wooden door within several minutes.

Moving down the south incline of the vast mound, the Death Merchant and his men heard the angry chattering of the L7A1 machine guns, and kept opening and closing their eyes to adjust them to the darkness. Yet all the time they were alert.

Toward the bottom of the slant the way became more steep, so much so that at times their feet were almost sliding and they had to brace themselves to keep from falling forward; the closer they came to the bottom the safer they felt, though each man realized that the feeling was only a false security, a self-protective mechanism.

"What about light?" McLoughlin asked as soon as they reached the flat surface of the hilltop. "The Provos will hardly leave on any lights for us."

"We'll first toss in grenades, then thermite," Camellion said. "We'll have enough light. Pass the word."

He looked up at the sky. A cloud had started to pass over the white face of the pitted moon, and the darkness grew more intense. But now the darkness was a friend . . . .

CHAPTER SIXTEEN

Totally unexpected by Keenan McGuire and the other Provos, the first rocket barrage caused their spirits to sink faster than Ted Kennedy's car off Dyke Bridge. The tremendous concussion hadn't helped him and the other Provos physically, the wave of pressure stunning them to semiconsciousness.

It was a fluke that concussion and flying chunks of rock—some as large as water buckets—hadn't killed McGuire and the other 62 terrorists. They were saved only by the immense size of the interior and the fact that most of them had been to the west. Some of them had been eating and relaxing, others stretched out on long grave-stones, cat-napping—all of them waiting for the two large cabin cruisers that would ferry them to the *Empress of the Wind*, a tramp freighter of Panamanian registry that was waiting thirty-five miles out, in the Atlantic. The *Empress of the Wind* was owned by the Libyan government.

For several long moments, McGuire, Clyde Lynch, Bridget Bowen, and the other Provos were staggered physically and emotionally, not only by the blast but also from the shock of the realization that they had been discovered and were under attack. With that recognition of discovery came a hideous pressure of extreme threat and fear, for in no way had they prepared for this incalculable danger. In the past there had always been some avenue of escape. But not now. They were trapped. Even more damning was the awareness that in another fifteen minutes they were to have left the inside of the Mound of the Hostages and started for the coast to the north.

"Keenan, maybe we could still reach the coast and . . . and . . ." began Bridget Bowen, whose pudgy body shook with fear. Concussion bells were still ringing in her head and blood flowed from her ears and nose.

"And do what?" McGuire said abrasively. "They found

163

out. The British know we are in this place. We can never make it to the cabin cruisers. I doubt if they even get to the coast. British patrol boats will capture them the instant they come within the legal limit."

He stopped speaking and stared around him. In the glow of dozens of Butane lanterns, their flames casting weird shadows on the high curved walls and ceiling, he could see that the Provos were disorganized. Damn them! They had said goodbye to yesterday and didn't dare think of tomorrow! Their fighting spirit had fled.

Cade O'Brian and Ruairi Paisley, both wiping their bloody noses, stumbled over to McGuire and Bowen, the panic of the condemned stamped on their faces.

"What are we going to do?" demanded O'Brian, his voice hollow. "My God! They must be all around us. How could they have guessed?"

"We have to run for it, run for the coast," Paisley growled excitedly. "We haven't a particle of a chance in this damned place. By all the saints! I was against coming to this place of the dead."

"We stay here!" McGuire's tone was calm and conclusive, the tone of a man who was staring Death in the face and accepting his fate.

The two men and Bridget Bowen saw a strange glint in his eyes, a fanatical glow that made Bridget remember a German police dog baring its teeth and growling at her when she was only a child of ten.

McGuire went on in a voice that made all three shiver, "If we tried to escape from here, we'd be out in the open. We'd be cut to pieces. It is better to remain here and take as many of the British with us as we can. There isn't anything else we can do."

Bridget Bowen's large milk factories began to rise and fall more rapidly. Dying was definitely not on her schedule. O'Brian and Paisley began to breathe faster. Damn it, death was forever! Imprisonment and detention were certainly preferable to death. One could always escape; at least the chance of freedom was always present. But Death was final.

Neither man, nor Bridget, had a chance to respond to McGuire's fatal pronouncement. In the gloom generated by the dust from the explosion, McGuire stared at the Provos moving around the raised stone graves toward the western end of the mound. He knew why: they wanted to put as much distance as possible between themselves and the smoking hole in the east.

"Get back, you idiots!" he screamed in fury. "Stay away from that end. Move toward the center!"

His warning was thirty seconds too late. There was a terrific explosion and a large section of the curved wall-ceiling on the west side became pure fire and crushed stone that instantly changed to a kind of natural shrapnel.

Forty Provos were knocked to the floor by the blast. McGuire and the three around him were staggered. Some terrorists screamed shrilly as stones of all sizes and shapes struck them. Twenty-nine terrorists died while shock waves sent a cloud of dust rolling toward the east.

"Put out those lanterns!" shouted McGuire, "and put on gas masks. Get down and stay down, you stupid sons of bitches. They'll be coming inside any moment!"

"Heaven help us!" sobbed Bridget Bowen. "They can come at us from both ends!" Tiny remembered bits of the past touched her consciousness, like fragments of a mirror reflecting some shattered fantasy life. She found it impossible to accept that within half an hour she would probably be a corpse.

The Death Merchant and his group of thirteen, now on hilltop level and to the east of the Mound of the Hostages, crept toward the southern edge of the opening. Three of the force would use Atchisson assault shotguns—Camellion, McLoughlin, and Sergeant Lucan Mahan, a fierce, bronze-faced professional who had spent his entire adult life in the British Army and was due to retire in eight months. But now the sixteen-pound Atchissons were slung across the backs of the three men, held in place by snap-slings. In their hands were BSA 9-mm submachine guns—weapons with 34-round magazines protruding from their left sides. Lieutenant George also carried a BSA.

Camellion stopped at the south edge of the opening and looked up at the top of the tear created in the twelve-foot-thick wall by the rockets. Irregular in shape, the opening was thirty feet across at its widest point and, perpendicularly, twenty feet at the peak. Stones had been loosened around the edges, some resting precariously, as if trying to decide whether to fall or stay put.

"I don't like it," whispered McLoughlin, who was behind the Death Merchant. "What we need is a gimmick. We've got to charge through twelve-foot-thick walls. And some of those stones on the ground are a yard square."

The Death Merchant studied the blocks of limestone that were at ground level in the opening. Some of the blocks were upended. Others lay on one side. Amid the blocks were chunks of broken rocks . . . all shapes and sizes.

"Those stones will also give us cover," Camellion pointed out, displaying consummate patience. "But we could use an edge. Find out if any of the Hell-Devils has a grenade launcher still attached to his assault rifle."

McLoughlin's quick check revealed that none of the Regulars did.

"We'll have to make do with what we have," Camellion said. He cocked his head and listened to the L7A1 heavy machine guns of the Super Puma firing projectiles through the west end hole. "We've got to show the Provos that the message of an eagle is never delivered by a dove."

"Well, that's a fact," admitted McLoughlin. "But at the same time, a wise hare does not carry tales to a hungry fox. And considering how we must be outnumbered, we sure as hell are the rabbits."

"Pass the word," Camellion said. "The only way we can do it is to rush the opening, get down behind the rocks, and start tossing grenades. But tell the others not to throw anything until I do."

"Six of the Hell-Devils said that they still have a few L-flares apiece," McLoughlin commented. "They'll help, if we live long enough to get to the center."

"We will," Camellion said softly, "but don't ask me how I know. Call it a gut feeling."

"I only hope we're alive to see the dawn," ventured McLoughlin, then turned to repeat Camellion's instructions to Lieutenant George.

Five mintues later, they charged the entrance, each man rushing straight in and getting down behind the first available rock large enough to give him cover. Ahead, straight west, there was only inky blackness. The IRA did not fire a single shot.

Camellion didn't waste precious time. He reached into one of his British Army supply bags, took out a fragmentation grenade, pulled the ring of the pin, and tossed the grenade as far as he could. The grenade exploded fifty feet inside the mound, but not a single piece of shrapnel came close to McGuire and his surviving terrorists waiting near the center of the mound's floor.

Thirteen more grenades exploded in rapid succession . . . thirteen blinking flashes of fire, thirteen explosions that vibrated the stones and made Camellion and the others hope that none of the large blocks above them would drop.

The Death Merchant leaned over to his left and whispered to McLoughlin. "Tell one of the Hell-Devils with an L-flare to throw it forward. We must see what lies just ahead."

"Sure we do, and I suppose you and I will take the point, right?"

"Wrong. I will. No point in both of us risking our necks. Hurry up. Have one of the soldiers throw a flare."

McLoughlin whispered to the man to his left. Private Arkell Carter pulled an L-flare from his bag, tore off the tab, and threw the flare with all his might. The moment it whooshed into blue illumination, sixty feet away, Camellion jumped to his feet and darted toward the interior. Crouched over, his eyes darting from left to right, Camellion saw in a glance that the entire floor contained nothing but raised stone graves.

Scores and scores of graves! All the same size—eight feet long, thirty inches wide, and forty inches high. Strangely enough, the graves were not placed in any particular pattern: some had been constructed so that they stretched east and west, others north and south, others pointing to random points of the compass. Some graves were very close together, others so far apart that the space of a small room was between them. Deliberate confusion. Maybe the druids wanted to represent that life is confusion, that only fools pretend to know what is in the mind of the gods; and so they constructed these graves in a random pattern symbolic of life's disorganization.

On McGuire's orders several dozen assault rifles and submachine guns opened fire, for McGuire had correctly deduced that the Death Merchant was the first of the attacking force. But the IRA chieftain had hesitated too long, thinking that the rest of the attackers would follow Camellion. Just as McGuire gave the order to fire, the Death Merchant was darting to the side of a north–south pointing grave. Several hundred high velocity projectiles rocketed toward the neatly formed pile of square stones that resembled an altar, projectiles of various calibers that struck the stones and glanced off with long, screaming whines. But none touched the Death Merchant, save two. A 9-mm slug and a 7.65-mm projectile ricocheted from the stone floor to the left. One stabbed into his left side, the other into his back. Camellion winced from the sharp, stabbing pain, but the Mermex material of his flak vest prevented the slugs from slicing into his flesh. The slugs would remain embedded in the material and would continue to be an annoyance until he removed the protective vest.

The Death Merchant went to work. He pulled tear gas canisters and K31 grenades from his bags and placed them in a row on the floor. He next took the ML9 transceiver from his belt and contacted the Silent Cobra and Lieutenant George. "When I start throwing grenades, do it. Got it?"

"We understand," George acknowledged with proper British precision.

"Got it, yes, and I think that in a few minutes we're all going to get it," McLoughlin said, with his own distinct brand of grisly humor.

"We can't die, Mr. Weaver," mocked Camellion. "Heaven won't have us and hell is afraid of us—out, good buddy."

He turned off the walkie-talkie, shoved it into its case, and picked up the first anti-personnel grenade, the circuits of his mind clicking. He had raced almost fifty feet; he could toss a grenade another fifty.

And unless I am badly fooled, McGuire will have placed his people toward the center. He'll have half facing the east, the other half the west, expecting an attack from both sides. Another thought floated to the surface of his mind. Silly humans, with their "if only" kind of mortality. It was the *fomes peccati* of the Latins and the *yetzer-ha-ra* of the Hebrews. Camellion laughed to himself. *Be as gods knowing good and evil,* so says the myth. But it forgot to add: *capable only of evil when man is left to himself.*

He pulled the pin of the grenade and, amidst sporadic firing from the IRA, tossed it over the raised pile of stones. He didn't hope to place any of the K31s in the midst of the terrorists—*but I'll sure be able to keep them down!*

The grenade exploded, thousands of slivers of steel shrapnel stabbing into the old stones of the graves close to the IRA terrorists, four of whom raised their heads just as the second grenade exploded. Three screamed, dropped their weapons, and covered their bloody shrapnel-shredded faces with their hands. The fourth Provo only dropped, straight down, as though his legs had suddenly evaporated. He was stone dead, his left eye coursing slowly down his cheek like the yolk of an egg. A single sliver of steel had pierced his eye and buried itself in his brain.

Camellion had toyed with the idea of letting the K31s explode in mid-air, above the Provos. He couldn't. The deadly shrapnel would reach not only the Provos but his own people as well. By throwing the grenades in the usual manner, the K31s would fall among the raised graves forwards, and the stones would absorb much of the steel slivers. At such a distance, the remainder of the shrapnel was not likely to reach the British, who would be coming in low with their helmet visors lowered over their gas masks.

During the explosions of the third, fourth, and fifth grenades, McLoughlin and the rest of the men raced forward, darting in by the flickering light cast by the burning L-flare, and dropped down behind raised graves near the Death Merchant.

Camellion called out, "A grenade each and a tear gas canister each!"—and pulled the pin of another anti-personnel grenade.

One after another, fourteen K31 grenades sailed toward McGuire and his terrorists. Every single one kept down, their faces buried in their arms. Unlike Richard Camellion, not even Keenan McGuire believed that Death is not darkness, but rather light, liberation, and freedom.

All this time, McGuire had been doing some rapid thinking. Only one man had charged into the giant hollow mound from the east, and from the time sequence between grenade explosions, there couldn't be more than eighteen or twenty men doing the throwing. And not one British soldier was charging in through the hole in the west end of the mound. Why not? The helicopter was no longer raking the opening with machine gun fire. Why? In a white-hot rage at being tricked, McGuire was certain that he knew the answer. The British ahead had been dropped by the chopper. Damn their souls to the deepest pits of hell! They were only the scouting party! Why, damn them! They had to be suicidal, trying to bottle him up like this until the main force arrived. By God! They would never succeed.

McGuire turned and whispered to Cade O'Brian who

was next to him. "We might still be able to reach the coast. Listen and—"

O'Brian turned and was stunned. "But you said—"

"Shut up and listen. There's only a handful of British pigs out there. Give the word. When I fire, we charge."

By the time the British had tossed five more L-flares the other IRA terrorists had received the order. McGuire triggered a short burst with his Czech Vz25 submachine gun, and the Provos jumped up and darted toward Camellion, firing short bursts.

The Death Merchant felt like jumping up nnd down for joy. He had assumed that they would have to go to the terrorists—*but McGuire must have guessed! Good! That little ole revolutionary is coming to us!*

Camellion and his men were more than ready, each man waiting with a fully loaded EM assault rifle . . . Each man except Camellion and McLoughlin, Lieutenant George and Sergeant Mahan, who each had their BSA submachine guns. In addition, the Death Merchant, McLoughlin, and Sergeant Mahan had unsnapped their Atchisson fully automatic shotguns and were ready to fire the weapons at an instant's notice.

K31 anti-personnel grenades could have decimated McGuire and his charging terrorists. The only reason that Camellion and his troops did not use the deadly grenades was that they would have had to stay down behind the graves to avoid the terrible steel slivers of shrapnel. With such a method, there was always a chance that some of the Provos would get through, catch them unexpectedly, and riddle them before they could fire back. Even so, because McGuire and his terrorists were firing short bursts as they darted forward and moved from grave to grave, Camellion and his force of thirteen were standing with both feet on the brink of eternity. Projectiles from both sides ricocheted off the tops and sides and ends of the raised grave stones. Scores of times enemy slugs struck close to the Death Merchant and other members of his force and sent rock dust and sharp chips flying against the hard plastic shields of their helmets.

In such a storm of flying slugs, some had to find human flesh. Many did! Two terrorists, Stephen Stormont and Oliver Curran, had the misfortune to jump up from the side of a grave and continue the race at the wrong time. In an instant, Camellion had stitched the two Provos across the middle with BSA 9-mm slugs, the impact of the hollow-pointed projectiles doubling the two men over as it pitched them back against the stones.

But the IRA terrorists were not amateurs in the game of death. Private Lyle Crowley, one of the Hell-Devils, uttered a sharp cry, jerked, and went down, his face and throat streaming blood. One 7.65-mm projectile struck him in the forehead and another hit an inch to the left of the hollow of his throat. Crowley was dead by the time his knees touched the floor. Norman Blacksmith, a twenty-four-year-old Hell-Devil, was the next to die, with a slug in his liver and two more in the right side of his chest.

In only three and a half minutes, Keenan McGuire and his twenty-seven terrorists were right in the middle of the Death Merchant and his men. The only edge that Camellion had was that his men were well trained, well organized, and functioned as one smooth running machine.

A wall of .280 EM assault projectiles tore into five Provos—three men and two women—who screamed, jerked, did a short fandango of death, dropped, and died, pools of blood forming beneath their lifeless bodies.

Private Ralph Weeks cried out, grabbed his chest, dropped his rifle, sighed, closed his eyes, and died. Three 9-mm projectiles from a German Erma SMG had bored through his chest.

A moment later, Lawrence Ogilvie died without as much as a murmur, the top of his head flying off from four Belgian FN subgun projectiles. With his braincase flew his helmet, four bullet holes in it.

There wasn't time for Camellion and crew to reload their automatic weapons. The Hell-Devils dropped their assault rifles and jerked out FN Browning auto-pistols. Lieutenant George put down his empty BSA chatterbox and pulled out a 9-mm Sig Sauer P220 pistol. The Death Merchant, Chris McLoughlin, and Sergeant Mahan picked up their automatic shotguns. At such close range, it was not necessary to aim the Atchissons; all one had to do was point the muzzles in the general direction, pull the trigger, and move the weapons slightly from left to right.

Blamblamblamblamblamblamblamblamblamblamblamblam!

Seven of the Provos couldn't have asked for more trouble if they had tried to smoke sticks of dynamite for cigars. The .24 caliber, 21-grain pellets tore into their bodies like tiny cannon balls. Jackets dissolved into clouds of cotton, nylon, and dacron poly fiberfill, and three of their terrorists died with holes in their chests the diameter of small water buckets, bits and pieces of cloth, leather, bits of bone, pieces of flesh, and a lot of blood bathing the air. The other four died with their faces erased and pieces of their exploded skulls going in every direction but down.

The seven terrorists were joined by Arkell Carter and Dearl Dwain Moore, two Hell-Devils whose time had come. Their executioner was Rosemary Keane, who stitched both men with an Israeli UZI, four 9-mm bullets slicing into Carter's stomach, six more cutting into Carter's gut and groin. Her pretty face twisted with hate, her pointed tits pushing out against the sage green reversible tanker jacket she wore, Rosemary threw herself down behind the side of a grave. Muttering a Hail Mary, she pushed her face down to escape stone chips flying up from the impact of several 9-mm parabellum slugs tossed her way by Tyler Burke and John Morgan.

At this point, it was no longer possible for the Death Merchant and his remaining force of seven to use the raised stones of the graves for protection. It was either stand up and fight to the death or remain crouched down and be slaughtered.

Three terrorists came at Camellion, who had leaped up and was ready to meet them within the confined space between two graves, none of the three realizing that they were trying to kill the First Disciple of the Cosmic Lord of Death.

Half a minute earlier, Cade O'Brian had tossed away his empty machine gun and had pulled his Heckler and Koch VP70 machine pistol that had an extra-long magazine containing 36 9-mm by 19 Parabellum cartridges. Now he tried to bring the muzzle to bear on the tall man wearing a gas mask behind a helmet face-plate. At the same moment, Mairin O'Dwyer, uttering strange half-laughing sounds, was positive that he could put three or four 9-mm slugs from a P38 Walther into Camellion. Between OBrian and O'Dwyer was Bridget Bowen, who was doing her very best to swing the long barrel of a Soviet PPsh41 submachine gun toward the Merchant of Death.

Such a deadly situation was not new to Camellion, who ducked to the right at the instant that O'Brian triggered the HK machine pistol, whose firing cycle was set on three-round bursts. The three 9-mm bullets burned past Camellion's left side, missing by several inches. It was the only chance

O'Brian would have. O'Dwyer, a bushy-headed, bushy-bearded piece of trash, and fat Bridget Bowen were doomed as well.

With astonishing speed, Camellion used the automatic shotgun the way a policeman would use a riot baton. He spun the Atchisson and pulled the trigger when the weapon was at a slant, with the muzzle tilted only a foot from O'Dwyer's arm and three feet from the left side of O'Brian's face. The last no. 4 buckshot shell in the shotgun exploded. Some of the .24 caliber pellets stabbed into the hand and forearm of O'Dwyer, who yelled and let the Walther P38 fall from his bloody hand. The majority of the shot tore into O'Brian's face. But the man didn't scream. He didn't have the time. His face vanished in a bloody splash of shotapart flesh and crushed bone, much of the mess splattering over O'Dwyer and Camellion, the rest falling to the top of a grave to the right. In another instant, O'Brian's legs turned to soggy spaghetti and Camellion reversed the empty shotgun, turning it so that the stock replaced the barrel. He stepped lightly to his right and slammed the big weapon upward to his left, a swift motion that knocked the PPsh41 in Bowen's hands to her right just as she fired, and slammed the side of the stock against the left side of O'Dwyer's chin and head.

The PPsh roared, but the slugs shot upward, hitting nothing but the ceiling. Bridget Bowen screamed shrilly with fear and rage while O'Dwyer, out cold, started to sink to the floor. She never really had time to know what was happening to her. Camellion released his right hand from the shotgun and smashed a *Seiken* forefist against the side of Bridget's temple. With a loud "Ohhh!" she started to wilt to the stone floor.

Camellion didn't wait to see the dumpy broad hit the deck. All around him men were cursing and struggling and trying to kill each other. He pulled out an auto mag, switched off the safety, looked around for Keenan McGuire, but didn't find the terrorist leader. Hearing a loud cry, he swung to his left in time to see Private Tyler Burke double over from a burst of machine gun slugs fired by Barry Drumm, a straw-thin terrorist, who wore glasses and was as bald as a doorknob. *The sonofabitch looks like a bongo drum with glasses!* thought Camellion. He raised the AMP and sent a .357 Magnum projectile into Drumm's right side the big slam lifting him several inches off the ground and pitching him over, then down, like a broken doll.

Where is that damned McGuire?

Hell-Devils Randy Powreles and Roy Kentrow were struggling with two terrorists. Not far from the four men, Lieutenant George and Sergeant Mahan were locked in combat with three Provos. Chris McLoughlin was occupied full-time with Ruairi Paisley, Clyde Lynch, and Rosemary Keane. The three terrorists might as well have tried to stop a buzzsaw with tissue paper.

McLoughlin had tossed aside his automatic shotgun, preferring to use only his hands and feet in combat at close range. Clyde Lynch, an FN Browning in his right hand, rushed at McLoughlin from the left, Ruairi Paisley, an HK VP70 machine pistol in his hand, from the right. To the left of Paisley was Rosemary Keane, her long, chestnut hair falling around her face and neck.

Weighing his chances, McLoughlin knew instantly that he was only a hair's-width from hell if he made a single mistake. He charged Lynch just as the bearded terrorist fired two shots point-blank at the broadest part of the Silent Cobra. Two 9-mm hollow-pointed projectiles stabbed into McLoughlin's chest, the two slugs instantly stopped by McLoughlin's Mermex flak vest. Yet the pain from the twin impact was similar to being hit in the chest with a hammer. An ordinary man would have staggered back. But McLoughlin, trained as he was, only winced and kept right on going, straight at the flabbergasted Lynch, who was so astonished that he was still trying to collect his senses when McLoughlin's left hand streaked out, fastened steel-like around Lynch's right wrist, and pushed the man's arm up and away from him. The FN Browning went off in Lynch's hand just as McLoughlin's right leg came up in a vicious *Mawashi Geri* roundhouse kick and his right hand shot outward, the momentum of his quick movement jerking Lynch forward and almost bringing the man to his knees.

McLoughlin didn't miss with his right hand, his four fingers formed into a *Yon Hon Nukite* four-finger spear, a spear-thrust that stabbed into Lynch's throat, the tips of his fingers crushing the top of the trachea.

With his windpipe turned into bloody mush, Lynch could only make choking sounds as he began to die. On the other hand, there wasn't anything wrong with Ruairi Paisley's voice. McLoughlin's roundhouse kick had not missed either, the tip of his boot snapping Paisley's wrist. The machine pistol went flying backward and Paisley howled in agony as Lynch began to gurgle like a stopped-up drain.

It had all happened so quickly that Rosemary Keane was suspended in limbo, dumbfounded, three seconds of amazement that cost her the most precious possession she had—her life.

"*Hi-yeee!*" McLoughlin let out a *Bushido* death yell and leaped high into the air with all the grace of a ballet dancer. His left arm shot out toward Paisley and his right hand went to one of the four Dwarf pencil-bladed knives he carried in a compartmented holster on the front of his equipment belt. As his left-handed *Yon Hon Nukite* stabbed into Paisley's throat, his thumb and forefinger closed on the hilt of the Dwarf and pulled the knife out of its holster. Up came his right arm, his hand snapped back, and the deadly Dwarf was on its way, propelled like a rocket by its heavy, rounded handle of steel.

McLoughlin's *Yon Hon Nukite* strike had been so powerful that his fingers crushed not only Ruairi Paisley's thyroid cartilage but also his carotid artery, the shock so terrible that Paisley died instantly.

So did Rosemary Keane! The thin, three-edged blade of the Dwarf buried itself in the hollow of her throat, an inch of the steel cutting into her jugular vein. For only a slice of a second, the ex-nun stood on wobbly legs while blood spurted around the blade and over the handle of the Dwarf, flowing down the front of her green tanker jacket. Reflex pulled her finger against the trigger of the Czech Vz27 pistol in her hand, the bullet striking the floor a few feet from McLoughlin, who had ducked down and was pulling two more Dwarves from their holsters. Rosemary Keane's knees buckled and she fell, her last darkening thoughts alternating between horror and beastliness, life and death.

Hell-Devils Randy Powreles and Roy Kentrow were greatly surprised when the two Provos they were fighting were suddenly "turned off." All four were evenly matched in height and weight and were struggling to disarm each other, when John Cooper's head exploded from a .357 Magnum projectile and parts of his skull and brain took off for parts unknown. Still keeping a sharp lookout for the elusive Keenan McGuire, Camellion was about to blow up Peter Smyth, the terrorist battling with Roy Kentrow. But McLoughlin beat him to delivering the death strike. Smyth cried out in pain and fear. His body jerked violently. His hands relaxed on Kentrow's wrists, His eyes rolled back in his head, and he dropped, the black handle of a Dwarf protruding from between his shoulder blades.

175

Sergeant Mahan and Lieutenant George were barely holding their own with the three Provos with whom they were fighting. While Joe Delaney was obsessed with trying to push a bayonet into Lieutenant George's stomach, Simon Teague and Jeffrey Willet were attempting to bring down Sergeant Mahan.

Mahan got lucky at the moment the Death Merchant was about to open fire with an AMP and McLoughlin was preparing to throw another Dwarf. He kicked Willet in the belly, a battering ram slam that took all the fight out of the terrorist. Camellion, his eyes darting around, lowered the auto mag and McLoughlin put away the Dwarf when they saw Private Kentrow and Corporal Powreles tearing across the short space to help Mahan and George.

At last the Death Merchant spotted Keenan McGuire, the biggest prize of all. The IRA leader was rearing up from one side of a raised grave thirty feet to the left of Camellion. Putting the Walther MP-K submachine gun over the top of the grave—no doubt to fire at Lieutenant George and the small knot of men to the east—McGuire also saw Camellion and the Silent Cobra. The Death Merchant fired the auto mag at the exact moment that McGuire, in panic, tried to duck down. The IRA leader was a microsecond too slow. The powerful .357 projectile struck the submachine gun with a loud whang and ripped through the Walther's right side, wrecking not only the mechanism but jerking the weapon from McGuire's hands.

By now, the three terrorists who had been fighting with Lieutenant George and Sergeant Mahan had been laid out cold. Camellion yelled at George and the other three men, "Get down! I've spotted McGuire. He's forty feet west of you."

McLoughlin had raced around graves and now was coming up from behind Camellion. Joining the Death Merchant, he whispered, "How are we going to take him?"

Camellion pulled out the second auto mag. "He'll try to creep west among the graves and lose himself." What else can he do? Let's try to block him with grenades. Then we'll rush him. Don't kill him unless you have to."

"Sounds good," agreed McLoughlin, who had pulled two 9-mm Berettas. "But the cylinder's probably in here."

"Cover me." Camellion placed both AMPs on top of a grave, took a K31 from one of his bags, pulled the pin, and tossed it fifty feet to his right, to the northwest.

No sooner had the grenade left his hand then he and McLoughlin dropped to protect themselves from the deadly steel slivers of shrapnel. The anti-personnel grenade landed at the end of one raised stone grave and exploded thirty feet to the west of McGuire, hundreds of steel needles pinging against the old stones. None touched McGuire, who had the feeling that he was in a world of unreality. Even the shuffle of his knees on the stone floor seemed to belong to some fleeting, artificial world, put together only by his own physical reactions and external stimuli, all of it forcing his body and brain to wither. All hope of escape was gone, and McGuire knew it, knew he was only prolonging the inevitable. Afraid to live but unwilling to die, McGuire pulled a Sig Sauer auto pistol and, crouched low, started across the short space to the side of another raised grave.

The second K31 grenade exploded, this one twenty-five feet west of McGuire. Most of the steel slivers shot upward. Other tiny needles stabbed into stones. Eleven struck Keenan McGuire on the left side of his body. Some bored into his hip, others into his left rib cage and the fleshy part of his left arm. Two stabbed into his left cheek.

The feeling was like being touched with the tips of blue-hot pokers. McGuire screamed in agony at the top of his lungs and rolled over on his right side, his mind in a whirlpool of fear and pain. The next thing he knew, the Sig Sauer was ripped from his hand and he was staring into the big, black muzzle of a long-barrelled stainless steel auto pistol of unfamiliar make and manufacture.

"Relax, me boy," Camellion said in a pleasant voice. "It's over. But for you, it's just beginning."

The accent of the voice was a puzzle to McGuire, who stared up at the gas-masked face through a haze of pain, fear, and wonderment. Then a second hurried up. He was carrying a Beretta in each hand.

"You're not B—British," McGuire croaked, looking up at Camellion. "You're not Irish. W—Who are you?"

"Death."

Weapons had been collected. Lance-Corporal Rodney Morgan, wounded in the shoulder, had been made comfortable. Lieutenant George had contacted Captain Kipp and reported that the battle was over and that Keenan McGuire and five other terrorists were in custody.

"We've broken the heart and back of the IRA in Ulster, sir," concluded Lieutenant George happily.

Captain Thomas Kipp replied that the armored column was only a mile from the Mound of the Hostages and would arrive shortly.

The six IRA terrorists sat butt-flat on the floor, their legs stretched out in front of them, their hands cuffed behind their backs. All six were in deplorable condition.

Keenan McGuire's body was one big pain. The two slivers of steel that had pierced his left cheek were particularly annoying, the tips of the needles protruding from the flesh so that he could feel the points with his tongue. He sat sullenly, his head down, blood dripping from his mouth. Bridget Bowen and Mairin O'Dwyer had swollen faces. Joe Delaney, Simon Teague, and Jeffrey Willet had knots on their heads from gun butts that had smashed them into unconsciousness. In addition, Willet was in agony from the kick that Sergeant Mahan had given him in his gut. His intestines had been smashed and he was only half-conscious.

Seven Hell-Devils had been killed. One had been wounded. Sergeant Lucas Mahan had a long cut on his right arm, but otherwise was unharmed. Lieutenant George had sprained his left ankle. Only Camellion, McLoughlin, Powreles, and Kentrow had come through the fire-fight unscathed.

The Death Merchant pulled a High Standard .22 pistol from a shoulder holster inside his fatigues, let it dangle loosely in his hand, and looked down at the captives.

"Where is the cylinder hidden?" Camellion demanded, his tone without menace. "I want to know what's in it, too. I don't care which one of you tells me, but tell me you will."

He gestured with the .22 pistol to emphasize his meaning.

Bridget Bowen stared up at the Death Merchant, the contempt in her eyes as terrible as venom from a bushmaster. "We are prisoners of war," she spat out. "We don't have to tell you anything."

Lieutenant George and Sergeant Mahan frowned, their sweaty, dirty faces becoming hard.

"You're all damned murdering terrorists," Lieutenant George said sarcastically. "Hanging you ten times over would not be sufficient punishment."

McLoughlin laughed, looked down at Bowen, and said, "I suggest you answer the man, hon. He'll slit your throat so fast you won't even know it until you shake your head."

The tear gas had drifted off long ago, and no one wore a

gas mask. Keenan McGuire looked up through bloodshot eyes, tiny knots of muscles in his cheeks twitching. He looked first at McLoughlin, then at Camellion.

"All of you—go to hell!" The words were pronounced with velvet smoothness, but icy cold.

The High Standard pistol in Camellion's right hand cracked twice. McGuire screamed. His body jerked. Then he fell sideways against Joe Delaney, who sat to his right. The Death Merchant had shot off the tip of McGuire's right ear lobe and had put a .22 bullet into the IRA chief's left knee cap.

Two more times the High Standard pistol cracked. This time it was Bridget Bowen who shrieked in agony and jumped, her fat face contorting in unbearable pain. She slumped back, moaning. Camellion had shot her twice in the stomach.

The other IRA captives—except for McGuire, who lay on his side, moaning—stared up in horror at the Death Merchant, disbelief on their faces.

"So much for the 'prisoner of war' nonsense," Camellion said, with a slight laugh. His voice changed to a tone as ruthless as his methods. "You're all murderers of innocent people, killers of children, killers of babies in their mothers' wombs. Don't expect any mercy from me. I have more respect for lice on a dying sow." His eyes went to Simon Teague, and the muzzle of the .22 pistol turned toward the quivering man.

"Wait!" yelled Teague. "I'll s—show you where the cylinder is. It's to the west. It—it contains a small atom bomb."

"If you're lying, I'll kill you very, very slowly, Camellion warned. "Get to your feet."

"Then I'll bring you back to life and do it all over again," added McLoughlin.

Walking behind Teague, with McLoughlin beside him, Camellion recalled part of a poem by Sara Teasdale he had once read—

There will come soft rains and the smell
of the ground,
And swallows circling with their
shimmering sound;
And frogs in the pools singing at night,
And wild plum trees in tremulous white;
Robins will wear their feathery fire,
Whistling their whims on a low
fence-wire . . .

> *No one would mind, neither bird nor*
> *tree,*
> *If mankind perished utterly. . . .*

Exactly! No one would give a damn—*neither bird nor tree.* But now was not the time to be philosophical. This mission was over. It wasn't likely that the Soviet Union would ever again risk bringing one of their subs close to the Irish coast.

Already the Death Merchant's mind was sorting out the pieces of the puzzle that Courtland Grojean wanted him to solve.

The Death of the General must be investigated! The message meant that General George Patton, the commander of the American Third Army in World War II, had been murdered.

Why? By whom? Supposedly, hundreds of millions of dollars in stolen Nazi gold was involved.

The Death Merchant smiled. He was looking forward to solving the General Patton Mystery. . . .